Need Your Number

Tampa Thunder, Volume 1

Mariah Goodwin

Published by Mariah Goodwin, 2023.

NEED YOUR NUMBER

First edition. April 7, 2023.

ISBN: 979-8988096313

Written by Mariah Goodwin.

This book is for everyone who unfortunately knows what it's like to be gaslit by toxic people. To those who have learned to love themselves after being made to feel unlovable. You are amazing. You are strong. You are beautiful. You make the world a better place. If you take anything away from this book please let it be that you are incredibly worthy of your place here in the world. Please do not allow toxic people to make you feel any different!

XOXO- Mariah

Triggers: There are some sensitive topics including choking and abuse. Make sure to take care of your mental health first when making reading choices.

Fiona

This is going to be the best internship ever! My favorite sport, time with my brother, and a chance at my dream job. Nothing will ruin this for me!

I put on my cutest sage green bell bottoms and white fitted bodysuit, and let my hair fall past my shoulders in their natural waves. The walk from my apartment I share with my roommates is only ten minutes to the arena. We live in Tampa, so it's hot but the walk has a nice breeze going today.

I spend the walk caught up in thoughts of my dream job - Social Media Manager for the Tampa Thunder hockey team. It's been my dream job since I went to a game with my family when I was fourteen. I love all aspects of social media for sports teams. Engaging and fun content can do wonders for a team's following and help bring in new fans. Over the years the Savannah Bananas have been killing it on TikTok and that's the kind of content I want for the Tampa Thunder! This internship running press for our local college hockey team will hopefully guarantee me an interview and a letter of recommendation!

Growing up in a house with a brother who plays hockey should give me a leg up to help me bond with the team. My brother, Luke, plays for the Tampa University Penguins and is hoping to be drafted this year. He is on a full ride scholarship. I know first hand how hard he has worked to get here. He's spent countless hours at the rink practicing solo and with the team. I'm excited to be able to spend time with him knowing once he hits the NHL, visits will be few and far between. Don't get me wrong, I am so excited to see him reach his dreams, but I will miss having him close by. My sister, Lucy, who is also one of my roommates, is my best friend. She loves hockey as much as I do and she's currently a junior studying to be a nurse.

Here we are, the arena where my dreams start to come true! I slide on my yellow sweater as I walk in and get hit with a gush of cold air. I head straight to the office I was shown during my orientation day. *Fiona Campbell, Press Intern* is what my door says. My own office! I can't help but giggle as I sit down and boot up my laptop and iPad sitting on my desk. I have thirty minutes until my official team introduction meeting. I spend the time logging into all the socials for the team and begin to jot down ideas for content on my notes app.

I head down to the press conference room and immediately notice the sounds of the team coming into the building. Loud, deep voices fill the hall. When I get inside I meet Marissa, my boss. She sits holding her coffee and offers me a welcoming smile.

"Fiona, please come have a seat. How's your first day going?" Marissa asks as I take a seat.

"I'm so excited to be here; this is a dream come true!" I exclaim.

"Good, we are glad to have you. I was just telling the coaches you have some great ideas to help get our fanbase to grow and fill this arena," Marissa tells me as she glances over to the man at the table I didn't notice.

Coach Jones is 6'3 and muscular; his beard and dark eyes give off the *stay back* vibe.

"I want my team morale to go up. We have a good team this year; I want the stands to reflect that," Coach said in a tone that was almost emotional.

"Yes sir, I understand. I have lots of plans to use all of our social media platforms to engage in the fanbase. As long as the team cooperates, I think we will see a big upswing in ticket sales," I told them confidently. Inside I was shaking in fear, but I know I needed to radiate confidence to win over the coach, and therein, the team.

"The team will be instructed in our meeting to work with you on the socials. My seniors need the press to help them with the draft this year and my younger players need to build rapport with teams and the fans to help them later on in their draft years," he informed me.

"Your brother is one of my best players, so I know you have a good understanding of the sport and I trust you will do the Penguins well. In turn I will get you a meeting with the general manager of the Tampa Thunder," he said looking into my eyes, knowing he just dangled my dream right in front of me.

"I won't let you down. You are going to be happy with my work and the work of the team!" I looked between him and Marissa, hoping he can't see the nervousness in my face.

"Ok, I'm going to go speak with the team and I will be back with them shortly." He turned and walked out.

I let out the breath I didn't know I had been holding in. I can do this. I have studied, researched, and followed sports teams for years. I know I can do this as long as the team cooperates with me, including my brother's best friend, Zane. The resident brooding, grumpy right defender. All the girls want him. He would be perfect to help increase our female game attendees.

The best thing about this internship is I don't date athletes, so I have no chance of getting wrapped into the hockey drama. Hockey players tend to have girl drama follow them everywhere they go. Zane leads the pack with most issues, with a crazy ex and puck bunnies following his every move. Luke told me about his best friend's issues with his ex during one of our sibling dinners recently. Focus Fiona! Stop thinking of some random hockey player.

Graduating from Georgia University last spring means I haven't had a chance to meet the team yet. Whenever I visited it was quick trips and we didn't hang out in groups, just us siblings. I was excited to meet these players who my brother calls family. Social media profiles helped me put faces to names already, though. Getting a glimpse at how they portray themselves online helps me feel confident in how I can promote the team successfully.

Lucy and Celisa, my cousin and other roommate, want to hit the bar to celebrate my first day! Slapshots is the local sports bar; it also is where Celisa works. My brother said he would meet us there after he finishes watching tape with the team. Hopefully I can find a distraction tonight to help me get my ex off my mind. I am desperate enough to go on an app but nowhere near desperate enough to go home with an athlete.

My ex, Justin, right wing for Georgia University Tigers hockey team, is the reason I have sworn off athletes. He's also the reason for my distracted mind as the team starts talking outside the press room doors. I do what I can to push off the thoughts of my cheating, verbally abusive ex right as Zane and my brother enter the doors.

Zane Miller, standing tall at 6'6 with the build of a brick wall, looks the part of a hockey defender. His shaggy, dark blonde hair falls in his face as he looks up, laughing at something my brother says, and pierces me with eyes that remind me of amber. His light brown eyes lock with mine for just a moment before I flick my gaze to my brother.

Coach Jones comes up to the front by Marissa and me.

"Gentlemen, it's time for a new season. We have a chance to win the championship if we play the way we have been practicing. You all know Marissa from the past few years of running our press dockets. This year we have an intern, Fiona. She will be working with you all individually and as a team to fix our fan base through social media. Fiona, go ahead and introduce yourself and then we will move to the plan for the season."

I stand frozen but notice my brother catch my eye and give a subtle nod. *He believes in me. That's what matters!* is all I can think as I begin my introduction.

"Hi, my name is Fiona Campbell. I am a recent graduate of Georgia University," I start.

Groans breakout around the room from the team at the mention of their rival, but my brother's small grin encourages me to move forward.

"Yeah, I know, rivals and all that. I am here to help revamp the team's social media and make this team one of the most followed, most watched, and most fan attended hockey team in the entire league. I know what I am doing, and I trust that you will respect my ideas and my time. If you have ideas, I would love to hear those as well." I end my introduction with a smile and subtle nod to Coach so he can take the floor.

Coach spends the next hour going over schedules for press and socials. My focus drops when I feel someone staring. I look up into the most beautiful amber colored eyes that only artists can dream of creating. He gives me a small smirk and a tilt of the head like he can't get a read on me. But why would he need to get a read on me? I need to focus on anything but the magnificent man in front of me. Every muscle in his forearm is showing while he relaxes in his khakis and Caribbean blue button up with the sleeves rolled. Do men know what rolled sleeves do to a girl? FOCUS!

I focus back on Coach's speech as it comes to an end. He gives out business cards to every player with my contact information so the players can reach out with their ideas and schedule. As the team files out, my brother comes up and gives me a big hug and rubs the top of my head messing up my hair.

"Luke! Stop, you're messing up my hair! It's my first day. How did I do, though? Was it good?" I asked him nervously.

"Fi, you killed it! You owned the room even with the rivalry distraction. I'm so proud of you, sis! Now make us famous," he states while he skips out of the room.

I turn to Marissa. "I am excited to begin. I'm going to head to my office and start setting up my content board. Is there anything you need from me?"

Marissa smiles and says, "No, let me know how getting started goes tomorrow. Don't forget we have a team who can help with editing if you need it." With that she walked away, leaving me in the room alone to ponder my thoughts.

I made it! I am in charge of a hockey team's social media accounts! I spin in my chair a few times, take a deep breath, and smile. I hear someone clearing their throat and jump up quickly.

"I saw you in here spinning. Just checking in to see if you were okay." Those words came from the smooth, deep voice of none other than Zane Miller.

"Yeah... um, yeah, sorry. I am fine, just lost in my thoughts. Thanks for...um, uh checking on me," I stammer.

Get it together, I tell myself. Zane gave me a smirk, like he's used to making girls flustered. I am not flustered because of him; I just was caught off guard.

"No problem. I will see you around, Fiona." He shook his head slightly as he spoke and then walked back out of the room.

I headed back to my office and thought about how awkward that was with Zane as I ate my lunch. I desperately wanted a McDonald's Coke and some Airhead candy, my go-to for comfort. Unfortunately, my chicken salad sandwich was going to have to do for now.

My office is amazing, with the wall across from the door being all glass that overlooks the ice rink. The wall behind my desk is a full bookshelf that I can't wait to decorate with photos and plants. The wall the door is actually on has a nice couch against it with a team photo hanging up.

I set up the wall across from my desk that doesn't look down at the rink as my content wall. I have about six Post-It notes up currently with different ideas. First things first are making some content of the players to help get the fans associated with the team. Especially the better-looking players. We could honestly use this social media campaign to attract some female attention.

I think back to the top five players with the biggest lady fan base and start there. Under each of the five players I have a to-do list: make an Instagram post, story, and a TikTok about each guy. Luke apparently is one of the five guys with the biggest lady following, so I guess I can start with him to kick things off. It's easier since he's my brother and I know everything about him, but making a thirst trap of my brother makes me feel slightly uncomfortable.

With a game plan in place, I text the five players I will be working with the next two days to get content filmed and ready to post. My focus begins to drift towards Zane again. Why is his gorgeous face and sexy muscles flashing through my mind? It's like a constant sexy man montage on repeat. I need to get laid asap. I text Lucy to set me up on one of those apps. Then I open my group chat with Lucy and Celisa to confirm tonight's plans.

Fiona: Can't wait for tonight, girls!

Lucy: How is it going? Drooling over any boys yet?

Lucy: Have you met Stuntz or Miller yet?

Celisa: YAY! First round on me!

Celisa: Share the gossip! Are they as sexy in person as they look on TV?

Celisa: Miller is HOT *fire emoji* He's got that dark, broody asshole vibe I love to hate.

Lucy: Miller is a fine ass male specimen. I would climb him like a tree if I could.

Fiona: Ooookay, I am done with you both lol. I did meet the ENTIRE team.

Fiona: And yes, I'm not too anti-athlete to admit there are some sexy ass men on this team. If only I didn't hate athletes so much.

Lucy: Tonight is going to be so fun!

I open the door to Slapshots, the hockey themed sports bar Celisa works at, and the energy instantly sweeps me up. The music is loud but not so loud you can't talk. It's modern inside but covered in tons of hockey merchandise and photos of all the players who have been patrons of this bar. I spot my cousin and sister sitting at a high top in the corner by the darts.

"You both look gorgeous tonight!" I exclaim as I take in their outfits. Lucy is in a cute pink bodysuit with jean shorts and white Vans. It compliments her toned body. She styled her blonde hair straight; it hits right at her shoulders looking stylish without looking like she tried too hard.

"Hi sis! Congrats on the first day!" She smiles; the smile reaches her deep blue eyes as she looks at me.

Celisa is sliding our shots over and I notice she decided on a tight black dress showing off all her curves. Celisa's long, almost black curly hair looks stunning and holds nothing to her dark brown eyes that resemble chestnuts.

"Shot time girls! I finally have a night off and I don't want to waste it sober!" Celisa giggles as we clink our shot glasses together.

Two drinks and four shots later I realize I probably should have eaten more than chicken salad today. I am tipsy by the time Luke arrives with none other than Mr. Dark and Broody. I notice his amber eyes catch mine as soon as they walk in. It's like a moth drawn to a flame.

"Fiona, you got 3 matches already!" Lucy exclaims, showing me the app she put on my phone earlier.

"Are you using a hookup app? Gross! " Luke snarks as he walks to our table.

"Not all of us can be campus wide heroes from slapping a puck on the ice!" I return the friendly banter. I notice Zane glaring daggers at my phone. It's like he's willing it to set fire.

"She's trying to get over small dick syndrome from Georgia," Celisa says matter-of-factly.

"Small dick who?" Zane says with a chuckle, looking at me with humor in his eyes.

"Oh, its Fi's shitty ex," Lucy says, with a knowing smile on her face.

I roll my eyes and grab my phone while telling the table, "Let's not talk about my lack of sex life anymore tonight. I need another drink".

I look over my whiskey and Coke, staring at Zane as he laughs at something Luke says. I need to really get laid. I can't keep staring at Zane while I have been in a drought. The drinks are hitting me. I should probably head out now before I have a hangover for work. I get up to leave and start to make my rounds to say goodbye.

Zane's jaw clenched. "Heading to your hookup now?"

I scoffed while slamming my drink down. "Excuse me? How is that ANY of your business?"

He set his beer down. "I just think it's unsafe for you to use apps. Just trying to look out." He thinks it's unsafe! That's ridiculous. He sleeps with tons of girls on campus all the time.

"I am not defending my choices to a playboy hockey player!" I roll my eyes. Setting my drink down, I storm off, not giving him any chance to respond.

Zane

She's stunning, I can't stop thinking about her piercing green eyes and tight ass. She dresses like a 70s hippy with her bell bottom jeans and tight tops. Hearing her laugh is like being wrapped in clouds. Fiona Campbell, sister of my best friend and teammate, this is going to be a problem. The moment I saw her in the press room she has been on my mind, it's like a moth drawn to a flame. I was surprised how well she held the room even when the team got rowdy about her alma mater.

Growing up in Nebraska makes me feel like an outcast around the local floridians. The way they all have a take no shit, dont care attitude. I have seen some of my teammates literally play chicken merging on the interstate with other cars, or yelling at a car to go faster that's already going 15 over. It's a whole new world down here... and I love it.

I grew up in a home with a dad who played hockey through college and a mom who played college softball. I have learned about the need to focus. My sister Penny played soccer through high school but didn't play in college. Penny and I are close. We talk multiple times a week and have a sibling date once a week. Since she graduated last year and started working as a teacher at the local high school we get more time together. Since our parents retired and our travelling she moved to Tampa to be closer to me. It was really sweet actually.

When I saw her in the bar tonight I thought this was my chance to talk to her but as I walked up I overheard them discussing her hook up app. Why would someone so hot need a hookup app? I probably shouldn't have even said anything to her, I just was warning her to be safe. Wasn't i? She looked pissed when she stormed off. I probably am going to need to apologize when I see her tomorrow.

Thinking about her face when I told her not to use those apps, she was pissed. Shes probably meeting up with whoever now. I rolled my eyes and sipped my beer. Why do i even care? I mean yeah she's hot as hell but I dont sleep around like she insinuated. Is that why i am mad? That has to be it, I'm mad because she insulted me, everyone always does that. Sure I hook up but not to the extreme everyone assumes.

9

Fiona is going to be in a great mood tomorrow, post hookup, that was a plus. I wonder what she would look like in my bed. I need to focus and get her off my mind. I don't need to get wrapped up with the social media intern I will have to work with all season. Plus she's my teammates and best friends sister. I need to get Fiona out of my mind for good. All the sexy outfits and her breathy laugh that makes me feel like i'm surrounded by sunshine needs to leave mt brain. Those long toned legs and tight round ass are not anything I need to think of while her brother is sitting next to me.

I finish my beer and listen to Luke flirt with a blonde puck bunny. I am about to tell him I'm leaving when I feel a touch on my arm. It's Celisa, Luke's cousin, she stares at me with her brown eyes fluttering her eyelashes. "Hi Zane, how are you tonight?" she says while lightly rubbing my arm. I turn to face her gently and subtly moving my arm from her grasp. "What's up Celisa, off tonight?" I ask knowing she is a bartender here at Slapshot. I hope that this conversation ends soon, I just want to go home and sleep. "I am off, want to have a drink with me?" she winks. Ugh she never gets that i'm not interested. "Actually I'm super tired and I'm going to head home in a minute" I say with a small smile hoping she gets the picture.

"Need a massage? I can come back to your house and help you relax" she leans forward reaching out and touching my forearm again. "Nope, i'm good thanks" I start to back up while i tell her. "Fine, Whatever Zane" she rolls her eyes as she says it. I bump Luke's arm as I turn to walk out "Heading out bye man" I holler as I stroll out the doors.

Tampa is humid and hot even at ten at night. My Apartment is only a block away from Slapshot making nights out convenient. As I step into my apartment it makes me miss home, I have pictures of my family on the wall. Time to shower and sleep, I am exhausted after being at the rink all day for practice and then our meeting with Fiona. Fiona, now she's back on my mind as I step into the shower. Thoughts of her take over as I put one hand on the wall to brace myself.

With the hot water running down my tired muscles I relax into the water. I grip my cock in my hand. I start to work my hand up and down as my mind begins to think of Fiona. I imagine my hand wrapped up in her soft dark waves while she's on her knees. She stares up at me with those piercing green eyes that are full of tears from choking on me.The sounds of her choking on my cock bring the blood rushing out of my brain. I picture her using her hand to help her handle all of my length. I start to grunt and my thoughts switch to bending Fiona over the vanity. I stroke harder with thoughts of us locking eyes in the mirror as I work myself in and out of her tight pussy. "Fiona...fuck" i grunt as streams of cum reach the shower wall. I finish rinsing off and head to bed. Falling asleep to thoughts of Fiona and her perfect ass.

Thoughts of how much I hate early morning practices enter my head as I reach over to shut off my alarm. I jump up and get dressed not interested in being late when I was just named Co Captain with Blake Stuntz. Stuntz is a draft hopeful he's a center and a really good one. He is a natural leader and amazing on the ice. Besides Luke he's one of my best friends. I hustle and make my protein shake then run out the door. My five minute drive to the rink doesnt give me much time to fully wake up and think of the long day ahead. We have practice, tape review, press bullshit no one likes, then we hit the gym as a team. Now they add in the social media extras we have to do, the only pro is getting to be around Fiona.

After practice we have thirty minutes until time to review tape with the team. I nudged Luke, "You down for Roasters?" I ask to see if he wants anything from the coffee shop outside the rink. A huge smile graces his face as he pushes his hair back "hell yeah, it's going to be a long ass day". We step inside the coffee shop, luckily there is no line, I place my order then step aside. Luke joins me on the other side of the counter saying "I got Fi something too, the girl will forget to stop and eat sometimes if she's not told".

As a hockey player i couldn't imagine forgetting to eat, we burn so many calories i feel like i'm constantly hungry. "Trying to win brother of the year bro?" I ask with a smirk, knowing I would definitely do the same for my sister. "Yeah man, with her on socials we are guaranteed to get some good exposure" he rolls his eyes and grins as he continues "more exposure is more puck bunnies in the stands". He laughs as our names are called and we walk back to the rink.

Everyone thinks I'm an asshole and a player, really I just don't want to settle down unless she's the one. My parents met in college and they fell in love fast, they both say once they knew they knew. My ex, Holly, really messed with my head last year and I'm not interested in that kind of drama this year. I just want to get through my senior year and focus on the draft.

Getting drafted is my goal for the season, I need to play hard and show I'm worth it. I want to play for the Tampa Thunder, it's my dream team! The coach looks for more than stats though, he wants strong players off the ice too. I need to keep my name out of any negative press, limit any drama, and keep my penalty minutes low. They also like players with a fan base so hopefully Fiona can help me get the image the Thunder want me to have.

Watching tape is a key part of most sports, you watch your team and your opposing team. You learn the strengths and weaknesses of both, you watch where mistakes were made so you have a plan for the next game. I focus on the game this week, the season opener. Their offense isn't strong. I don't see us struggling to keep them away from our goalie Davis. This game should be cake meaning my penalty minutes will be low and my stats will start out good.

"MILLER!" suddenly noticing my name being called and i spin around. I turn to see a head of dark wavy hair and soft green eyes looking my way. "Hey, what's up? Sorry I was lost in thought" I tell her trying to explain why I didn't answer her the first time. "Do you have time in twenty to meet and go over your social media plan? Maybe start filming content, Coach said you can skip tape today" she answers confidently, like she could read my mind and knew i was going to tell her i have tape review now. I roll my eyes "well then i guess i will be there in twenty since you cleared my schedule". I grimace knowing that it came out more snippy than I intended. She straightens herself standing taller "I didn't clear your schedule, I made a plan with the coach for my part of the job. If there is an issue you can take it up with him Miller" she turned and stormed off. Her walking away in her cute yellow converse and tight legging onesie thing that compliments her toned thighs and tight ass. I stand in the hall watching her walk away, knowing I was a dick and it's going to make life a lot harder.

I go sit in the players' lounge to kill time and finish my coffee. I look up to find Blake Stuntz sitting in the chair next to me, staring, like he's waiting on me to speak. "What?" I say with an eye roll. He gives me a small smile "Just wondering when you are going to get the stick out of your ass.". I'm not playing these head games today "What is that supposed to mean cap?". "I heard you being an asshole to Fi, that's Luke's sister man. Be careful I see you looking at her. She doesn't date athletes so don't waste your time and she's not the girl to fuck with. I'm not telling you what to do with your dick, but I am warning you it could end badly." he stands up and walks away. Leaving me with that insightful speech.

What the hell, a lecture from cap already today. I didn't look at Fiona any special way... Did i? I mean I'm not going to pretend I don't notice how stunning she is. But plenty of girls around campus are hot, not just her. I don't look at her any different than I look at the girls in the bar at night. Does the thought of just her face make the blood rush to my dick? Yes. Does that matter? No because I haven't gotten laid in a while and I'm sure that's the only issue here. Cap probably just sees horniness on my face.

Now what I want to know is what he meant by Fiona doesn't date athletes. She works for a hockey team and has a hockey player brother. Like what could have caused her to swear off all athletes. Also how did Stuntz find out? Maybe she mentioned it in their meeting this morning. This feels like a challenge now, but she hates me and cap already warned me to stay back. I just need to know why she decided to make that kind of pact. Maybe I can get her to open up about it, or I can ask Luke. Luke seems like the better option considering she doesn't seem to like or trust me at all right now after I was a dick twice.

Fiona

What an asshole, I thought to myself as I walked back to my office. I didn't purposely make him miss a tape review; it was the time the coach assigned for him. Plus, I didn't think anyone actually liked reviewing tape, Luke complains all the time about it. I look around my office at the daisy rug and house plants I brought in this morning. I wore my lucky sneakers today, yellow low top converse. They pair perfectly with the black jumpsuit I picked today. It shows off my waistline and makes my legs look great. I don't have a huge chest, but this jumpsuit is just low cut enough to look good but professional.

My brother brought me coffee and a blueberry muffin since he knows I will forget to eat. I begin to look at my content ideas for Zane so I can hopefully find something we can film today without needing to spend too much time together. Luke says that Zane is a good guy and isn't the asshole player he's made out to be. But my past two interactions with him have proven that wrong. First the comments on my hookup app and then he wants to be an ass because his coach scheduled him to work with me during tapes. Not really proving himself to not be that persona he's described as.

My current issue is that even though I was mad and annoyed last night, I still couldn't get him out of my mind. I can't stop thinking of his arms in that rolled up button down, and the way his pants sat tight on his legs showing off his muscular legs and round ass. My face reddens as I remember I went home and got myself off to thoughts of him.

Lying in bed all I could think of was him tossing me on the bed, hooking my legs over his shoulders and eating my pussy until I cum on his tongue. I touched myself to thoughts of him flipping me on my stomach and fucking me from behind while playing with my tits and clit. I bet Zane has a big thick cock that would fill my pussy up completely. I went to bed satisfied but also lost in thoughts on Zane. I really needed to hook up with someone so I can get him out of my head.

I started to get an ache between my legs remembering last nights "self-care" session. It's what my roommates and I call our masturbation time.

As I start to think of Zane pinning me against the wall of my office and fucking me during our session, there's a knock on the door.

I take a minute to recompose myself and remember Zane maybe God like in looks he's also a complete asshole. Most importantly he's an athlete. An absolute no go for me, especially a hockey player, my ex ruined that for me forever. Another knock comes to the door, time to get this shit show over with I think as I open the door.

I open the door and step to the side inviting Zane into my personal space. "Wow this is really nice, the view of the rink is amazing" he says as he looks around. I give him a nod and sit at the table by my content wall "Thanks, ready to get started?". He sits across from me "of course, but before we start, I just want to apologize for being an asshole last night and this morning, I'm not really an asshole, I'm not sure what is wrong with me". I give him a small smile not making eye contact "no problem, water under the bridge, let's get started!"

I open my tablet up and turn on the keyboard that I have for it. "So, Zane Miller, heading for the draft, senior, ladies' man. tell me about yourself; hobbies, superstitions, favorite snacks, what's your family like, goals in the NHL, goals your senior year, and your major" I look up at him and continue "I won't be using everything this just gives a good starting point of getting to know the real you and lets me think of how to create your online presence." He lets out a long sigh and makes eye contact with me. His eyes are stunning. I could get lost in them.

"Well, my only hobby is hockey honestly, but I do like to surf every once in a while. I'm not great at it. My only real superstition is I must have 2 airheads before a game, I know it's weird. It's something I stared back in the mighty mite league. I want to play for the Tampa Thunder. My goals this year are to be a good co-captain and get the team a championship. I am majoring in sports management" His answers are short and not too full of emotion, but I type them up in my player profile I created. He catches my eye and continues "My family is amazing, all athletes in college except my sister, Penny. Penny is one of my best friends I love her so much she comes to almost all my games. My parents make sure to catch as many games as they can in person when they are in town. They are my entire support system; I wouldn't be here without them. I love them." This was the most amount of emotion I have seen from him, it's like another person talking to me. "I am close with Luke and Lucy too, so I understand. I hated being away at college the past 4 years." I give him my first genuine smile during this meeting, and he smiles back.

I write up some ideas quickly "I think we could do a cute TikTok about your airheads, see what flavors everyone likes etc. I also would love to maybe get some surfing footage we could use to let people see you off the ice." I write some more and then say, "also I need you to do some charity work any ideas where you would like to volunteer?" He stares at me for a moment before collecting himself "I do a beach cleanup yearly; we can do that. Everything else sounds good to me." I realize I am actually smiling now, he's not so bad, I guess. "I love cleaning up beaches too, I haven't been in a while. When's your next cleanup so I can plan to be there to film and help of course" He leans forward "The next one is in 2 weeks, it's at cocoa beach, I usually go over and stay the night so I can get some surfing in."

"Perfect! One weekend, two different types of content! I can drive over the same day, I will just get a hotel." I love cocoa beach, but I don't want to seem overly excited. "Sounds good, but you can just ride with me, and we can save gas if you want." He's obviously trying to be nice by offering me a ride, but why not I could use that time to do some other content editing.

This has been a really productive meeting; I am about to ask him to meet me tomorrow to film some on ice stuff when another knock comes to the door. "Come in" I almost yell as my brother comes in with a vase of daisies "Thank you Luke, you didn't have to do this!" He looks confused "Um, I didn't, I love you but why would I get you flowers, these were delivered, and I offered to bring then up" just now noticing Zane he adds "Miller! What's up man?" Zane just looks up and nods then goes back to glaring at the flowers.

"Open the card!" Luke begs while I reach for the envelope. I open the card, reading it my good mood instantly sours and my face falls, but I quickly regain my composure. "That's a weird reaction to getting flowers Fi" Luke says as he snatches the card before I can stop him. "WHAT THE FUCK! He's still doing this shit! You moved, when is he going to stop with the bullshit" my brother says with a pissed off face his empty hand balling into a fist. I reach for his arm to comfort him "It's fine, I'm not letting it get to me, he's just being an asshole, trying to mess with my head no worries I'm fine." I grab the card, give Luke a hug and remind him I'm working, and we can talk later. He hugs me back and heads out obvious anger radiates off him.

I forgot Zane was even here until he reaches up and swipes a tear from my cheek "I'm not sure why I did that I'm sorry, I don't know what he said or who he is, but you deserve to be treated like the absolute queen you are." Zane gives me a quick hug and walks out the door. Leaving me to feel my feelings alone. He's good with emotions which is weird for a hockey player, but he does have a sister he's close to, so I am sure that helps him to be better with emotions that the average college guy. I start to cry again right as my phone dings with a bunch of group chat messages.

Luke: Fi got flowers from that asshole ex with a shitty card. I will kill him.

Celisa: What did that asshole say?

Lucy: Yes, tell us! I will stab him in the left nut for you girl.

Fiona: The flowers are my favorite kind, but the card said "Hope you are enjoying your new internship! When you are done playing "independent" I will be here to pick up the pieces. My heart is always yours Fiona, stop playing games and get back here in my jersey where you belong. See you in a few weeks at the game! Love, Justin"

Lucy: What kind of delusion is he living in?

Celisa: We need to beat his ass. We are all going to the game against GU with you! I don't want you alone.

Fiona: I'm fine guys, its empty threats he won't talk to me in person. I will see you at home!

Why did Luke even tell them, I would of told them when I got home. Wouldn't I? It's not that I want to hide things from my best friends, but they worry too much. I am fine. I finally got the courage to leave Justin after 3 years and it was the best decision I have ever made. He was verbally and emotionally abusive to me. He tried to control my every move. I would be lying if I said I wasn't worried about the game against GU coming up. He will be there, and he expects me to be in his jersey. I don't think he will be dumb enough to confront me though. If I leave the arena after most of the team that should put me in the clear.

I pull out my phone and send a text to Zane "Hey its Fiona, can you meet me after tapes tomorrow to film some on ice footage?" Now that I have handled that I start to write up my content plans for the seniors. I flip my phone to silent, turn on my playlist and get started.

I look up when I hear laughter in the hall. Checking my phone, I see its already 430pm. I must have just zoned out and focused on working. Needing to head home and eat something, I clean up my office and get ready to head home. I throw the flowers away because I don't want that reminder in my office. It feels good though, kind of freeing. With a smile and my head held high I go to the car.

Getting home I shower and make some mac and cheese, my favorite comfort food. No one is home yet so it's the perfect night to head to sleep early. Cleaning the dishes and putting the leftovers in the fridge for the girls when they get home. My bed looks so inviting, I am exhausted. I climb in and bundle up under my favorite fuzzy blanket.

My eyes snap open, I was exhausted, why cant I fall asleep. When I close my eyes all I see is those amber eyes and that shaggy blonde hair. Thoughts of Zane are flooding my head. This time I'm dropping to my knees and taking his huge cock, choking but I keep sucking hungry for all of him. In my thoughts, he grabs me up and tosses me on my bed saying he's hungry right as he slides me to the end of the bed. With my legs hooked around his head he licks my pussy and starts to rub my clit at the same time. I cum on my fingers as I imagine it being Zane's tongue, I'm cumming all over. I get up, clean myself up, then get bundled up in bed again.

What does it mean that I keep coming back to him when my thoughts are quiet? What is it about him that keeps me wanting his touch? Maybe it's the thought that I know he's off limits. If he wasn't an athlete I would of already fucked him out of my system. I drift off the sleep my brain still flooded with Zane Miller.

Zane

Walking down to the ice hoping Penny calls before I need to meet Fiona. I think yesterday will bring a positive change to our friendship. I didn't question her I just gave her the support I hope I would be able to give Penny in that situation. I don't know how Luke hasn't killed her ex. He better not do any shady shit at the game cause I have a feeling Luke's nots going to keep a level head. This will be our first game against them since they broke up.

My phone rings taking me from my thoughts of the situation with Fiona and her ex. "Penny, how are you doing?" I take a seat on the bleachers. "Good? You okay brother you seem off this morning" she questions my tone. "Yeah, I'm good, just want to check on you. Are you coming to the beach cleanup?" trying to cover up the weird vibe from earlier. "Of course, I will be there, I never miss a chance to do something good with my brother. I will meet you there Saturday morning." I can always count on Penny to show up when I need her. "Great. Just a heads-up Luke's sister, the social media intern, will be riding with me there to get footage of the cleanup and me surfing" I can hear her chuckling as soon as I say it. "Interesting, you have never invited anyone but me to your cleanups, that's your time, it's not for publicity its for you." I see Fiona walk up, quick to end this conversation "It's no big deal, Pen, I will see you there. I love you" with an exchange of I love you we hang up.

"Sorry about that I wasn't trying to eavesdrop" with a small smile Fiona walks up. She looks hot in her leggings and crewneck team sweatshirt; her hair is up in a ponytail with her hair falling in curls. "No worries. That was my sister Penny, she's coming to the cleanup so you will meet her then, she's a mess but I love her." I lace up my skates preparing for our content filming. I'm surprised to see Fiona putting on skates, hockey skates at that. Nothing is hotter than a girl in a pair of hockey skates. As she starts skating around the rink, I have to use all my willpower to keep the blood from rushing straight to my dick. She looks sexy as hell out there on the ice. Stepping on the ice, I focus on why we are here, content.

After about an hour of skating circles around each other, literally, we call it a successful day. We got footage of; me skating, doing some trick shots with the puck, my favorite celly (celebration) skate moves, and some of her interviewing me while we skated around. She even tossed me an airhead while she filmed asking what my favorite flavor was and having me ask what everyone's favorite flavor is for engagement or something. It was relaxing and actually more fun than I expected. We say our goodbyes and I head home for the night.

The next week flies by as we prepare for our first home game. September is when things start to get busy on campus. The parties are going in full swing, i don't party but i have had to go get my teammates. People are starting to mention the game and how excited they are for us to open the season. The posts Fiona has been making has the school buzzing with talks of our first game. So far the most popular one is of me and the airhead, but close second is Luke and Stuntz recreating a TikTok dance on the ice. I have to admit it was creative and funny. I haven't seen her much since our day on the ice, but its game day so I'm kind of excited to see her today. Then next week its beach cleanup, and the last weekend before we start having games almost every weekend until the season is over.

Walking into the rink in my suit, I stop seeing Fiona and another girl filming us walking in the doors. I vaguely remember a message saying they would be doing this. Something about a girl on TikTok, Monica Something, that does this and it always goes viral. I give them a small nod and say hello and make my way to the locker room. Im not sure why seeing her smile at me pregame made me feel so good inside, but it cant be a good sign. Time to get ready for the game, we need this win.

We skate past Fiona whos filming our entrance on the ice. I get distracted seeing most of the players smiling and joking with her, when I just skated out and nodded. I have no reason to feel jealous, but I do. Before I have time to process these feelings, I skate around the boards looking into the stands for the first time. The arena is sold out, like not a single open seat. It's a high female turn out but I will take it. I realize that's 100% due to Fiona when I notice how many girls are waving airheads in the air when I skate by. I giggle to myself and when I skate by Fiona again, she tosses me an airhead, white cherry my favorite, as she beams at me with her gorgeous smile. I dont get to catch her eye much during the game, Stuntz and I stay focused helping to keep the team with their eye on the prize.

NEED YOUR NUMBER

We win the game, it's our first win in front of a sold-out rink in my 4 years here at Tampa University. The energy is the arena is INSANE. I can barely hear my own thoughts as we all celebrate then skate off the ice. Luke comes and slaps my back "2 assists and a goal, that's killer for a defender! You were on another level tonight, whats the secret?" I wanted to say Fiona but instead "The arena man, the crowd was killer tonight, the vibes were amazing!" Luke smiles "Hell yeah, Fiona is killing it, I cant believe we were sold out! See you at Slapshots." I nod turning to showers and get ready. Walking out to my car I see Fiona and wanted to stop and say something, anything, instead I just walk straight to my jeep.

Slapshots is packed wall to wall with people in Penguins gear. I saw lots of girls in my number, just not the girl I wanted to see. I really needed to sort these feelings out before we head to the beach this upcoming weekend. Right as I decide to find someone to help me get her out of my head in walks the subject of all my thoughts. In a tight silver dress that shows off the prefect amount of cleavage and has her toned legs on display for the world to see. Her hair is down now but its cascading down her back begging to be wrapped around my fist. I'm getting a boner in a bar full of people because of someone's hair, this is fucking pathetic.

Four beers later, a blonde puck bunny was hanging on my arm trying to flirt but I couldn't stop staring at Fi. The way she tossed her head back and laughed, she looked breathtaking. The sound of her laugh drifted over to me and was like music to my ears. I excuse myself from the table and step out onto the patio with my beer.

"You okay man? You should be happy, theres a million puck bunnies in there with your number on if you don't like that blonde." Luke claps me on the shoulder waiting on me to tell him whats wrong. How do I tell him I have a thing for his sister, and I want to convince her to give me a chance. "Sorry Luke, I have a girl on my mind, shes not interested. I think she thinks im a player, when really I just want to settle down and find what my parents have." I take a big sip of my beer. "Well man I love the player life so i cant help you, but if shes worth it she will come around, and if she doesn't then shes not the one. For the record I suck at this kind of advice, Lucy is the one who could help you out." He claps me on the back again and heads inside.

23

I finish my beer on the patio when I hear the door open again, I don't want anyone to recognize me so I don't turn around. I hear footsteps come to a stop at my side right as I hear "Miller, why is my brother telling me you are out here sulking over a girl? Whats going on? Is it about Fi?" my eyes fly open and I choke on my beer "what? What are you talking about luc? Are you drunk?" She giggles "Zane I see how you look at her, I saw you watching her while a desperate puck bunny hung on you, I heard how you treated her after he who shall not be named had those flowers sent." I let out a long sigh "What do I do Lucy? She doesn't date athletes, I don't think she even finds me attractive. I am not this player like everyone thinks, I want real love like my parents had. Your sister is breathtaking, smart, driven, funny, everything I never knew I needed in my life" She takes a moment before saying "Fi went through some shit with her ex, he was horrible, shes scared. She does find you attractive, but after Justin that's not really enough to make her break her no athlete clause. I will drop some subtle hints and you just keep being charming and let her see the REAL you. I know you aren't a player, I see you flirting but you almost never actually leave the bar with anyone, I know you aren't what you are portrayed to be." With that she hugs me quickly and runs back inside.

I head out shortly after, climbing into bed with thoughts of Fiona and I. I can see her climbing on me letting me cup her beautiful tits with my hands as I flick her nipples with my tongue. I pull one nipple in my mouth sucking while I roll the other between two fingers, then switch. She would moan and start getting wet between those gorgeous thighs. With one hand I would slip my hand and feel her slick wet slit. Sliding one finger in and rubbing my thumb on her clit, she would begin to rock her hips. I can practically feel myself slipping inside her warm tight pussy. As I pump my dick with my hand, I continue to imagine her riding me. Fiona would be moaning my name as I filled her with my big cock. One hand wrapped in her luscious hair and one rubbing her clit she would climax at the same time as me. With thoughts of her pussy being filled with my cum, I shoot all over my stomach while moaning her name. As I catch my breath I get cleaned up. I fall asleep hoping I get to see her again in my dreams.

I wake up to a text;

Fiona: I didn't see you at the arena and you seemed busy at the bar. Congratulations on a great game. I got some amazing footage of you, your skate around the rink looking at everyone with airheads is going viral.

Zane: Thank you! Viral Wow that's crazy, all the props go to you for catching all the good footage.

Fiona: Thanks, have a great Sunday see you around this week! Cant wait for Friday!

With that I pull up the team TikTok. We are already at 15k followers! I watch all my videos seeing the puck bunnies flooding the comments, I roll my eyes. The video that really catches my attention though is the walk-in video. Most of the guys were smiling, joking, flirting, and then I walk in with a subtle nod. I really wasn't being very charming; it was worse than I thought. I would be ready next game. I also plan to be charming and a great sport for any content she needs, except dances, I'm not dancing.

I did as I said I would the rest of the week. I participate in most of the content shoots without complaint. I even tossed a few ideas out there, if Lucy is right and there's a small sliver of a chance, I could win over Fiona I'm going to try everything. This road trip together will be a great opportunity to talk and connect. I am hoping I can get her to open up to me and in turn I can give her a chance to see the real me.

Fiona

Today's the day - road trip time! I love road trips! I mean honestly who doesn't? The snacks, the playlists... all the vibes are just perfect!

Zane has been amazing this week. He's really putting effort into the content I have needed. I'm not sure what's changed but he's not the asshole I thought he is. I'm hoping this road trip keeps us in a good place. Dare I say he's actually become a friend? We joke around, and I don't want to murder him all day anymore. Even my brother has noticed the changes in him. Zane's lack of partying has taken Luke's wingman away. Not that I have any right to care if he's partying, it's nice to know he's not.

The entire Tampa U Hockey administration is amazed at the progress I have made. The first home game was sold out, we sold more merchandise that night than all of last season before playoffs. My own personal win is that the concession stands sold out of Airheads across the entire arena. The campus is alive with talk of hockey. This letter of recommendation is as good as mine!

Lucy comes waltzing in my room as I finish packing. "Hey Fi, I hope you have a great time! Maybe try and enjoy yourself a little bit. Zane and you both deserve some time to relax".

I look at her with a smile. "I am going for work but I will do my best to make sure I take a breath and actually enjoy myself."

She gets up and walks out saying, "And Fi - give Zane a chance to show you he's not this asshole you think he is."

What does that even mean? I have been giving him a chance. She knows I don't date athletes. If that's what she's hinting at, she's ridiculous! We are friends. I am giving him the benefit of the doubt that the person he's been showing me is the real him. I'm going to see the off-the-ice Zane and I'm sure it's going to be fine. What's the worst that could happen?

A black lifted Jeep pulls up and I instantly know it has to be Zane because of the two surfboards on the roof. He hops out and grabs my bags, loads them in the back, then opens the door for me.

"Thank you. Are you excited?," I ask.

He climbs in and puts his seatbelt on. "I am! I love surfing and the beach cleanups are important to me. The time off the ice is refreshing."

I look over to find a small smile on his face. He looks over quickly and his smile grows, but his eyes are what gets me. Those amber eyes could melt my panties right off, if they didn't belong to a sexy hockey player, of course.

He notices me staring. "You good Fiona?"

Quickly, I look away. "Yeah, I'm fine. Sorry, what's the playlist vibe? Let's get this party started!"

He hands over his phone cord. "Well, Penny always says passengers are the DJ, so here you go. Let's see what you got."

Our hands brush when I grab the cord and I swear I could see sparks flying. I focus on picking the perfect playlist, giving myself time to mentally will the aching between my legs away.

An hour into the drive we stop at the gas station and I get a fountain Coke. It's not McDonald's but it will do. We both grab some snacks and check out separately. When we get back in the Jeep, I pull out my Airhead and Zane gives me a weird look

"You didn't have to get me Airheads, I got myself some while we were in there."

I give him a laugh and say, "Actually, Zane, these and McDonald's Coke are my comfort foods. That's one of the reasons I loved your Airheads superstition so much!"

He now is sporting a full ear-to-ear grin. "Who knew we had so much in common? Any other comfort foods you like?"

I think. "I love pierogis, strawberries, and my mom's chicken and yellow rice."

With a quick look in my direction he admits to never having pierogis before. Which is honestly a crime; they are so yummy and just fill my soul with warmth. Conversation naturally ends and I'm surprised to hear him singing along to songs from all ten albums of Taylor Swift.

"Want to get dinner at the restaurant next to our hotel?", he asks as my stomach growls. "Yeah that sounds good. I could go for a drink and some food.", I reply.

We pull up to the hotel and he offers to go check us in. The hotel is on the water and absolutely breathtaking with the views of the beach. Zane looks stressed out as he walks back out of the hotel lobby.

"What's wrong?", I ask as he looks at me with stress practically radiating off him.

"Well, apparently there was a pipe that burst and there's only one room left; it only has one bed. I can sleep on the floor, or we can try and find another hotel," he says, obviously worried about how I'm going to react.

"No, it's fine. The beach clean-up is walking distance from here. We are both adults; I'm sure we can handle sharing a bed for the night." I'm trying to convince myself more than him, I think.

"Let's get our stuff upstairs and then head out. I can use that drink right now," I say with a smile trying to get him to relax.

The room is amazing; the view is beautiful from our balcony facing the beach.

"I'm so sorry Fi, I never would have booked us the same room, especially one bed," he said, looking like someone kicked his puppy.

I touch his forearm. "I wasn't kidding when I said it's okay. We will be good we can be professional. Plus This view is amazing and I know it will all be fine."

We both get changed for dinner. Zane is wearing khaki shorts that fit his muscular thighs perfectly and a navy-blue button up short sleeve with a light orange floral print. It accentuates the colors in his eyes more than I care to admit that I noticed. I put on a yellow sundress that shows off my curves, a pair of wedges that help show off my legs, and my hair loose down my back.

As we walk over to the restaurant Zane looks at me. "You look stunning tonight, Fiona. Just thought you deserved to hear that."

I can feel my cheeks reddening. "You don't clean up too bad yourself. Nice to see you outside of hockey gear," I say breathlessly, as I try to keep my mind from checking him out again.

Our waitress tries to flirt with Zane multiple times but he doesn't seem to notice. I get his full attention the entire dinner as we discuss our childhoods, siblings, favorite hockey players.

"So, Fiona, what's your career end goal?", he asks, actually caring what I want to do, unlike Justin, who just wanted me to be a trophy wife.

"I actually want to work for the Tampa Thunder. I know that is, like, a huge dream, but it's what I really want. I want to be the mastermind behind their social media."

Zane looks up with a chuckle. My face falls, thinking he's laughing at me.

"No, no, I'm laughing because my end goal is to play for the Tampa Thunder. It's my dream team. I just thought it was funny we had something else in common."

We are a few drinks in when Zane asks about Justin. "So it's not my business, but can I ask what happened with your douchebag ex? I know we play his team next week."

I take a deep breath, considering telling him it's not his business, but instead I say, "Justin and I dated for three years. He wanted me to be a trophy wife; I obviously didn't want that. He wasn't supportive, he became emotionally abusive, constantly manipulating and gaslighting me. After graduation I got the internship lined up, broke up with him, and moved the same day. I didn't want to give him a chance to manipulate me to stay."

Zane looks at me like I'm the strongest woman he's ever met. "Fiona, that's amazing! I'm so proud of you! My parents met and fell in love in college, so I haven't dated much because I want what they have. But Penny dates and I always worry about her. I'm glad to hear that you were strong enough to leave."

Hearing that Zane is proud of me and that he wants what his parents have brings tingles to my heart. He's supportive of my career, he loves his family, he's hot as hell, the protective vibes he gives off could melt panites... why can't I just go for it? He's not Justin. He's caring, kind, and sure, he can be a grump, but he remembers the little things. If he treats me so great when I'm his friend, I can only imagine what it will be like to date him.

He pulls me from my thoughts as he pays the bill. I thank him for dinner as he places his hand on the small of my back and he guides me through the crowded restaurant. I expect his hand to drop once we get outside but it doesn't. The fire I feel where his hand is is enough to make me want to fan myself. I notice he maneuvers me to the other side of him. When I give him a questioning look, he simply states, "Men walk on the side closest to the road; gentleman rules and all that." With a smile we go back to comfortable silence.

Walking into the hotel lobby, once those bright lights hit me I realize I'm way more drunk than I thought. I trip as we enter the elevator, but Zane catches me easily. Suddenly I find myself pressed against his chest with his arms steadying me, as I look up at his perfect kissable lips. Right as I'm about to say fuck it and kiss him, the elevator door pings open to our floor. Saved by the bell, literally.

As we enter the room I give us some space saying, "I'm going to go get ready and dressed for bed. I will be out in a few. Can you set an alarm for whenever we need to hit the beach for surfing?"

I grab my bag and hear Zane behind me. "Yes Fiona, I will set an alarm. We will surf, get breakfast, then head over to the cleanup. See you in a minute."

As I shut the door, I swear I can hear him breathlessly say, "Fucking elevator." I smile knowing he felt it too. He felt the sparks, like we were one kiss from setting the elevator on fire.

I wash my face and get the makeup off. I don't have a complicated skin routine, but I don't want to break out either. I quickly put my hair in a loose braid to keep it from getting knotted. I immediately regret not packing sweats and a t-shirt. I take my bra off and put on my light yellow shorts that sit low on my hips and hit high on my thigh. My black tank leaves a small sliver of skin exposed and is low cut but fits perfectly. If I knew I would be crawling into bed with Zane, I would have worn something that covered more.

I decide to yell out the door to him, "For the record, when I packed my pajamas, I was going to sleeping in a room alone. I didn't pack this expecting to be sharing a bed."

With that, I finish up in the bathroom. His eyes look hungry as he checks me out. He stares then quickly heads into the bathroom to shower. I think he's trying to hide a boner, but I could see it. The outline in his pants make me feel like I definitely wouldn't be disappointed in any bedroom activities. I hear the shower start and after a few moments, I can hear the telltale sounds of him grunting as he strokes his cock. After a few minutes I hear the moans getting faster. As I squeeze my thighs together, trying to get the ache and wetness to go away, I hear him moan my name as he finishes.

Drunk or not, a man has never came saying my name. I don't know if it's the drinks we had or the elevator tension, but I am soaked between my legs. The only cure for my kind of tension is Zane. I need to get my head clear before he comes out here. With that thought, he comes out of the bathroom in a pair of boxer shorts and nothing else.

Zane

My God, my heart stops as all the blood flows straight to my dick when she steps out of the bathroom. She's wearing short shorts that showcase her toned legs and tight ass perfectly. It's like a wet dream come to life as my eyes slowly travel up to see she has a tank top on that shows just a little stomach and is low cut. I know she didn't pack knowing we would be together but damn, this is my own personal hell, to have her like that lying in bed with me when I won't be able to touch her.

I step into the bathroom being careful not let her see the raging boner I have. "I'm going to take a quick shower."

I step into the steamy hot water and start stroking my cock. Images of Fiona flash through my mind: her sexy shorts, her perfect ass, her tits that would fit perfectly in my hands, images of her laughing and smiling. It doesn't take long to get myself to climax. Before I can stop myself I cum all over my hand with her name on my lips. Fuck. FUCK! I really hope these walls are thick and she didn't hear me. Or maybe it's good she hears me so she can know what she does to me. I decide not to put on my shorts, I walk out in just my black boxers.

By the look on her face as her eyes take their time looking at me from top to bottom, lingering on my cock, I can tell she heard me in the shower. Her cheeks are flushed and she looks guilty as she looks up.

"Good night Zane. See you in the morning," she says.

I climb into bed next to her being careful to honor the space currently between us. Thoughts of her and I flash through my mind while sleep evades me. I finally focus on her breathing and sleep finally comes and takes me.

I slowly wake up with something soft in my hand. I squeeze. It's Fiona's perfect tit. At some point in the night she moved over to me and we are now spooning. Her tit is out of her tank top and in my hand, nipple erect. She starts to wake and slowly presses that tight ass against my painfully hard erection. As she moans quietly and wiggles back even more, I'm about to cum just from her touch like a fucking high schooler. As I start to figure out how to untangle us so she won't have to wake up uncomfortable, the alarm goes off.

With a gasp she startles fully awake, pressing back further as I reach and hit the alarm with the hand not on her tit.

"Oh my God, oh my God! I'm so sorry Zane! I don't know how I ended up over here."

I grimace. "Fiona, hun, it's fine but please, for the love of God, please don't grind back anymore. I'm about to embarrass us both by creaming in my pants from your touch."

I begin to untangle us as she says, "Oh, I'm so sorry! This is embarrassing! If it helps, you are... um... bigger than anyone I have ever been with."

She turns bright red, stammering, "Wow, why did I just say that? It's not a lie but also, I just - well I don't know, I'm flustered."

I get up from the bed as she locks eyes on my boxers and the tent inside of it.

"I'm just going to go get dressed," is all I say as I grab my wetsuit and head to the bathroom.

I think of everything I can to ease this massive hard on: grandma's feet, taxes, sweaty hockey gear stench. It seems to work. I rinse my face and get dressed. It's about to be a very long day. At least she complimented my dick during her awkward apology.

When I come out of the room, she's in her bathing suit with linen shorts and a crop tank top.

"I'm going to bring my boards to the water if you want to meet me down there when you are ready."

She gives me a small smile. "Yeah let me get my things together, then I will be down."

As I go to walk out the door I turn around. "Fi, don't overthink any of this. We were asleep, we had been drinking... use whatever reasoning you need, but don't let it eat you up inside. Let's have a great day!"

With that I step into the hall, leaving her to calm her thoughts.

About twenty minutes later she joins me on the beach looking flushed but a lot more relaxed. I would be willing to bet she got herself off before she came down. Which is incredibly hot, but now is not the time to be turned on.

I ditch the wetsuit since the water's not that cold yet, opting to surf in my board shorts. I head to the water and start to get in the surf zone. I figure if she needs anything specific, she will let me know.

After about an hour of tearing up wave after wave, I am watching Fi focus on everything she films. The way she studies the waves, the sunlight, the angle she is shooting me its entrancing seeing her like this. She splashes through the waves for the perfect shots. The look of her tits in that swimsuit as she's bouncing around should be illegal.

I sit on my board as she snaps a bunch of shots. "Did you get anything good? Or do you need more footage?"

She looks at me, confused. "I got tons of good stuff; you are great out there. But I'm surprised you are done already."

My smile grows wider. "Oh I'm not done, but you are going to put your phone and camera down and come try surfing."

She looks at me like I have five heads. "I don't know how to surf! This is your thing! It's okay, I will just start editing while you surf."

"Nope! You are going to come give it a try. I think you will love it!" I don't give her time to argue I start to head back to shore.

I switch to my other board I brought for this moment. It's longer and easier for beginners. This should be fun. I think learning something new will be fun and give her a chance to relax a bit after last night and this morning. I know she's feeling the sparks between us, I just can't pressure her. I need to let her relax around me and hopefully she will find herself in a position like I'm in. Where the idea of never giving us a chance is scarier than the idea of our friendship we worked hard for go up in flames. All I want is to treat her like the princess she is. I want to drink McDonald's Coke and eat pierogis - whatever those are - while we watch TV.

I feel like Fiona and I could have what my parents have if she would drop the no athlete rule. I focus back on Fiona and see some guy talking to her. I see fucking red. I want him away from my girl. My girl, oh I'm so screwed.

"Fi, babe, you ready to get out there?"

She looks over, smiles, says something to him, and starts heading to me.

"Babe? Really caveman? Afraid someone's going to try to whisk me away on their surfboard?"

I roll my eyes and laugh, "I'm just trying to keep you away from assholes with only one thing on their mind."

We head to the water after practicing how to pop up on the board a few times. I push her board out into the water. I can tell she's terrified, so I decided to help.

"Close your eyes, close them. Feel the water moving beneath you, feel how the board goes with the waves. Let your mind clear of all the negative things you have rolling in there."

I can see her body relaxing. "I'm going to push you into the wave and you're going to stand up when you hear me tell you."

She lets the quietest, "Okay, I trust you." It makes me feel something, hearing she trusts me.

I push her into the next wave .

"Up! Up! Up!" I see her struggle, but she gets up. "Yes Fi, go girl!"

I swim into shore. She rides the wave all the way to the shallows where the waves break. Before I can fully steady myself, she throws herself into my arms.

"I did it! It was exhilarating and relaxing at the same time! I want to surf all the time. That feeling was amazing!"

With her arms around my neck and her legs around my waist I lean back so I can see her face. I gently push the brown locks of hair that fell out of her braid.

"I saw you Fi, you killed it! I'm so proud. I told you to get out of your head and just relax."

I continue to hold her, neither of us rushing to break apart. She looks at me and her voice, almost coming out as a whisper, says, "Thank you for everything. Showing me how to trust myself, how to trust someone else, how to relax. Thank you for this experience."

I stare at her kissable lips as I whisper back, "Of course. It was my honor to be a part of this moment with you."

Not wanting to break apart but knowing we need, to I add, "Do you want to go again? We have another thirty minutes before we need to get ready for the beach cleanup."

We spend those last thirty minutes caught up in pure bliss. We talk, laugh, and in some parts, just surf in silence. Fiona really let go and freed her mind today. She learned to trust herself, trust her decisions, trust me. Surfing is all about trusting the ocean to give you the proper sign when to go, then trusting yourself to know how hard to paddle and when to pop up. I'm so grateful to get to be here with her as she hits this moment in her life. The joy she's radiating brings me so much unexplained happiness.

Back in the hotel room I let her shower first, so she has time to get ready. She left me her laptop so I can flip through the images and videos. They are amazing! It's like she captured the focus, peace, and happiness I have when I'm on my board. She sees me in a different light than anyone else ever has. I think I'm falling for someone who won't date athletes.

I finish doing a quick scan of the content she got and look at the few photos and videos I got of her and smile because she looks like a pure ray of sunshine.

We gather our stuff, dressed for the clean up. I'm wearing navy board shorts, a white tank top, and white slip on sneakers. Fiona is in a different bikini with jean shorts and a cropped Penguins hockey tank top, and sandals. I shoot a text to Penny to let her know we are on the way as we load up the Jeep. I open Fiona's car door for her and we head out. I remind Fiona my sister is coming and to just ignore any off-the-wall comments she makes. We ride in comfortable silence.

At the beach cleanup I come around and open the door for her and help her get her backpack of gear. My sister pulls in next to us. I lock my Jeep and open Penny's door, then pull her into a hug.

"Always the gentleman, brother. Good to see you!", she says with a smile.

I lean forward, whispering, so only she can hear. "Don't say anything crazy, Pen. She works for the team."

She skips over to Fiona, completely ignoring me. "Hi, I'm Penny, this weird thing's sister. It's nice to meet you. I hope he's not giving you too much trouble."

Fiona grins back. "Nice to meet you too. No, he's not too bad. He taught me to surf today, which was amazing!"

My sister looks behind Fiona, giving me the "hmm, interesting look". Penny knows I have never taken anyone out to surf with me that's not family.

Once we check in we get started with clean up. Fiona films the first half of the day, interviewing me, interviewing Penny, getting sibling footage. The event organizer lets her interview him about my years volunteering here, the work the organization does, and more. Once she has enough footage she puts her stuff in the Jeep and begins to help with clean up. I watch as she shuffles through the sand looking sunkissed and gorgeous. I stare daggers any time a guy comes up to talk to her but try to be sure she doesn't catch me.

"So you love her?"

I almost choke on my water as my sister comes up from behind me.

"What? Are you crazy? We aren't even dating," I inform her - again.

"I see you watching her. You are protective, you care about her. Dude, you took her surfing! That's your sacred just-you thing. So when are you going to grow some balls and ask her out?"

I grimace, then tell her about Fiona's shitty ex and her no athlete dating clause.

She listens and says, "Figure it out, brother. The way you look at her - it's how dad looks at mom. But don't wait for her too long if she's not going to change her mind."

After that the three of us spend the rest of the afternoon joking around and sharing fun stories until it's time to leave. I walk Penny to the car, opening the door for her.

I open the door for Fiona then get ready to head back to Tampa. A quick stop at McDonald's for a Coke and we are on the road home. Fiona edits while I drive with music blasting. The silence feels comfortable. The drive goes by too fast and soon I'm in front of Fiona's apartment, opening the door and hugging her goodbye. I get lost in thoughts of her while I drive home.

I am so screwed.

Fiona

The moment I walk through the doors the girls are waiting. "You look so tan girl! How was it? Did you guys finally bang?" Lucy shoots off question after question. "You do look tan! I'm sure they didn't bang Luc, she doesn't date athletes and she not really his type" Celisa says that with the weirdest tone. He's obviously attracted to me, right? Ugh why do I even care, I'm not going there. "Hello earth to Fi" Lucy says. "Well, we didn't bang but sparks were flying" I'm not sure why I say it, I feel this pang of jealousy with how Celisa made her comment. "I'm getting wine, tell us everything!" Lucy runs and grabs a bottle of wine and 3 glasses. Then I spill the details.

I tell them about telling him about Justin and the way he opens doors and walks on the farthest side of the road. I tell them about the bed mix up and they both scoff. They we get to the shower part of the story, "I am laying in the bed, and I can hear him jacking off in the shower. At the end he moaned my name clear as day, then walked out with just boxers on like I didn't just hear him practicing self-care." My cheeks flush red as I sport a sheepish smile. Lucy starts fanning herself "Girl tell me you said something to him when he came to bed!" I smile "I didn't, we just went to bed but when we woke up, we were spooning, his hand was holding my boob, and he had some serious morning wood. He woke me up and said and I quote "if you rub against me again, I'm going to embarrass myself by cumming in my boxers." This time is Celisa with commentary "Well let's not get too excited you aren't really sure he said your name and come on morning wood happens to every guy no matter what." What the fuck, where was this attitude coming from. "Right, anyways he took my surfing that morning. We filmed content then he actually taught me to surf! He got some videos and photos I will show you later. After my first time going by myself, he picked me up and held me and whispered in my ear how proud he was of me for trusting myself and trusting him, but the way he said, it felt like it had more meaning." This time I don't give then a chance to comment and I continue on "I met his sister, she's amazing, she made a comment about how he never takes anyone but family surfing with him because it's his special time. Then she kept making jokes about how protective he was of me." Lucy looks up obviously tipsy "I told him at the bar to be careful or he would fall even harder for you" as she says it she slaps a hand over her mouth and looks away. At the same time Celisa and I both look at her stunned, "Excuse me, as my sister you did what?" She looks at me shyly "Listen he's been crushing on you since the say you guys skated alone, that's why you haven't seen him partying or with any girls around. He wants you! All I did was tell him to protect his heart, because I love you and I think he would be perfect for you, but I know you aren't interested in hockey boys. I was trying to warn him to get his feelings under control, so his heart didn't shatter, I'm sorry Fi, I wasn't trying to hurt you." I blink back the tears forming in my eyes "No its okay, I understand, I wish I could just be with him, he has shown me he would treat me good, and he is obviously interested, I just have to live for me right now." She reaches over and pulls me into a side hug.

"I'm going to bed goodnight, welcome back Fiona" Celisa says as she heads to her room. "I think she's had a crush on Zane, and it's never been returned so now seeing him falling for you has her hurt" Lucy informs me. "I don't know what to do Lucy. I'm so confused, he is amazing, but I don't know if I'm ready. Plus, the draft, he wants Tampa but that's not a guarantee" I say with a small smile. Lucy pulls me into a hug "Fi, if you want to find a problem you will. Maybe take some time to think about it, decide if all those fears are worth possibly finding your soulmate."

I take a long shower and lay in bed lost in thoughts when my phone dings:

Zane: Thanks for this weekend I had a great time I hope you did too.

Zane: PS you better give me pic creds when you post your surfing photos.

Fiona: I had an amazing time, thanks for letting me tag along. Of course, got to give credit where its due

Zane: Good night sunshine. I know we don't have any content to filming leading up to these weeks game against GU but hopefully I see you around.

Zane: I if don't see you then remember not to get in your head about him being in town. You are stronger than letting him get to you.

Fiona: Good night, Z.

Flipping to another text I send the screenshot to Lucy who just sends back a message that says "Swoon with a heart eye emoji" how helpful. Sleep continues to evade me, so I go post the picture of me surfing on a decent size wave looking the happiest I have ever been. The caption was a sun emoji and then I wrote "pic credits to the best @zanemillerhockey". Less than a minute later he liked it and commented "Best photographer ever, oh and you weren't too bad yourself sunshine" he ended it with a laughing emoji.

I must have fallen asleep not long after because I wake up to my phone full of notifications. Comments on my photo range from how happy I look to am I dating Zane to am I single. I also have a winky face text from Lucy, and I'm sorry text from Celisa, and a text from Luke just saying, "is there anything I should know". I choose to ignore them all and get ready for the day.

I blow dry my hair straight put on some light makeup and then head to find something to wear. Today is mostly editing so I don't need to go on the ice or be in meetings. I choose a pair of black jeans with rips in them and a vintage penguins' that's figure forming; cute and comfy is the vibe. I slip on my yellow converse and head out the door.

Stopping at Roasters I notice a few girls looking at me, I choose to write it off as a misunderstanding. It's not until one of them walks up to me I realize they were looking at me. "Hi, you're that surfer girl, right? Are you dating Zane? No one's seen him out in a while, so we were just wondering" the blonde says. I give them a polite smile "no we aren't dating I'm not sure why he's not partying anymore, wish I could be more help, have a nice day." Well, that was weird, I guess girls are checking his tags often, I giggle at how ridiculous that is.

When I get to my office, coffee in hand, I see a small bag. Inside is a handful of airheads and a new penguins' shirt with my brothers' number on it.

Fiona: Thanks for the goody bag I love it.
Luke: What goody bag?
Fiona: The airheads and shirt with your number on it?
Luke: Not from me, sorry sis
Fiona: LUCY!!!
Lucy: What?
Fiona: I just got a goody bag, airheads and a penguins' shirt
Lucy: That's nice of Luke but weird flex
Fiona: Luke didn't send it

Lucy: Oh Zane, He wanted to do something nice but didn't want to be a Justin and give you something with his number

Fiona: That was very thoughtful, thank you

Zane: They were giving us family and friends shirt today, but I didn't want to assume you wanted my number

Fiona: Thank you! Seriously I love it.

I get focused on my edits for the week. After a few hours the arena is quiet. I start dancing in my office to my "swiftly" playlist while I put together the content wall. After about 5 songs of dancing and singing, I hear clapping. I turn around so fast and find myself running smack into Zanes broad chest. "oh, my lord you scared me." "Sorry I was just coming to drop something off on my back to watch tapes." As I start to say "you got me enough al" he shows me a McDonald's coke "ok fine I will take one more gift today. You didn't have to do this you know." He smiles huge "I know I didn't, but I wanted to, well I got to go I just wanted to give you that." As he walks out a sophomore player, Marshall, almost runs right into him "watch it bro." I holler at Zane "Glad to see you kept some of your grumpiness, thank you again!"

This week flies by with lots of content going out with our game against big time rivals GU this weekend. I have team content, tons of senior content, we have the mascot out interacting around campus. We did a free t-shirt scavenger hunt based on videos we posted this week. It went viral and this game is sold out already. The concession stands have doubled their airhead inventory. We are all set to have a successful rivalry game.

It's now Saturday morning, game day. I wake up and take my time drinking my coffee. I start to drift into thought of running into Justin and what I'm going to wear today to help keep the peace. Lucy comes out and I talk to her about my stress and the negative thoughts going on and before she can talk me down my phone pings.

Zane: Stop with the negative thoughts' sunshine, I know you are in your head about him right now. Don't let him effect your life any more than he already has. Wear your brother's jersey because YOU want to or wear a penguins shirt with no number because YOU want to. DON'T choose based on keeping the peace with him.

My eyes start watering and I smile. "Okay well now you have to show me" Lucy says grabbing my phone. "I need to give this man a chance" I decide out loud. Lucy jumps up "fuck yeah about damn time. This was seriously the sweetest thing he could of done. He knows you, he knew you would be in your head today." I grab my phone rushing to my room to get ready.

Fiona: Thank you, lets talk after the game there's something I want to give you! Good luck, crush them today, for me!

Zane: You got it sunshine, see you!

I spend the next hour doing my makeup and hair, a heavier makeup but nothing crazy, then my hair in big curls down my back with small braids around the crown to keep it out of my face. I decide on black leggings that fit perfect and a penguins' shirt that fitted. Of course, I complete the outfit with yellow vans and airheads. I wanted to tell Luke about Zane and I, but too late now.

I rush over to the stadium to prepare for entrance photos. Everyone comes in looking nice in their suits, but one suit catches my eye. Blue suit with yellow tie and the man wearing it, he's hot. Zane walks up giving us a wink and tossing me an airhead. I don't have time to talk to him now, but I can feel the air between us charged with sparks.

I head to the front row seats where Celisa and Lucy are. The boys skate out every Tampa U fan including us holding up airheads for Zane. My eyes are glues to #27 as he stops at the boards and tosses me another airhead and winking. Luke skates by and we all give him the 'I love you' sign. "Here comes GU, are you ready?" Celisa questions concerned. "I'm ready" I state completely not ready. I lock eyes with Zane right as Justin skates up pulls on the shoulder of his jersey in front of us almost to taunt me for not wearing daring wear another jersey that's not his. Which wasn't why I didn't wear a jersey, it was out of respect of not talking to Luke yet.

Zane

Fiona wants to talk after the game. I don't know what she has to give me but I'm excited. I'm trying to keep my head focused on the game. It's important neither Luke nor I let Justin get to us. We can't afford to be put in the penalty box. Skating past Fi and her friends, I drop her an Airhead and shoot her a wink. She looks gorgeous in her Penguins shirt and tight leggings. All I want is to claim her as mine in front of this entire arena but we aren't there yet.

I catch her eye right as her douchebag ex skates by and I can see him raising his jersey sleeve to her.

Luke skates up to me. "I'm going to kill him, I swear to God. Can't he just leave her alone?"

I knock his helmet lightly. "Just try to keep your cool, man. I know he's the world's biggest asshole." We continue warmups and then line up for the national anthem.

As we are skating to line up, I overhear, "Look at her! She is so hung up on me, she didn't even put on her own brother's jersey and he plays for the team she works for. I got her bitch ass wrapped around my little finger."

I stop by Luke and Stuntz. "Listen this isn't the best game to do this, but I just overheard Justin talking mad shit about Fi, and I can't let it go. I'm going to lay him out over and over every chance I get. I'm sorry, I know we need the win."

Luke grabs my helmet. "I don't know what's going on with you two but don't hurt her dude. Let's talk after the game."

Stuntz taps us both on the helmet. "Do what you need to do, but don't cost us the game." As he skates off he says, "Make him pay. Fiona doesn't deserve his harassment!"

Its fucking on! The first period flies by with Luke cross checking Justin and cussing him out right at the end. Luke is just swinging punch after punch on Justin. We barely pulled them apart but Justin just smiled. Maybe I shouldn't have told Luke exactly what he said right as the whistle blew, but he kept asking. Justin goes out of his way to skate past Fiona at the end of the first period doing the jersey lift again.

"Fuck this - I will be right back," I tell Stuntz and skate to Fiona. Justin is still close enough to see us. I bang on the boards and yell for her to meet me at the press door by the locker room.

I hear her friends yell, "GO GIRL!"

Thankfully they seem to be on my side. I quickly skate to the door as Luke catches my eye and nods. I know that's his way of approving of me going to Fi, and letting me know we will talk later.

I stop at my bag in the locker room then head to the press room.

"Hey Zane what's wrong?" I hear Fiona almost out of breath.

I shove my jersey at her. "Listen I want you, I always have. I just told your brother I want to be with you. I NEED you in my number, but I won't force you. Take this and decide if you want me or not. I'm about to kill Justin out there! All I can think of is he hurt my sunshine. I got to go; I know you want to talk after the game, so I will see you then." With that I run back to the rink doors.

As the second period begins, dumbass tempts me again. "Looks like whatever secret meeting you guys had scared her off. She doesn't want you man, she's always been mine."

I grind my mouthpiece so hard I'm afraid it's going to break. I look subtly to the side; he's right, she's not there. Did I scare her off? Fuck I didn't want to do that but my emotions got the best of me. I shake my head, trying to focus. I need to beat this fucker then I will deal with Fiona.

So far, it's a shutout, even with Luke getting put in the penalty box again for slamming Justin into the boards. We have two goals so far. I'm happy with that as long as we keep them from scoring. The energy in the arena is another level tonight! I focus on not looking over to where Fiona was sitting. I can't afford to lose focus. With thirty seconds left we score again, with an assist from yours truly.

As the buzzer goes off, I hear banging on the boards behind me.

I turn around and it's like a dream. There's my sunshine, standing on her seat with my jersey on and my number painted on each cheek. I skate over, taking my glove off and putting my hand on the glass.

She reaches up and I barely hear her say, "You are worth every risk; I couldn't imagine myself in another number! Now go kick some ass!"

NEED YOUR NUMBER

With that I skate to my team and Luke taps me on the back. "I'm happy for you man, you will be good for her. Now let's go shut this game out!"

As we skate back out Justin's teammate yells, "J, isn't that your bitch in the stands now wearing #27 and has his number on her cheek?"

Justin looks over. "What the fuck, that little whore! No worries - once I see her in person, I will fuck her face down until that number rubs off."

With that, my gloves are off and I'm slamming him into the boards, beating his ass. Luke is there too. He heard it just like I did. Stuntz and Marshall finally pull me off and I get a five minute major penalty, but it's worth the look on Justin's stupid ass face.

"Stay away from my girl, you stupid fuck," I say as I skate to the penalty box, making eye contact with Fi and nodding to let her know I'm okay.

I come out with eight minutes left in the final period. We score two more goals, one being another assist from me. We are on fire tonight - the crowd, the rivalry, everyone hating Justin... it was just the perfect recipe for a shutout! We beat our rivals in a shutout, we have never beat GU in a game where they didn't even score once! The crowd is going crazy! I search the crowd for my sunshine. She's on her seat waving and points towards her office. Probably letting me know she's going to upload any content she got tonight while we shower and have our talk with Coach.

About an hour later I text Fi letting her know to just meet me at the rink doors where the team comes in. When I step out I didn't expect to see Douchebag Magee trying to talk to her. I linger back though, knowing she can hold her own. I don't want to take the power from her. I read somewhere that victims of emotional abuse need their next partner to not take their power from them.

I can hear him raising his voice but she is calm and direct with him. I'm about to step in when she turns around and sees me. I wasn't sure if I should kiss her with Justin being there. I didn't want our first kiss to be uncomfortable. But before I can decide what to do, she runs and launches herself at me. With her legs around my waist, she looks at me with those perfect kissable lips and I forget who's around.

The kiss feels like it lasts forever yet it's not long enough. The sparks are flying while I kiss her like she was giving me the oxygen I needed to stay alive. Her lips are soft and she lets out the smallest moan when I lightly bite her lip. When we finally break our kiss, she buries her head into my shoulder, and I carry her to my car. I set her down, opening the door for her to get inside. As we drive off I see Justin standing in the same spot, angry. I was so distracted I didn't even look for him as I walked to the car.

"So, what did you want to give me tonight?" I ask Fi. I hold my hand on her thigh as we drive.

She smiles shyly. "Well, I was going to meet you wearing the team shirt with your name on it, then kiss you - but I think this worked out better."

I give her thigh a small squeeze. "So, sunshine, where are we headed?"

Without making eye contact she just says, "Your place?"

My breath catches in my throat as I try and not get turned on more than I already am, seeing her in my jersey.

It's her first time at my apartment. It's nothing special, but it's clean and decorated, thanks to Penny. When we go inside and sit on the couch. I pull her into my lap so she's straddling me. "Sunshine, what changed your mind? Was it seeing Justin? I won't be mad, I just want to know where your head's at."

I give her a small smile.

"No Z, I texted you to meet before the game even started, remember?'

I take a second and remember that's right, because I got the text before we did our walk in photos.

"I decided to take a chance on us when I realized you know me better than most people in my life. You knew I would be panicking about Justin and the game. You knew just what to say to talk me away from an emotional breakdown. You let me have my moment with Justin. You gave me the chance to be strong without you. That's why I chose you, because I would want to walk side by side through life together supporting each other in the grand moments and picking each other up in the lowest moments. I want you, Z. Not because of anyone else; because of who you are."

I am so overwhelmed with her answer, I just stare. She giggles and leans in. "Now's the part where you kiss me and make me forget I was ever anyone else's."

My heart skips a beat as I lift us both off the couch and carry us to my room. I kick the door closed, pinning her to the wall while she's wrapped around me. I start kissing her neck. She moans, grinding herself against me .

"I have been dreaming about this, Z."

I keep her pinned while I move to the other side of her neck trailing kisses down. "Oh yeah, sunshine? Did you touch yourself while you thought of me? That morning we surfed. Did you touch yourself to thoughts of us?"

I pull back, looking into her green eyes.

"Yes. I touched myself in the hotel that morning and many times in my room. Thoughts of you invaded my mind I had to take care of myself. I would ask if you think of me when you jerk off, but I heard you in the shower, so I know you do," she says with a seductive smile as she grinds against me.

I toss her on the bed and take off my shirt. "Be a good girl Fi, and take off my jersey. I want to fuck you in it, but right now I want the full view of your banging body."

As she makes quick work of the jersey and bra, I am in the middle of unbuttoning my pants when I see her perfect tits. I have gotten off to thoughts of these erect nipples and palm sized tits more times than I care to mention. Fiona clears her throat and I focus back on stripping down. In just my boxers I lean down and start kissing her neck again, while I take one of her tits in my hand, rolling her nipple between my fingers. She moans and I can feel myself getting even harder, which I didn't know was possible.

Fiona

The minute he called me a good girl, I swear I became wetter than a slip and slide. This man is going to be the death of me. He is squeezing my tits just enough as he rolls my nipples between his fingers. As he drops his mouth and sucks on my nipple, I gasp.

I'm grinding into him moaning, "Please Zane, more I need more, please."

I'm about to orgasm just from having my tits played with, which is insane, considering I always faked it with Justin. As he alternates to my other tit, he slides his hand between my legs and growls into my ear, "Go ahead baby, take what you need. Grind away on my hand while I play with those gorgeous tits."

He takes my nipple back into his mouth and I climax against his hand with my leggings still on. He leans up.

"Such a good girl Fiona. Let's go ahead and see what you have going on under these leggings."

I slide my leggings off and as I pull my navy blue lace thong down my legs, Zane stares at me like he hasn't eaten in months and I'm a free buffet.

"Spread those legs for me baby."

I spread them as he strokes himself through his boxers.

"Look at that sweet wet pussy, already dripping for me," he says, and with that he drops to his knees and drags me to the edge of the bed.

"Tell me if I need to stop," is the last thing he says as he hooks my legs over his shoulders and begins to kiss my thighs.

"You.. uhh.. You don't have to do that. No one has ever done that before. It's ok," I stammer.

He pauses his kisses. "You mean someone skipped out on the most delicious part of you? I won't be skipping this, baby girl. Lay back and relax. Let me take care of you the way you deserve."

I can feel him drag his stubble between my legs. Suddenly his tongue is between my lips and he's licking me from top to bottom. I have never felt so aroused and stimulated. He uses his hands to keep my thighs spread and my pussy open for himself. As I start to get used to the sensation of him licking up and down, he sucks onto my clit. I gasp and start to sit up, grabbing his hair. He reaches up with one hand, easing me back onto the bed.

"I'm going to cum, Z, it's too much!" I can feel him chuckle as he continues to suck on my clit and slowly slips one finger inside.

"Your pussy is nice and tight for me. It's wet enough I could probably slide my thick cock right in without issue."

He goes back to sucking and fingering me, and as soon as he adds a second finger I explode. I didn't even know you really could orgasm twice, especially without actual sex.

I try and catch my breath then look up into his amber eyes.

"Zane, I want to pleasure you too. Let me suck your cock." As I say it, I reach out and start stroking through his boxers.

Breathless, he says, "Okay" and he drops his boxers.

I get on the floor and down on my knees and start stroking him with my hands, unsure how this is even going to fit in my mouth or pussy. I can't wrap my hand around it.

Zane's hand fists in my hair. "Be a good girl and put it in your mouth, sunshine."

As I suck, I also use my hand at the base since he's so big. He tightens his grip on my hair, fucking my throat faster and faster. I look up at him with tears in my eyes and moan as I keep taking more and more.

"Fuck sunshine, I'm about to cum," he says, slowing up.

I grip his ass cheeks with both hands, pulling him to me as I continue to suck his big thick cock. He tries to pull out of my mouth as he grunts with orgasm with my name on his lips. But I keep myself locked on him and continue to suck and swallow until I know I got every last drop.

He helps me up and kisses me thoroughly. I feel like I am floating. He walks me back to bed and places his palm against my clit and begins to rub. As he rubs, he slides two fingers inside.

"Yes baby, rub against me while I finger this pretty pussy."

Right as I'm about to climax again he stops.

"Z, please, I'm so close."

Instead of continuing, he lays me back then stands back up, reaching for his pants. He pulls out a condom, ripping it open and rolling it on.

He climbs on the bed; my heart starts pounding out of my chest.

"Shhh baby girl, I can hear your thoughts running a mile a minute. Relax that pretty little mind."

He lines up with my opening, easing in just the tip.

"Be a good girl and relax for me. I know it's big but this tight pussy was made for my cock."

He edges in little by little, talking to me and lightly playing with my nipples and clit as he goes. Finally I can feel his hard body against me so I know he must be fully in.

"Sunshine you are so tight, fuck, it's so perfect. I feel like I'm about to cum."

I start to move.

"No! Wait, give me a second or this is going to be a super fast round of sex."

I giggle and start kissing his chest until finally he starts to rock in and out. I moan as he pulls all the way out and then slams back in.

"I think you are rearranging my insides, your cock is so big!"

He chuckles, making me tighten around him. Once he can tell I'm comfortable with his size, he throws one of my legs over his shoulder and begins to fuck me harder.

"Please, Z, please" I beg, needing to cum again.

"Not yet, sunshine. I will tell you when you can cum." He drives into me with his thumb rubbing my clit at that exact moment.

My eyes are starting to roll back in my head right as Z says, "Okay baby you can cum."

I explode.

We orgasm together and I can feel my pussy clenching his cock repeatedly. As we both try and catch our breath he goes and takes care of the condom. He comes back with a warm washcloth and starts to clean me up. He takes his time, with slow gentle swipes, making sure he got all the sticky wetness. Then he presses a small kiss to my forehead and goes to his dresser. He gets himself a pair of boxers and brings me a hockey shirt and a pair of boxers to wear.

"There's a spare toothbrush, a brush, and some makeup remover, from Penny, on the counter. Whenever you are ready you can go get ready for bed. I will be right here waiting to cuddle you."

He really does think of everything. I give him a sweet kiss on his swollen pink lips and head to the bathroom. I wash off my makeup and brush my hair and put it in a braid. While I brush my teeth, I take a second to really take in the past few hours. So much has happened and I don't regret any of it. I take a minute to text the girls, letting them know where I am so they don't worry. I slip on the clothes Zane gave me and head back to the bedroom.

I come out to Zane in bed scrolling on his phone, and noticed he put a cup of ice water and a charger on my side of the bed. For someone who can be so grumpy he really has the sweetest heart. It's like he can read my mind.

He looks up and says, "It's been a long eventful day for us both. Why don't we get some rest and we can talk over breakfast before I take you home to gossip with the girls."

I laugh, knowing that's exactly what's going to happen when I get home. "Ok goodnight, Z."

He lays down next to me. "Goodnight sunshine, get some sleep."

At some point I wake Zane up by grinding against him.

"Round two?" he chuckles as he reaches around and slides my shirt up to play with my tits.

I keep grinding against him and I take his hand from my tit and guide it down. It's when his breath catches that I realize he didn't know I had slid the boxers off already. I am ready for him while he starts playing with my clit, I reach behind me and touch his balls while I continue pressing my ass against his forming erection.

It's my turn for dirty talk. "Come on babe, give me that thick cock. My pussy is wet and ready."

It must work because I can feel him get super hard against me. I get ballsy and guide his cock between my lips, letting his cock feel how wet I am. When I start rubbing against him I realize his tip is bumping my clit with each pass. It doesn't take long before I reach back and grab Z by the hair, pulling his head closer to mine and look him in the face while I cum from just his cock rubbing me.

"Fuck me, you are so sexy." He leans back and I can hear the drawer open and close. Then I hear the distinct sound of foil ripping. He reaches between us, rolling the condom on to his cock. Once he's fully sheathed I reach down, line him up, and rock hard and fast, taking almost all of him in me at once.

Zane slowly flips me on to my stomach, pulling me up by the hips so I'm resting on my elbows with my ass up. He begins railing me from behind. He's going hard and deep.

He reaches down and undoes my braid quickly. I don't understand why until he wraps my hair up again. He pulls my head back by my hair, and he leans forward.

"This pussy is mine, and only mine, do you understand me?"

I am about to orgasm as I yell out, "Yes this pussy is yours and only yours. Please let me cum, I'm ready."

With that he tells me to start rubbing my clit and as I'm about to climax he says, "Be a good girl and cum for me"

I orgasm so hard I almost black out. Zane kisses me sweetly all down my back and arm as he pulls out. I'm too tired to move.

He comes back with a washcloth and uses it to clean me up again. But he also starts brushing my hair and throws it up in a quick braid.

Giving me a sweet goodnight kiss, he whispers, "I might fuck you hard and rough, but you are my sunshine and I will always take care of you. "Penny taught me to braid so if you ever want me to braid your hair, just ask babe."

That's the last thing I hear before I pass out in his arms after our midnight quickie.

I wake up slowly. I am spread out across Zane's chest. My leg is across his lap with his hand holding me in place. He must be waking up too because his thumb is starting to rub small circles on my thigh. As he mumbles in his sleep he leans down and kisses my forehead.

"Good morning, beautiful. How did you sleep?", he asks quietly.

I smiled up at him. "I slept well. I was exhausted! How did you sleep?"

He continues rubbing my thigh. "I slept great! Waking up next to you was even better though."

Before I can respond he pulls me fully on top of him and tries to kiss me.

I lean back. "Zane! I have morning breath."

He pulls me to him. "I don't care, I want to enjoy waking up with you in my bed."

He begins with sweet kisses working up to more as he nips at my bottom lip to get me to let his tongue in. I feel his cock hardening below me and I start to grind. With one hand behind my head Zane uses his other hand to palm my ass as I rub myself on him. As I moan with pleasure I reach and pull my shirt off and throw it next to me on the floor. Z stares at me like he's never seen me naked before. I love the way his eyes roam my body as he smiles like he has won the lottery.

I move to get off him and he holds me in place.

"Where do you think you are going?"

I look down at him.

"Well, to do what I have planned we both need to lose our bottoms," I say with a wink.

We both strip down to nothing. I reach into his drawer and grab a condom. I take his cock into my mouth a few times before I slip the condom on him. I climb right on top, grinding myself against his hard length, his tip hitting my clit. I moan out in pleasure.

I lift myself up and guide him to my opening. I'm so wet that he slips in easily for the first few inches. I start bouncing to help ease the rest of him in. Finally I feel myself sitting flush on him, so I know he's in completely. I feel so full I don't think I could take another inch. I start bouncing myself up and down while Z palms my ass, staring into my eyes.

"I love watching those sexy tits bounce around while you ride my cock, sunshine."

His confession makes me blush. I can feel us both getting closer to climax. Zane grabs my hips and begins thrusting harder and faster.

"Now baby, cum with me," he growls and with that we both collapse in post-sex bliss.

"I need to get back to the apartment," I say as I get up and walk to the bathroom.

I put on last night's leggings and the shirt I wore to bed. I brush my teeth and head back into the bedroom.

"I want you to stay but I know you need to see your friends and I should probably study," Zane says.

I give him a kiss and smile.

"Kissing me doesn't make me want to take you home, Fi. Can I at least take you out on a date Tuesday?", he asks.

He gets dressed while he waits for my answer.

"Of course we can go on a date Tuesday!"

With that confirmation he takes me home and walks me to my door, leaving me after a nice make out session in front of the door while he grabs my ass. So glad we didn't have neighbors outside.

Inside the door Lucy and Celisa are waiting with their coffee cups.

"Okay spill it, all of it! Did you finally bang? What about Justin? Are you guys dating?" Leave it to Lucy to bombard me the moment the door is shut.

I tell them about running into Justin outside the arena and how I told him to fuck off. I told them about the first kiss, jumping into Zane's arms and just getting drunk on his taste as we made out and he carried us to the car.

Stopping to make my own cup of coffee, I say, "Then we got to his apartment."

I bite my lip, blushing. "Are you sure you guys want all the details?"

They both almost yell, "YES!"

I tell them about the couch conversation about Justin. "Then I told him, 'Now's the part where you kiss me and make me forget I was ever someone else's.'"

Lucy starts to fan herself. "Ok girl, that has to be one of the hottest things you have ever said."

I give them all the details of the night, stopping to answer their questions. I tell them about all the orgasms, the oral, the way being called a good girl almost had me orgasming from the words. I tell them how he cleaned me up and braided my hair for me. I even tell them how I initiated the hottest sex in the cowgirl position this morning.

When all the details are out, I lean back and finish my coffee. "I have never been more jealous of someone else's sex life as I am right now! Girl you better never let this one go!" Lucy exclaims before asking, "So are you guys official?"

Celisa looks away and I can tell she's still bothered by this situation.

"No, but we are going on a date Tuesday and I'm sure we will be having that conversation soon," I contemplate.

"I bet your relationship launch on Insta will be KILLER," Celisa says, trying to be supportive.

Zane

I have been so busy since the game Saturday, I haven't gotten to see Fiona. Tonight's our date. I'm taking her to Sparkman Wharf, a container park on the water. They have tons of food and dessert options along with live music. It seems like the kind of place Fiona would enjoy, much more than a fancy restaurant.

Fiona texted me earlier saying she was running late to work due to a hair straightener malfunction. I'm not sure what that means. I swing by Roasters Coffee Shop and grab her favorite coffee.

When I get to her office, I can hear her shuffling around paperwork of some sort.

"Knock, knock. Coffee delivery," I say as I walk in and hand her the drink.

"You are a lifesaver! I was in a rush; I look a mess and I forgot to charge my laptop."

I scan over her outfit. Jeans with a cute Penguins shirt and her yellow Converse. Her hair is up in a bun.

"You look great babe; I have a few minutes. Do you want to talk about what is causing you to be so stressed?" I grab her hand, giving it a small kiss.

"Honestly?" She looks up, blushing. I gave her a reassuring smile and nod for her to continue.

"I'm not sure where we stand; I know we have both been busy the past two days. But I have just been letting my mind go crazy with ideas that you aren't that busy and you were out with other people because we never talked about exclusivity."

I tried to stifle my chuckle. "Babe, I know you have some issues with trusting but I wasn't partying before we got together so I'm definitely not partying now. Plus, after giving you my jersey to wear in front of everyone I thought you knew - you're the only girl for me. You are my girlfriend, my girl. My everything."

With that I can see her visibly relax as she gives me her classic jumping hug. It's becoming our thing.

I nuzzle my head into her neck and tell her, "Post us online, tell your family, shout it from the rooftops... do whatever you want to do, I'm all yours! I have to go. I will see you for our date."

I set her down and give her a kiss. As I walk away she slips something in my pocket. When I'm in the hall I look and see that it's an Airhead with my number written on it with a heart around it.

As I walk downstairs, I check my phone and decide to help her see it's just her. I think they call it a soft launch or something. Penny told me about it. It's where you post something about your significant other on social media/Insta, but you don't post who they are. I know the perfect post to make. I shoot a picture while I'm stepping onto the ice of me holding up an airhead towards Fionas office.

Zane: Check Instagram, sunshine

Fiona: Oh my, did you soft launch us? I love it!

Zane: See you tonight!

Before I can put my phone away, I get a text from Penny.

Penny: Why is there a photo of you holding an Airhead with your number inside a heart On your instagram? That looks like you are holding up while you are on the ice.

Zane: You are the one who taught me about soft launching, asshole. I'm trying to make my girlfriend comfortable knowing she's the only one on my mind. You know how puck bunnies can be.

Penny: Clever, brother, hope I get to see Fiona soon!

Zane: I knew you saw the jersey switch at the game. I was waiting for your text.

Penny: Well, brother, you did a good job. Is that Fiona's office in the picture? If so, you KILLED the soft launch.

Zane: It is. Talk soon! I must get to practice.

In the middle of practice Luke skates over. "Let's shoot some pucks after practice so we can talk before this date you have tonight."

I give him a nod right as Coach yells my name. I am still in trouble for the five minute major penalty I got on Saturday, even though I explained how justified it was. Coach likes to keep our penalties low though, so he's still punishing me - just less intensely as he usually would.

NEED YOUR NUMBER

Practice seems to drag as I think about Fiona and our date tonight. I just want her to be comfortable and happy. I look up at her office periodically knowing I can't see in but I hope in those moments she's looking down at the ice. I also spend a little bit of practice thinking about my upcoming exams and what I need to work on to prepare. Our next two games are pretty cake teams. As long as we stay focused, they should be easy wins. Then we move to a stretch of three away games. Being away from my girl is going to suck.

This season is it for me. We need to win that championship to put Luke and me in a good place for the draft. With any luck we will both get drafted to the same place. I also hope it's close to Tampa since this is where my girl is. I wonder if she would be willing to move with me and work for whatever team I go to. I won't ask that of her though. I know how badly she wants to work for the Thunder. We will make the distance work until I can get traded back down here if I don't make it during the draft. My thoughts are stuck on what is going to happen with the draft when Coach blows his whistle to tell us practice is over. I go to the locker room to take my gear off before I go skate with Luke.

My Insta is blowing up with notifications and tags asking who the mystery girl is, how long we have been dating... some puck bunnies even comment they don't mind sharing. I almost throw up reading that. I'm about to respond when I see a certain ray of sunshine uploaded a new post. I'm so glad I turned on notifications for her.

It's a picture of her holding up her coffee cup towards her windows looking over the rink while we are practicing. The caption says, "Thanks babe (with a yellow heart emoji)".

I quickly like it then head out to meet Luke.

I'm smiling like an idiot by the time I hit the ice. Luke has his phone in his hand when he looks up at me. "The two of you make me sick with your posts."

I can't help but laugh. Luke joins me in laughter and the tension seems to melt away. He stops in front of me and I can just feel the brother lecture coming. I have given it to guys for Penny before.

"You are my best friend, so I know you deserve someone good. I want that for you. But she's my sister, she has to be my concern. I hope that you guys can be happy together and help each other dominate the hockey world.

I know that you will protect her, but I hope you also protect yourself. She's been through shit with Justin, and I don't want to see her heartbroken again. I can't handle seeing the shell of a person she becomes with heartbreak. But I also don't want her issues with trust - and with athletes especially - break you. I don't want her to break your spirit, like your ex did. You are both grown adults so I support you both, but please be careful with her heart."

"I will do my best to keep her happy and spirit intact. I love you, brother." I pull him into a bro hug. A few taps on the back later we separate.

"Okay let's hit some pucks. We have a championship to win this year!" And like nothing ever happened, we are back to joking and skating while performing different stick drills. We practice for about an hour before I excuse myself to go study and get ready for our date.

I get home, shower, and make myself a snack. I am really grateful to get an apartment so close to the rink and campus as a student. A lot of the players live in the athlete dorms but I decided on the apartment so I could have my own space.

I get my books out and start to study. My classes are pretty simple this semester, but I still want to be sure I am doing well in them.

About an hour into my study session my mom calls. "Hey bug, how are you? Are you eating well? How are your grades?"

I roll my eyes, knowing where she's going with this, but I decide to play along. "I'm good, nothing new over here. I'm staying fed and my grades are good. It's an easy semester for me." I close my book.

"Oh nothing new? I was just on Instagram and saw a pos,t then when I called your sister, she said I have to ask you. So son, tell me about her."

I chuckle, knowing her call wasn't a plain check-in call. I proceed to tell my mom all about Fiona. The beach cleanup, surfing, parts of the jersey issue, etc.

"Well, I love her TikToks of you, and taking her surfing means she is special to you. I can't wait to meet her. Just be careful. Holly really hurt you and I don't want to see that happen again!"

I grimace at the sound of my ex's name. "When are you guys coming to Tampa?" We continue our conversation for another thirty minutes discussing their travels. I love that they could retire and travel together. They deserve it.

After we hang up it's time for me to start getting ready anyways. I organize my books and get my kitchen cleaned up. Just in case Fiona and I come back here, I want to be sure the apartment is clean.

I go to my closet to find something to wear. I decide on off-white shorts with a light blue button up with the sleeves rolled. I style my hair gelled back slightly so it's still shaggy but out of my face. I don't shave, so I have some stubble. I put on my white Vans and get ready to pick up Fiona.

I drive to her apartment, which is also just off campus and not far from me. While I drive, I decide to stop quickly at the flower van that's set up a few blocks away in a trendy area of Tampa called Hyde Park. I make her a bouquet of daisies and baby's breath. Simple but beautiful, just like my girl. I went back and forth about whether I should do flowers or not, but just because her jackass ex sent her threatening flowers doesn't mean she doesn't deserve "just because you are beautiful" flowers.

Getting to Fiona's, my heart pounds while I knock on her door. Lucy answers.

"Come in, she will be out in a second. Nice flowers! Also loved your post earlier." She winks and walks over to the kitchen bar. We have a few minutes of small talk but nothing awkward because Lucy and I have always gotten along. We used to see each other all the time with Luke before her nursing school schedule took over her life. They say the hockey schedule is hard, but nursing students have it rough. We both look up when we hear footsteps down the hall.

"You look amazing, sunshine, like everyone is going to be jealous I get to take you out," I say, pulling her into a kiss.

Her hair is straight and hanging down her back, hitting just below where her bra would be, with minimal simple makeup. She's wearing a white sundress with a cut out in the back to make it look like there's a bow. Finishing her outfit is her yellow Converse, and I absolutely love it. Unlike other girls, she wears what she loves, which gives her this confidence that's almost empowering.

"So, lovebirds, where are you headed?" Lucy asks, sipping on her wine.

"I'm taking her to Sparkman Wharf. I figured the food truck style dinner and dessert, and the live music would be a simple and fun, no-pressure kind of night out we both need."

Fiona smiles. "I love that idea. This is going to be super fun; I have been wanting to go there since I moved back!"

Fiona runs to grab her purse when Lucy stares me down. "I know Luke did this already but you have both been hurt. Be careful, but not too careful. I hope you are each other's soulmates cause I couldn't imagine anyone better for either of you."

I nod at her right as Fi walks out.

Fiona

Zane showed up with flowers and it was precious. He gets extra first date points for taking me somewhere I really want to go. I'm not really a fancy restaurant kind of girl. I really just wanted to do a chill night and that's exactly what I'm getting. I am so excited to try a few of these different places they have here. Zane has his hand on my thigh the entire drive. I snap a picture of it, posting it on my story with just a kiss emoji.

I tuck my phone away and start singing to the lyrics from my playlist. Once we get to Sparkman Wharf, I immediately take a picture of each of us in front of the Tampa sign. I also get someone to take one of us together. This place is what social media creator dreams are made of. There are lots of places to take pictures and create content. I am in awe as we walk around taking tons of pictures and scoping out the food options so we can circle back. I don't know the last time I had this much fun just hanging out with someone.

The food was amazing and for dessert we got these cute little popsicles! We ate at the tables over by the stage and listened to the band play. My face hurts from smiling so much. We talk about our families, college and the struggles of senior year; we discuss hockey, and plans for the rest of the week.

Everything with him feels so natural; there's no awkward tension. I don't feel like I have to put on a fake face to keep him happy. I struggled with that with Justin. He really made being happy hard. I couldn't pick the place we ate or suggest we take a million photos. I definitely wouldn't be wearing my Converse because it would turn into him screaming at me. I don't know why it took me so long to leave but thank God I did, because now I'm in Tampa with my family and I have Zane by my side.

He finishes his popsicle then asks me to dance.

"I'm not a good dancer. I will probably step on your toes" I say. As he grabs my hand, he pulls me into him and begins to sway. This moment is one of those they say will 'alter your brain chemistry'. It's like we are alone dancing out here with no one watching. We dance for multiple songs before we finally separate.

We get back in the Jeep and Zane says to me, "I had a great night Fiona. Thank you for coming."

I squeeze his hand. "This is the best first date I have ever been on. Honestly, it is the best date I have ever been on in general."

We keep holding hands. "I'm sorry I can't come over; I have so much I need to get done tonight. Maybe tomorrow after we go to the bar with Luke I can come over?" I give him a reassuring smile.

"Of course sunshine, I understand. We get busy; it's totally cool. I look forward to seeing you tomorrow at the bar though."

Zane walks me to the door again, and again we have a PG13 make out session out front. The chemistry between us is orgasmic. The smallest of kisses can almost get me off.

"Good night, beautiful. I will text you; be sure to check Insta later. I have the perfect picture to post." With a wink he walks back to his Jeep.

I go inside and pour myself a glass of wine. Sitting at my desk, I get some last minute edits done for my meeting in the morning.

Lucy pops her head in. "Have you been on Insta?"

I grab my phone. "No should I have?"

She jumps on to my bed. "Check it. I will wait!"

Opening the app, I see Zane's post first thing and I just stare at the screen. It's the perfect picture. I am obviously laughing as the sun sets but I'm holding my wine glass up at the perfect angle that my face is blocked. The caption reads, "Sunsets are beautiful but this view - it's breathtaking (sun emoji)".

I notice I have tears. "It's amazing, he's amazing. No one has ever said such sweet things to me before."

Lucy hugs me and drops a kiss on my head. "Sis, you deserve every single moment of his love and attention. Stop doubting yourself."

I like the post and spend the next hour smiling like a fool as I work on revising the content we filmed this week.

I go to bed late because I am up editing the last of the away game prep. The guys worked really hard to do some TikTok dances, lip syncing to funny viral sounds, and of course our usual "hot hockey guy" content. The game scheduled for this week is only 2 hours away, so the team expects a decent number of fans to come along. I will be going to this one but the two games after I won't be attending due to them being out of state. I decided not to travel out of state unless it's playoffs or the championship. I don't feel like I need to be at all the away games and I am not a huge fan of planes. I get ready for bed to prepare for this meeting with Marissa to go over my progress.

I woke up late, so I have to skip a coffee run and head straight to the meeting, so I don't see any of the players because they aren't off the ice yet. I go over our content plans, showing all of our videos and the roll out time for each of them. Marissa is impressed and the athletic director, who decided to sit in today, said she was incredibly impressed as well.

"Would you be willing to teach courses for the other social media interns? You would be reimbursed," the athletic director says.

I am shocked. "Yeah of course! I'm pretty busy but maybe each sport can shadow me here for a week and watch from planning to rollout. Then I can spend a day during that week at their sport to help guide them."

The athletic director stands, smiling, and reaches to shake my hand. "Sounds good. I will email you to work out the specifics. I am very impressed with what you have done so far with the hockey team. If you ever need a job, our athletics press department will have a place for you."

I shake her hand. "Thank you so much!"

Marissa and I discuss a few things and then she congratulates me on such a big recognition and the job offer if needed. I'm so lost in my thoughts as I walk to my office, I don't even notice the McDonald's Coke or Lucy holding it.

"Did the meeting go bad? I thought your content looked amazing!," she says looking concerned.

I shake my head. "Actually, they offered me a full time job after my internship and asked me to train the other sports for a raise in the next few months!"

"That's amazing Fi; congrats!" She hugs me and then walks in my office.

"Thank you, and thank you for the Coke! What's going on? What brings you to the rink? She gives me a small shrug

"No reason. I was just in the area and wanted to swing by and say hi. But I should probably head out. See you tonight!" She runs out the door.

How weird, I think. I look at the rink and see the team heading to the locker room. I know that means I might get a chance to see Z if he's able to step away before they start tapes. I start posting and begin the never-ending task of responding to comments and interacting with followers. After about 30 mins I hear knocking and see Z walk in.

"I heard your meeting was good! Marissa was raving about you impressing the athletic director." He wraps me in a hug.

"Thank you! She asked if I would be interested in being paid to train the other sports social media teams. I said yes, then she offered me a full time position here at the end of the year. I thanked her; I don't want to completely disregard the offer in case I don't get hired by the Thunder."

His lips take mine softly then slowly gets rougher as he grabs a handful of my ass, making me moan.

"I am so proud of you babe! You are going to do great things and the Thunder would be stupid not to take you."

He holds me against him and kisses my forehead softly. "I have to get back to tapes. I will see you tonight; I just wanted to congratulate you!"

My day flies by. I think the meeting results really put me in an amazing mood. I am being extremely productive. I even go online and order Zane some tape for his new hockey stick he just got last week. I take a quick scroll through the socials for the Tampa Thunder. They definitely could use more content. I have so many ideas to help them control the NHL hockey social media scene. One day, I tell myself, I will get my shot!

Heading home to get ready for the bar, I start to overthink. What do I wear for my first official group outing with my boyfriend that I haven't even posted online? I look at multiple outfits before deciding. I pick a forest green romper that shows off my legs and looks great against my skin. I keep my makeup simple, allowing my eyes to be the focus on my face. I wear my hair in loose curls that I have pulled back with a small clip. I decide on a cute pair of white strappy sandals to keep the outfit looking cohesive.

I don't see Zane when I get to the bar, but I do see Luke. I decide to head over and wait for everyone at the table.

"Hey, brother. How are you? How are your classes going?"

Luke pulls me into a side hug. "Classes are good. I'm keeping my grades up. How are you? I heard congratulations are in order!"

I smile. "Thank you, and I'm good. The team keeps me busy, but it's the best job ever. Things are good with Zane too, if that's what you want to ask next. Also, I know what you are thinking. I'm telling mom and dad next week when I see them."

He gives me a knowing smile and bumps my shoulder. "I'm glad you are happy sis. Like I told him, try not to hurt each other. You both have shitty ex's and have had your heads messed with. Just be each other's peace, not chaos. I will always pick you, but I do love him like a brother. Just be careful."

Tears well in my eyes. It's not often I have moments like this with Luke and I know he feels guilty not being in Georgia to protect me from Justin.

"I love you," I say. "I will do my best not to hurt him. He treats me really well, and I don't want to lose him." We hug again and get back to small talk, both of us wanting out of the touchy feely moment.

Once everyone arrives, we get our drinks and play a few rounds of darts. It's turning out to be a lot less stressful than I expected.

I head to the bathroom with the girls, girl code and all. We giggle about how Zane has repeatedly complimented my outfit but also said he misses my Converse. Lucy and Celisa know how special that is for me because Justin hated my Converse, so I stopped wearing them for a while. They gush about how Zane stares at me like I hung the moon. But all the good feelings end when we step out of the bathroom and look at our table.

When we come out we see five or six girls at our table. Luke seems to be eating it up. Zane seems to be ignoring them, but one particular blonde I have seen before keeps reaching out and touching him even though he keeps moving away. He looks up at me and gives me an apologetic smile. I'm not mad at him because he keeps trying to get away from her. We haven't discussed how we would be together outside of our close group of friends, but something just comes over me.

I walk over to Zane, throw my arms around his neck, and kiss him. This kiss is one that says *stay away - this man is mine*. I work my hands into his hair as his hands slide down to my butt, pulling me closer to him. We get lost in the kiss, forgetting where we are, until Celisa whistles and brings us back to reality.

"I am so sorry! I don't know what came over me," I tell Z with a sheepish smile.

He puts his arm around me at the table. "Don't ever apologize for publicly claiming me as yours. I love possessive Fi."

The rest of the night goes by without any issues. We have fun hanging out, joking around about their classes and the away game this weekend.

After another beer, Zane whispers in my ear, "Are you ready to leave babe? I want you all to myself before we get busy the rest of the week."

I look up and smile. "Yes, I am ready to get some alone time with my man."

We say our goodbyes to the group and head to his Jeep. I don't miss the glares and giggling coming from the girls who were with Zane earlier. But I'm the one leaving hand in hand with him so I'm not going to even react.

When we get to the Jeep, Zane opens my door then picks me up and sets me on the seat. I wrap my arms around his neck and he steps between my legs.

He kisses me. "That was," kiss on the neck, "the hottest", kiss on the other side of my neck, "thing," kiss on my collarbone, "to see you," kiss on the mouth, "possessive like that."

I wrap my legs around his waist and pull him to me. "Kiss me Z. Show me how much you liked it!"

Zane takes my mouth in his, pulling my bottom lip to give it little nips, which make me ache between my legs. He has his hand wrapped in my hair, tilting my head back just enough to give him better access to my mouth.

"We should probably head out before this turns into something illegal," he growls and as he steps back, I can tell how hard he is.

Feeling adventurous, I decide I'm about to surprise him with something I have never done before - car head. I think that's what I heard Celisa call it before.

When he gets in, I reach over to his pants before he has a chance to put his seatbelt on. "What are you doing Fi?" he asks me with a slight shake in his voice.

"Relax. I want to do something special for you, something I have never done for anyone else," I tell him as I work his zipper down. His cock is hard and throbbing when I wrap my hand around it and begin stroking.

As I lick my lips I whisper, "I always loved the idea of being in public, the thrill of knowing you could always get caught."

Before he can answer I have my mouth on him and begin sucking. I swirl my tongue around the tip, flicking it over the slit that's dripping precum.

Zane's moans give me the courage to start going faster and, being daring, I lightly scrape my teeth as I go down. He sucks in a deep breath, grabbing the back of my head.

"FUCK sunshine, I don't think I can last much longer."

That was all the encouragement I needed to take him all the way back. I start to gag, and my eyes begin to water.

"I'm about to cum, baby," he murmurs.

I keep sucking and working him with my hand. He loudly moans my name as I stare up at him with my eyes glossy and I swallow every drop. I give the tip a little extra love as I pull back from him smiling and wiping my face with my hand.

"Keep that up babe and I'm never letting you go," he winks, and we head to his house with smiles of content happiness on our faces.

Zane

Driving home all I can think about is how lucky I am. I just got a blow job in my Jeep while we were in the parking lot of the bar. It was incredibly hot; all I want to do is throw her against the wall and fuck her senseless. Fi mentioned being into the chance of getting caught. It makes me wonder what other kinky things she might be into.

Once we get home, I want to find a way to bring it up. I give her thigh a little squeeze, trying not to focus on how soft her tanned skin feels. I can feel the muscles in her legs, imagining them clamped around my head as I eat her pussy. She's as turned on as I am; her face is flushed and she keeps squeezing her thighs together.

I decide to take a page from her book, sliding my hand up her leg, stopping at the edge of her romper. She has a slight shiver, but she doesn't tell me to stop. Slipping the romper to the side, my breath catches audibly in my throat because she has no panties on. She looks up at me with a smile and winks. The temperature in the Jeep feels like it went up ten degrees. Sliding my hand between her thighs, I start to run my finger between her soft pussy lips. She's soaked with arousal

"Is all this wetness for me, sunshine?", I ask her.

She spreads her legs and turns her body towards me, giving me better access

"Yes," she says breathlessly.

I slip two fingers in and she tightens as I pump my fingers in and out of her.

"Touch yourself. I want to see you make yourself cum," I tell her.

It's hard to concentrate on driving, but even when we pull up to the apartment, I don't take my fingers out of her.

Fiona reaches down and begins to circle her clit, making her grind on my hand as my fingers continue to slide in and out.

I slip in a third finger and whisper, "Be a good girl and cum for me baby."

That's all it took before she tosses her head back, her mouth forming an 'o' and she moans my name loudly through the Jeep.

I walk around the Jeep and open her door, allowing her a chance to adjust her romper before she gets out. I wrap my arm around her and guide her up to my place. I unlock the door and lead her inside, dropping a kiss on her forehead as she walks past me. I lock the door and then the tension instantly becomes too much.

I grab her hand, pulling her into me and smash my lips against hers, hungry for a taste of her. I pick her up as she drops her purse on my floor.

The apartment is dark but we don't even notice. I pin her against the wall and begin giving her kisses down her neck, stopping to nibble on her ear. She likes that because she bucks her body against mine.

"Fuck me now Z, please I need you," she groans into my ear.

With her legs still wrapped around me, I struggle but finally succeed to get my pants undone. I pull her romper to the side, holding her ass up with one hand and letting my hard cock slide between her folds. I know she loves it when the tip moves and hits her clit.

"Z, please, I'm on the pill and I'm clean, please, I need you in me now. I can't wait."

I waste no time lining myself up with her entrance. "I'm clean too, and I have never fucked anyone bare."

My mind is gone the minute I slide into her. The feeling of her warm tight wet pussy around my cock is more than I can handle. We are both sweating as I fuck her hard and fast against my living room wall. She claws my back over and over while she moans and begs for more. I know she's about to climax when she grabs my hair tight and pulls me into her.

I continue to ram my cock into her. You would think we were going to make an 'us' shaped hole in the wall. When I cum, I lift her off my cock and carry her carefully to the bedroom and set her on the bed.

"Two orgasms already tonight, Z - the Jeep and once on the wall. You spoil me," she says with a smile so big it looks like she's squinting.

After I clean her up with a warm washcloth, I sit on my knees pulling her to the end of the bed.

"Time for my dessert," I inform her right as I pull her legs over my shoulders. "This pussy looks so sweet." Then my head is buried between her thighs. I run my tongue up and down her wet slit before pushing it inside her just a little, making her moan. She takes a handful of my hair as she holds my head in place as I start sucking and flicking her clit. I use one hand to reach up and rub her nipple between my fingers. The other hand holds one of her legs helping me to have good access to that delicious pussy. She cums all over my tongue and I lick up every drop.

"Fuck, that felt good babe," she says as she tries to catch her breath. I pull her into me, holding her close.

I have never been cuddle me kind of guy, even with my ex. Tonight though, with her cheek on my chest and her dark hair spread across the arm I have wrapped around her, and her leg tossed over mine, it feels right, like this is how it's supposed to be.

"Can I ask you something? You don't have to answer if you don't want to," Fi says timidly.

"Sure, what's up?", I murmur into her hair leaving a light kiss.

"Luke told me about your ex. He said she messed with your head. What happened? You don't have to tell me though if you aren't comfortable."

I take a deep breath. "Holly was my girlfriend for about 4 months during hockey season. She originally seemed great but once the season really kicked off, things were bad. She would beg me not to go to away games, threaten to cheat on me when I left, she would post on social media about being at parties when I was gone, call me crying right before the games... It was a huge mental game with her. I lost my focus, spent a lot of time in the penalty box, and my stats took a shit for the season. When we finally broke it off, she admitted to cheating almost every away game. I wasn't in love with her, so it's not like my heart was broken. But I would be lying if I didn't say my head was messed up from it and I had trust issues. Honestly you are the first girl I have actually wanted to be in a relationship with. You were worth trying to win over."

She rolls over and is straddling me. "Well, you have ruined anyone else for me so you don't have to worry about me," she says with a wink. "But really I am so sorry she treated you like that, I hate her for you."

And she strips her shirt off, showing off her perfect tits. Her nipples are erect and begging to be sucked. I take this moment to bring something up.

"Fi, I want to try something when you are about to orgasm. I think it will make it more intense. We can have a safe word if you want to stop."

She slides her panties to the side and begins to grind against my cock still inside my boxers.

"Okay, the safe word is 27," she says with a wink. Damn this girl is going to kill me one day. She pulls my cock out and guides it into her pussy. She bounces up and down as I play with her tits with one hand and squeeze her hip with the other.

I flip us over, sliding all the way out and then slamming back in, hitting her deep inside. My thumb rubbing her clit while she starts playing with both nipples. Watching her rub her nipples, moaning, has me pounding into her faster. I keep rubbing her clit until she begs me to let her cum. Right as I feel her tensing up, I wrap my hand around her throat, squeezing just a little.

"Be a good girl and cum on this cock." I look down in time to see her squirting all over me.

"OH MY GOD! Did I just pee on you? How embarrassing! I am so sorry!" She's about to start crying.

I chuckle and keep fucking her really wet pussy. "Babe calm down, you squirted. It's okay, actually it's more than okay. It's fucking hot as fuck."

She looks confused. "I have never done that before. Usually Justin would just fuck me missionary until he came. That What we did? was different, but so good. Will you choke me again when I cum? I want to keep trying new things."

I am putting her legs up in the air by my head while I pound into her repeatedly. "I'm about to cum, Fi." I reach down and wrap my hand around her throat, and we orgasm together.

As we both come down from the highest post orgasm ecstasy I have ever felt, we stay cuddling. After a while I get her cleaned up. She goes to the bathroom and brushes her hair and teeth. She puts on a pair of boxers and one of my shirts. I should get some pajamas for her, but I selfishly love seeing her in my clothes. We climb into bed and fall asleep wrapped up together.

When I wake up in the morning, I slide out of bed and shower before I take Fiona home. I have class before afternoon practice and she has to work.

By the time I am out Fiona is dressed and ready to go. I make quick work of getting dressed so we can leave.

On the drive back to her place I ask her if she would be willing to go to dinner with Penny and me on Friday. Although she said she would love to, I feel nervous. I want her and Penny to get along. They got along at the beach clean up but things are different now.

Rushing to class, I try and think if I have to call Penny before she starts teaching. Probably no, so I just shoot off a text letting her know we are good for Friday evening.

Thursday is my favorite day because we have afternoon practice with most of the team having morning classes. It also is the day I meet with Stuntz to go over captain stuff.

Class goes well - I get an A on my test, which I'm grateful for, knowing midterms aren't that far out. I took summer classes the past three years and that's when I did my heavy courses to be sure they didn't land during the season. I'm not on scholarship, but I still wanted to be sure I'm always in good academic standing so I can play.

Practice flies by. I see Fiona in passing while she's filming with Emerson Davis, the goalie, and I am heading off the ice to my meeting. Blake Stuntz is the best center in the league, but he doesn't let his ego get him. He is fair with the team and has helped me work on my skills as a leader. We discuss any players who need some one-on-one attention from us. Sometimes we help with skills on the ice, classes, and personal stuff in the players' lives. All those things play into how we perform, and we support the team in any way we can.

The rest of my day passes without much going on. I hit the gym with Luke, and we discuss the team we are playing this weekend. I spend the rest of the day at home cleaning, doing laundry, and studying. I am working on my paper when I get a knock at my door. I open it and no one is there. When I look down, I see a coffee, a couple of my favorite energy bars, and a bag of Airheads. The note attached says, "You always spoil me. I know we both are busy today, so here's my treat for you. XOXO – your sunshine".

I work on my surprise study snacks until it's time for bed. I can't help but wonder what Fiona is up to right now. I know she's having a girl's night though, so I don't text her except to say good night. I get in bed but find myself missing Fi's touch. I won't have a chance to have her sleep over for a few days and that sucks. Hockey season makes relationships difficult sometimes.

It's Friday afternoon and I head home to shower and change so I can pick up Fiona on time. With simple jeans, short sleeve button up, and my new black Converse, I head out the door. Fiona wears her straight with the front braided. Her long yellow dress hits at her ankles, showing off her strappy white sandals. I love how she dresses like the ray of sunshine she is.

When we get to the restaurant, Penny immediately wraps Fiona in a hug. They spend the whole dinner exchanging stories about me, talking about college and Fiona talks about her siblings. Penny tells Fi about her class and how she likes teaching at the local high school. Penny went to college in the panhandle, moving to Tampa when our parents retired and sold our childhood home in Nebraska. She figured if I was in Tampa, she would move close to me. I actually loved that she did that since we have always been close. Like Fiona with Luke, she even used to skate with me.

With dinner over, I feel relaxed knowing one of the most important people in my life approves of my girlfriend. I wouldn't let Penny tell me who I could or couldn't date but I do care about her opinion.

"Your sister is amazing! She is so funny and smart. Meeting her at the beach clean up is different than meeting her as your girlfriend. Hopefully she likes me, because I love her!", exclaims Fiona.

I kiss the hand I'm holding as we drive. "Of course she likes you, who wouldn't?"

I hate having to drop her off instead of her sleeping over, but tomorrow is game day so we have to arrive at the rink early so we can travel in the team bus to the game. Fiona is going to the game too, but she is driving herself. After a long kiss at the door we say our goodbyes and I head home.

Fiona

It's game day so I have a lot to get done before I get on the road. I pack up my bag with my camera, chargers, memory cards, and laptop. I am sure to check the team's social media sites, since content was prescheduled. I just want to be sure it posts. There will be a decent number of fans at this game since it's not too far away, so I told them to tag Tampa U Penguins for a shot to be featured. I want to help increase our visibility.

Now for the hardest part, what to wear. I want to be cute but comfortable. It's my first game as Zane's girlfriend but I'm also working, so I need to dress nicely. I decide on the cutest outfit - black bell bottoms with rips, a long sleeve Penguins shirt with Miller across the back, and my white Converse. My hair is up in two space buns with simple makeup. I am ready to be wandering the arena with the team. I hope I can get some good footage from the Penguins press box.

During the drive I decide it is the perfect time to call my parents about Zane.

My mom answers almost immediately. "Hey sweetie, how are you? Are you heading to the game? I miss you."

I smile. Hearing her voice always makes me feel good. "Hey momma! How's it going at home? I promise to come over for dinner soon, but that Clearwater traffic kills me." I don't bother explaining how driving over the bridge to one of the most popular beaches is a traffic nightmare.

I then launch into dating Zane. I tell her how he treats me and give her chances to ask questions. She warns me to protect my heart; she doesn't want me to hurt again. Overall, the conversation is good and she asks to meet Zane soon. I promise to bring him over. They don't leave the house much since Dad has been in remission for thyroid cancer. That's one of the main reasons Lucy went into nursing, I think. She used to want to write fantasy novels. Dad is doing better, but we all worry.

Arriving at the arena, I find Marissa and check in about what I am going to be trying to record. I go around filming some shots in the locker room during Stuntz's speech to the team. I didn't see Zane, but he might have been with one of the trainers. I give Luke the 'I love you' sign then head back to the stands.

In the stands I go around filming the different areas of our fans. I see the Airheads in most of their hands, which makes me laugh. As I head down to the team box, our team takes the ice to warm up. I can see Z scanning the area for me. The minute he sees me I turn my back to him, letting him see my shirt. As I turn back around, he's pumping his stick in the air - a sign of celebration in the hockey world.

I get some great footage of the game: Stuntz scoring, Luke coming in with an assist, Davis, the goalie, making an amazing block, and Zane checking the other team's player into the boards. With each goal you saw our fans holding up Airheads or Snickers, which I just mentioned in a post a few days ago were Davis's favorite candy. We may not have had many fans at the beginning of the season but the ones we have now are amazing!

The team is 3-0 so far; a hat trick if you want to call it that. I want to wait for Zane after the game, but I really need to get on the road since it's a two hour drive back home. I shoot him off a text letting him know I was heading out and he played a great game. On the way to the game I have someone take a picture of me with my back to the camera and the arena in the background. I shoot that off to him too; I know it will make him smile.

I'm on the road for about an hour before I get a text of the smiling emoji with the heart eyes. He loves the photo and tells me to drive safe. I'm tempted to drive to his apartment and wait for him. I wouldn't mind another sleepover with him. I focus on my drive home with car karaoke to all my favorite songs. Luckily it's late so there's no traffic.

I get home around midnight. I shower, put on one of Zane's shirts, and get into bed. I'm asleep not more than two hours until I get a call from Zane.

"Hey Z is everything ok? Did you guys make it back?", I murmur half asleep.

"Yeah, babe we made it back. I left something for you at your door. Can you grab it?", he tells me sweetly.

I get up in just my shirt and panties and head to the door. When I open it I almost drop my phone.

"Are you up for a sleepover? Emphasis on sleeping though because I'm exhausted. I just wanted to be with you."

He pulls me into a hug before I answer.

"Yes of course come in! I will give you the tour tomorrow when we are awake," I say, then I lock the door and guide him to my room. I climb right into bed while he strips down into boxers and gets in beside me. We cuddle with my back to his front and he kisses my cheek softly

"Fi, you being there with my name and number across your back made me feel amazing. Thank you!"

I whisper back, "I felt like I needed your number on me for the game." With that we both drift off to sleep.

We wake up around 9 when Lucy comes walking in exclaiming, "OH MY GOSH! I should have knocked. I am so sorry!"

We both chuckle and make sure the blanket is pulled up over us.

"We just slept. I just didn't want to be without Fi," he tells her, making her eyes fill with love as she smiles at us.

"That's so sweet, keep this one," she jokingly tells me.

"Planned on it. Now what are you here for?"

"Oh, I was just grabbing one of your sweaters I think would look cute with this dress." She waves her hand showing off her teal dress.

"Go ahead. Give me details later." I send her off with the 'I love you' sign.

"Do you all do that? I have seen all four of you using that sign randomly even when Luke is on the ice," Zane asked.

I press my back further into him, getting comfortable again. "Yes it's a family thing we started when my dad was sick and we couldn't go in his room. We would sign "I love you" through the glass door."

He kisses the top of my head. "That's sweet, baby. Do you have any plans for the day?"

I snuggle into him. "Well I was hoping to spend it with this sexy hockey player I know."

"I'm just studying but I would love for you to come spend the day with me," he tells me.

We both get up and get dressed. I put on a cute pair of sweats with a matching crop tank top. We stop at Roasters for coffee and muffins before hitting his apartment. I get my laptop out and start editing while he studies for his classes. We work in comfortable silence. Every once in a while we will talk about something then go back to working. It doesn't feel weird being in silence and I don't feel forced to fill the void which is nice. The day is going great until the sports channel begins their talk about the NHL draft.

We listen as Stuntz, Luke, and Zane are all discussed with game video playing and the announcers talk about their pros and cons. I'm not sure why, but it's like a cloud has covered us suddenly. I knew he was entering the draft, but I guess it was easy to forget there was a chance he wouldn't get Tampa. He could be picked by any team across the country, while I am here. I could follow him, but I don't know that I want to feel like I am following a man.

"Earth to sunshine, are you ok?" he asks, concerned.

"Yeah, sorry, I guess sometimes I forget how the draft works - that you don't have a guarantee of playing for Tampa," I tell him, shrugging.

We discuss how much he wants Tampa and that we can do long distance until he can get traded. He doesn't mention me moving with him ,which kind of hurts, but I think he's trying to be respectful, knowing Justin demanded I move with him. The talk of the draft really puts a damper on the mood of the day.

I come up with an excuse about why I need to head home. I even have Lucy pick me up so that Zane doesn't have to stop studying to drive me home. The tension between us when we kiss goodbye is high; you can almost feel it in the air.

When I get in Lucy's car I instantly regret leaving. I feel like I'm running away, which I am. Lucy tries to talk to me and I tell her about my feelings. She agrees he's trying to not be like Justin and advises me to not let this distance between us last too long.

I know I'm being ridiculous and selfish, but I spend the entire week going out of my way to avoid Zane. I just need to think, and I don't know how to talk to him about it. I know he notices though, because Luke and Stuntz have asked me what's wrong since practices haven't been good with Zane not being focused. I just don't know what I want - do I want to follow him where he goes? Try out long distance? Also, we haven't been together that long so I don't know how to process how strong my feelings are.

Zane has been giving me space, texting me every morning and night reminding me he's here for me whenever I am ready to talk. He doesn't give me any ultimatums or send texts cussing me out, like Justin would. He knows

I'm going through something, and he sends his support without making me feel forced to decide.

The guys leave on Friday for Saturday's game because it's in Virginia. I regret not going to see Z before he left. I am such a shitty girlfriend. I tell him to text me after his flight and get back to my edits, trying not to focus on how it's all hitting me how bad I fucked up. Zane never even asked what the plan was, he never demanded an answer, and I am over here having a breakdown. I am treating him terribly and messing his game up. I need to fix this asap.

I reach out to Lucy and tell her it's a sister 911. We decide to meet at a local wine bar. I tell her everything with tears in my eyes. I don't want to lose the best man to ever enter my life.

She grabs my hand, squeezing it lightly, sending me comfort. "You just need to find a way to show him you are as committed as he is."

I begin to think. I figure out the perfect thing! Now it's just getting it all done before his plane lands. Lucy and I sit together, having another glass of wine and get started.

When Zane lands, he is going to find that I officially hard launched us on Instagram. He has wanted to do this and officially announce that we are a couple, but I kept putting it off. I know that Z and Holly had issues during away games with commitment. I don't want to be another woman in his life who messes with his head. I want to show him no matter where he goes, I am here for him. I will support his career and be by his side, starting with announcing to the internet we are officially official.

I use the picture of me in his jersey with his number painted on my cheek on my Insta. Then if you swipe through the post, you see us on our first date, me at the away game in his shirt, and my favorite is a picture of us kissing and he's holding me in the air with my legs wrapped around him. The caption is "I thought I needed his number, what I needed was him" . I quickly tag him, then hit post. Now it's just a waiting game.

With each notification I almost jump with anxiety thinking it's him. As I wait for his text, I scroll the comments. Some are nice, talking about how cute we are, and they love us together. The puck bunny comments are mean - commenting on my looks and how we won't last, but I just ignore it. If I am going to be with someone on his way to the NHL, press is going to be a part of our lives and everyone knows most comments on the internet are mean.

I head home and take a shower trying to clear my head. I don't want to focus on how I have been distant all week over something stupid, just to profess my want for us to be together on the internet without texting him first to let him know where my head was at. All I could think at the time was I wanted to make a grand gesture to show my devotion. All of a sudden my phone pings with a text from Lucy telling me to check Insta now.

Right there, front and center, is a picture of him holding me not kissing, me in his number at the GU game, a picture of us cuddling in bed, a picture of us surfing and he tagged me. The caption "I need you in my number sunshine *sun emoji*".

When he gets to his hotel we talk a bit on the phone before I fall asleep. Time feels like it's moving slow without him here. I shoot off a text telling him to hurry home because I want to apologize in person and in bed.

We text a few times before the game Saturday and I remind him I can't wait for him to come home. The team ends up having a complete shutout game. Stuntz has a hattrick, Luke scores twice, Zane has two assists, and Davis doesn't let a single goal in. Zane texts to tell me he hid a key under his mat, and he expects to see me at his apartment when he gets home. I pack a bag, knowing they won't be home until after two AM.

The awkward moment being alone in your boyfriend's apartment for the first time. Like do i just sit on the couch? I dont want him to think i am snooping. Would he even think that? I could try something sexy like posing sexy for when he gets home. I am exhausted so I decide to be spontaneous, and I get in his bed wearing only his jersey. I know when he comes home, he will be tired but I think seeing me with no panties on and his jersey hitting right below my ass is going to give him a jolt of energy, but until then I fall asleep.

Zane

Boarding the plane for the away game while Fiona is being so weird is not an ideal situation. All week she's been distant with me since we talked about the draft. I'm not sure if she's upset about the draft, because we both know there's a high chance of me being drafted and there's a chance I'm leaving to whatever city I'm drafted to, or if she feels like it's a Justin situation where she will have to follow me where my career takes me. I don't mention her coming with me when we talk, because I really don't want to come off like I am putting my career first. Her dream is to work for the Thunder, and I don't want to interrupt that. All I can hope is that we can put this behind us and start to figure things out.

I have played terribly all week with being unfocused, but as Stuntz reminded me, I can't let anyone affect my game or I won't have a career to worry about. This feels eerily similar to when Holly and I would fight before away games, but I know the draft would be an issue regardless of where this game was happening. I really like Fiona; I don't want to lose her over something that's not even an issue yet.

While on the plane I listen to music, hoping to clear my head. Every player is different when traveling. Some like to talk and play cards, others listen to music, some scroll social media mindlessly if we are on the bus and have service. The game is midafternoon tomorrow, which is nice because we will be able to get home by like 2 am. I left a key under my mat for Fiona. I'm going to text her after the flight to tell her; I hope she uses it.

Even Penny doesn't have a key to my place because I like to keep my space private. For some reason though, I wanted Fi to have a way to come over if I'm away. I selfishly want to be able to come home after away games to her in my bed. I know it's too early, but I am starting to think I am falling in love with her. Is it too early? My parents fell in love fast, so maybe it's possible I am in love with her. But Fiona - she's not the type of girl to just fall in love at the drop of a hat. I will just keep working on winning her over. Starting with us going out on another date. Maybe meeting each other's parents or becoming Instagram official. Just something to help keep us moving forward.

When we land and I have service, my phone is blowing up. I immediately text the family group chat to let them know I landed and I am safe. But before I even have time to check my Instagram notifications, three different people come up and congratulate me. Even Coach looks at me and gives me an approving head nod as I get off the plane and on to the team bus that's waiting. As soon as I am seated, I pull up my Instagram, needing to know what everyone is talking about. When I see the post causing this commotion, my heart almost explodes with happiness.

I'm tagged in a post from Fiona. She just publicly confirmed our relationship with a few photos of us over the past month and my favorite one - her being in my number. It brings a huge ear-to-ear smile to my face, seeing the caption. I decide to make my own post, since I don't want to call her while we are on the bus. I post my favorite pictures of us and let her know I need her in my number.

When I get to the hotel, we talk on the phone a little before she falls asleep. She texts me to hurry home because she wants to apologize in person. The fact she wants to do it face-to-face shows she really is a good person; she was just struggling with how to handle the situation. We exchange texts in the morning before the game.

We end up having one of our best games and shut out the home team! Not a single goal got in and I had two assists. Luke scored a few times, but the MVP was Stuntz. He ended the game with a hat trick - three goals in one game! We shower and head to the airport, finally heading home.

Before the plane takes off I send a message to Fi, letting her know I hid a key for her under the doormat and that I would love to see her when I get back. I hope it doesn't come off as demanding but I really want to come home to my girl. Especially not seeing her much all week and with the tension we have been having, it would make everything better to be with her.

I spend the entire plane ride and drive back to my place obsessing about whether or not she will be at my place. I consider calling her, but if she's at home asleep I don't want to wake her. Even if she's at my place I don't need to wake her up. Just crawling into bed with her there will be enough for me. I am exhausted but on edge as I walk up to my apartment.

When I get inside, I see the key on the counter by a set of car keys. She came! Suddenly I am full of excitement. I'm going to get in bed and crash, but in the morning I'm going to worship her body. At least that was the plan until I walk in the room and see her.

She is laying there in my jersey, the blanket kicked off her. Her long waves of hair splayed across the pillow and her perfect lips in a kissable pout. I walk over and plant a kiss on her cheek.

Fiona stirs slightly, murmuring, "Hi babe I missed you," and she gives me a sleepy smile with her eyes closed.

"I missed you too sunshine," I tell her while I rub my hand lightly on her thigh. I drag my hand dangerously high and freeze when I realize there is no band from her underwear. This girl is going to be the death of me. She is in my jersey with not a single thing on underneath.

"You found my surprise I have for you," she murmurs and subtly lifts her ass into my hand.

"Fi, you have to stop, or we won't be going to sleep anytime soon," I say, as I move to keep rubbing her leg, letting my fingertips lightly graze her inner thighs. She moans lightly and spreads her legs.

"Baby, I need you to actually look at me and tell me yes. I need to be sure you are okay with this. I don't want to take advantage of your sleepy state," I say, taking my shirt off. She sits up and reaches for my sweats, pulling them and my boxers down in one swift motion.

"Is this enough of a yes for you, babe?", she asks. Before I can respond, her mouth is on me. She is wasting no time, sucking me hard and fast, stopping to flick her tongue across the tip and licking up the precum I am releasing. With my hand wrapped in her hair, her eyes moist from choking on my cock, and the subtle drag of her teeth, I am climaxing with her name on my lips.

"Such a good girl swallowing every drop", I say, and with that I grab her hand, taking her to the bathroom. I bend her over the vanity and when I reach down, I confirm what I already suspected: she's soaking wet. "Is that because of me, baby?"

She nods her head.

I line up and bury myself inside her. Seeing her in my jersey is doing things to me I didn't know it would. I feel protective and possessive. Like I want to own every piece of her and protect her from all the bad in the world. When she looks into the mirror and makes eye contact with me, I gently pull her hair, tilting her head back. "Keep looking at me, baby. I'm about to cum and I want you to follow me."

I let go, giving her ass a smack. I can feel her getting more tense, so I start going harder and faster.

"Now Fiona... FUCK, SUNSHINE," I almost yell as we make eye contact, climaxing together.

I set her up on the counter and do something I have never done. I begin to feast on her before she gets cleaned up. I am licking both of our mess out of her tight wet pussy. It should be gross, but something about it turns me on, cleaning my girl up with my mouth. I suck her clit and alternate flicking my tongue over it and up and down her slit. She grabs my hair and orgasms all over my tongue. I grab a washcloth, cleaning her up. Then I carry her to bed. I take off the jersey .

"I can keep you warm tonight," I wink. Climbing into the other side of the bed also naked, we drift off to sleep, exhausted from our strenuous bedroom activities.

Waking up on my side, with Fiona's ass pressed into my groin, I can feel myself growing harder by the minute. I start trailing kisses down her neck and up around her ear. She stirs, grinding herself against me. The arm that's currently around her is the one I use to start lightly palming her tits one at a time, giving her nipples a little love as I alternate between the two. Moaning, she pushes back harder and then leans forward a bit. Just enough so that my cock was able to move between her thighs. She is wet when I start thrusting forward slightly.

"Z, I need you" she moans, and that's all I need to adjust slightly and guide myself into her.

I'm not going to last long. I can already tell because this angle makes her extra tight. I reach down and start rubbing her clit. I want to be sure we both are satisfied. We climax pretty quickly, but this felt different than last night. This felt emotional and intimate.

"That was amazing, Z," she says as cuddles into me.

"Let's go shower babe, and then we can start our day."

I take her hand, leading her to the shower. I take the soap and help wash her body, spending extra time where I know she's sore. She doesn't wash her hair - something about my shampoo sucking - but she does put in a little bit of conditioner. When we get out, she grabs clothes from the bag she packed and I brush her hair and throw it in a loose braid for her. I throw on some basketball shorts and a shirt and have my Tampa Thunder hat on backwards.

As I make coffee Fiona explains her feelings this past week. The way she felt torn between wanting me to mention her following me to wherever I get drafted and not wanting me to. She makes it clear that no matter what she wants to make this work. I decide to invite her to my family's house for Thanksgiving. Then she invited me to her parents for Christmas. I feel like we are making progress.

We move to our usual Sunday activities; she's editing and I'm studying. I like the routine we have together.

"Hey Z can I ask you something?" She gives me a sheepish smile.

"What's up babe?" I turn, intrigued.

"Do you think since we are like, officially together, that you would maybe possibly want to do a matching Halloween costume?"

She looks down.

"Yeah, babe that sounds cool. Why are you so nervous to ask?" I smile at her reassuringly.

"Justin never wanted to and he yelled at me for asking once. I know you aren't him, but I just still get nervous sometimes."

We have two weeks until Halloween, two away games to get through. I know we will be ok as long as neither of us lets our pasts get to us. Communication isn't always our strong suit, especially with our emotions, but here is to hoping we can get through it.

"I am sorry he was such a shithead. If you want matching costumes, let's do it. I want you to be happy, babe. If I ever make you uncomfortable with how I talk to you then you need to tell me so I can fix it please," I tell her.

We spend the rest of Sunday together watching some rom-com she found on one of my streaming services. I learned she loves popcorn but only with lots of butter. She also talks the entire movie and usually I find that annoying, but with her I just found it endearing. After the movie she starts to gather her things, leaving the key on the counter.

"The key is for you Fi. I like you being able to come over even if I'm not home, especially on away game nights," I tell her.

She adds the key to her keyring. We have a long goodbye with lots of making out, just the way I like it. As she walks down the hall I holler out, "You can bring stuff here if you want. Some clothes, or even just hair stuff you like for when you sleep over. No pressure, I just want you comfortable."

The day flew by with us just relaxing and spending time together that I don't realize how tired I feel. I go lay down for bed and start thinking about if I was possibly rushing things. I don't want her to feel pressured. It's not like I am asking her to move in. I just want her to be able to wash her hair if she wants. Or use the brush she likes. Maybe she wants to sleep here on a weeknight so she could have an extra set of clothes. I'm not sure what I want except for us to be together whenever we get the chance. This weekend she's going to watch the away game at Slapshots with the girls. I'm hopeful that she will end up back here so I can see her when our flight lands.

Fiona

He is amazing! Honestly, Zane just makes me so happy. I think about him giving me a key and inviting me to bring some stuff to his house so I can be comfortable when I stay there. I try not to let myself feel pressured. I know he has only the best intentions. Plus, it would be nice to be able to wash my hair using my own hair products when I stay the night.

When I get home, I shower and then go talk to Lucy.

"Hey, Fiona. Those Instagram posts were epic! 'He needs you in his number.' Swoon!"

I giggle, swatting her arm. "Thanks! Last night was amazing, and honestly so was this morning," I wink.

"Boo! No fair - you get a super hot man, amazing mind-blowing sex, you've already graduated, AND you have a great job!" She jokingly frowns.

"Want to go to the beach tomorrow? You don't have classes or clinicals. We can have a sister date." I lean into her lovingly.

"YES! Please, that sounds fun! But don't forget about the game day party at Slapshots this weekend," Lucy reminds me. Then we flip on our favorite vampire comfort show.

I shoot a text to Marissa before bed just to clear if it's okay that I don't go in tomorrow. She doesn't mind as long as I get caught up Tuesday. I let Z know my plans so he doesn't get worried when he doesn't see me around the rink. I'm working on this thing called communication.

I head to bed but I don't sleep nearly as well as I do when I am in bed with Zane. Something about him puts my wild, anxious brain at ease so I can sleep.

Waking up, I check my phone for any texts before getting up.

"Beach day!" I can hear Lucy yell from the kitchen.

Getting up, I throw on my cute yellow bikini with a black coverup dress on top. I braid my hair into two Dutch braids and grab my floppy hat. I don't usually burn but I like to protect my skin. We get our cooler packed, grab our beach bag, and head out the door. It's not too busy for a Monday in October and it's warm out, which is nice.

I give Lucy all the details of Saturday night and Sunday morning. I tell her how amazing he treats me in bed and out.

"I'm so fucking jealous! You are averaging three or four orgasms every time you go over there, you lucky bitch!" Lucy exclaims.

I just laugh, knowing it's true.

"After how your dickhead ex did you for three years without one orgasm, you deserve it. Karma is repaying you tenfold."

Trying to move on from this conversation about Justin. I ask her about school. I know there is nothing easy about nursing school. She gives me the details of rotations and which professors she has, and how they teach. She wants to go to the ER, which sounds like a lot to me, but I know she enjoys the rush. I know she will succeed in whatever she puts her mind to. I make sure to tell her how proud I am of her. She's strong, but she needs to know I am here for her if she needs it.

"So Luc, are you seeing anyone? Any casual hookups you want to dish to me about?"

She gives me a guilty look, then says, "Nope. I am so busy; no time to see anyone."

Usually she has a few hookups a semester, so either she wants to hide who it is or she is really, really focused on her classes (which doesn't seem to be the case). Recently I heard her say this was her easiest semester to date, leading me to believe my darling sister is hiding something. I will let her keep it a secret for now, though.

Flipping the subject, I say, "What are we doing for Halloween? I have a boyfriend who's willing to match me so I want to do something fun!"

This perks her up.

"There's a few parties over on frat row. I don't usually go over there but it could be fun for the night!" Lucy says.

I hate frat row. It's always super rowdy, but I can let loose for the night. Why not?

"Sounds good. I need to figure out our costumes."

We spend an hour debating costume options until I think of the perfect one.

Driving home, I'm in one of those weird, after the beach moods. Like where you want to take a post-sun nap, then wake up and have a sandwich.

We listen to my playlist, signing along until we get to the house. Before we go our separate ways inside, Lucy reminds me of the game day watch party at Slapshots again. I agree to go, then head to my room to take that nap I was fantasizing about.

I wake up hours later and realize its 10 P.M. I must have crashed after I showered. I see that Zane has texted a few times. I try to call him while I go make a snack and get ready to go back to bed. Since he didn't answer, I send over a spicy picture of me on the beach. My boobs are almost out, I am laughing in it, and you can see my ass partially. I want to give him something nice to wake up to.

In the morning I am kind of surprised I don't have a text from Zane, but I just decide not to dwell on it. I put on a cute yellow dress and my beige cardigan, paired with white Converse. My hair is up in a high ponytail that's curled. I put on some light makeup and a few sprays of my perfume. I shoot Zane a good morning text and let him know I will see him later.

This is my first time at the rink since we publicly confirmed our relationship. I don't know if I expect anyone to treat me differently, but I hope they don't. I just want things at work to stay how they are.

When I walk through my office door, I am scooped up from behind. I let out a little scream but quickly realize it's Z.

I swat his chest. "You about gave me a heart attack!"

He sets down the two coffees he has. "Sorry, babe. I brought you coffee."

I smile at him, leaning up to give him a kiss. He reaches over, closing the door.

"That photo was a tease, baby girl. I made myself cum before I got up because I wasn't making it here without getting off to that picture first" Without warning he locks the door, then walks me to the side of the office where the rink is.

My stomach drops. I know it's one way glass and my door is locked, but I know whatever is about to happen is going to be wildly inappropriate. The idea of being caught, of being seen, has my panties soaked. I can see how hard Z is through the sweats he wore into the rink. My heart is pounding out of my chest and my skin is tingling in anticipation.

I am backed against the glass when Zane drops to his knees in front of me. "Are you wet for me, sunshine?"

I can't form words, so I just nod. He pulls my dress up around my waist, revealing my panties and their wetspot.

"Mmm… I can already see how soaked you are. Is it the idea of being caught? Is it that someone might see or hear us up here? Is it the anticipation of what's about to happen?" I am still at a loss for words.

"Come on baby, use your words."

All I can get out is a quiet, "All of the above."

Without notice, Z throws one of my legs over his shoulder and slides my thong to the side. He proceeds to give me the best oral of my life, right there in my office against a window. I moan into my hand as I orgasm to keep the sound down. He stands up and wipes his face on a tissue from my desk while I fix my dress.

"Bye sunshine, I will see you later." He winks and drops a kiss on my forehead, then leaves to get ready for practice.

It takes me about thirty minutes to process what just happened. I slowly drink my coffee he brought and decide I need to get focused.

I grab my laptop and get to work. By the time I am 100% caught up and ready to head home it's after 6 P.M. The players have left and there's just a few of us in the admin who are still here.

As I head out to the parking lot, I see Zane leaning on my car.

"Hey Fi, I just wanted to see if you want to get dinner," he tells me, like he hasn't been waiting for a while.

"Sounds good," I reply, and he opens the Jeep door parked next to me. I climb in.

We go get Cuban sandwiches, something Tampa is known for. They are delicious and always hit the spot. We spend all of dinner laughing and enjoying our time off campus. I snap the cutest picture of him burying his face in my neck from behind me while I'm laughing. I share it to my stories with the onscreen message, "My lucky number is #27". Being a social media couple is new to me. I think in the three years I was with Justin, I shared like ten photos. There just wasn't much happiness to show. Now I am always smiling and feeling full of bliss.

It's suddenly Friday afternoon and I am not sure where the time has gone. Work has been so busy since dinner on Tuesday that I barely had time to breathe. I am about to grab lunch with Z before he has to report to the plane for this game in North Carolina tomorrow. I am going to watch from the bar and then head to his house to wait for him to get home.

We get the best Chinese food from our favorite place and then take a short walk around the pond by the rink. I take a moment to really appreciate the little things with him.

"I will be wearing your number tomorrow so you better impress me," I say with a wink, nudging him with my shoulder.

"Don't worry babe, I plan on impressing you when I get home too," he laughs. "But honestly, I had no idea how much I needed to see you in my number until I saw you at that game in my jersey. Your support means so much to me."

Trying not to cry, I decide to joke and say, "Well, always remember I need your number." I'm not sure he understands that moment from our first interview in my office.

He surprises me by saying, "My jersey number of course," with a wink.

I give him a hug and kiss then we go our separate ways. I head home and he heads to the airport. When I get home, I quickly shower and head to bed. Zane texts me late, letting me know he landed, and he would call me before the game. I fall asleep not long after getting that text.

The next morning, I get up and work on the teams' social media. I make a few posts about where to catch the game on TV. The team did a fun TikTok dance on the ice that I post, hoping it will get the Penguins on everyone's mind. I keep busy until Zane calls and we chitchat for a bit. I wish him luck on the game.

I get ready for the game watch party, deciding on Zane's jersey, tucked in the front of my jean shorts and my yellow Converse. I wear my hair in a big ponytail. It's curled and teased slightly for volume. I shoot a picture to Z, then head over to Slapshots.

Celisa is slammed behind the bar, but I give her a wave when I come in before I head to Lucy, who got us a high-top table. The atmosphere is amazing! It's so cool to see all the fans here cheering on the team. Some people recognize me and come and say congratulations or they nod at me when I walk by. Overall, people are really sweet about it.

But the blonde we have come across a few times here keeps pointing at me and giggling with her friends. Or she glares at me, then turns her head when she notices I noticed her.

"Ignore her. She's just mad about Zane's post before the game," Lucy says, taking a sip of her drink - some kind of fruity something.

I immediately pull out my phone, unsure how I missed his post. Then I see it.

On his stories is the picture I sent him. "I have never met a more amazing, beautiful woman. I love you in my number."

I am so lucky to have him!

"He loves you," Lucy says, nonchalant.

"No, he doesn't, it's too soon. We are just enjoying each other right now," I say, not entirely convinced myself.

She shrugs and we go back to watching the game. Zane plays a strong game; the other team struggles the whole game to get past him.

We win again! It's not a shutout, but we won! The guys played hard. I know they will be exhausted when they get home.

Zane looks at the camera during his after game interview, sweating.

"You are having the best season of your college career, Miller. Is there a certain someone helping inspire this?" She flirts with him while asking.

"Well, Katie, you follow me on Instagram, so I am sure you know the answer, but to anyone who doesn't follow me, yes this is my best season yet. My girlfriend inspires me to work hard. She's a literal angel on earth. She knows I want to play professionally, so she pushes me to be my best on and off the ice."

After the interview, it's all eyes on me in the bar. My face flushes and I hurry and say my goodbyes to Lucy and Celisa so I can head to Zane's.

As I walk out the door Blondie says, "He will never actually want you. You're one of those phases. You will never be important to him."

Usually I would be the bigger person but fuck this!

"Well, I have weekly dinners with him and his sister. She invites me to girls' nights. I have a key to his apartment. He's taking me to meet his family over Thanksgiving. But I guess it's just a phase. There is an entire team; go be a puck bunny to someone else."

NEED YOUR NUMBER

And I walk out with my head held high, going straight to Z's apartment. Sure, I exaggerated my friendship with Penny, but fuck Blondie, shes such a bitch all the time for no reason.

Once I arrive, I see there's a bag of Airheads waiting on me with a note.

Fi, since you won't be there for me to give you one in person, I decided to leave you a bag. – Z

I open the bag and go shower and get ready for bed. Shooting a text to Zane, I let him know to fly safe, and how proud I am of his game tonight.

Zane

That interview has my phone blowing up, my parents texted wanting to meet Fiona, Penny texted asking about our plans this week she wants to do dinner, Fiona texts but doesn't mention the interview, and lots of puck bunnies who took my confession and are using it as a challenge to try and get me. But what really kills me is the text from Lucy, who never texts me, it's a video link.

Fiona told that girl off, the blonde girl, Nicole, was a one night stand last year and she always hangs on me. I don't like her, and I push her off more often than I should ever need to. I was proud of her for defending herself, but laughed at the way she used Penny and the key to show she was worthy. I just claimed her on national television, and she uses the key as her point instead of using the interview to her advantage. I close the video chuckling and get in my jeep to head home.

Fiona is fast asleep in bed when I get home snuggled under the covers. Stripping out of my clothes I crawl into bed with just my boxers on. I am exhausted so I just lean over and kiss her, so she knows I am home. She murmurs something I think is English before falling back asleep. I lay in bed for no more than ten minutes before I succumb to the dreams calling my name.

I wake up to the smell of bacon. I reach over for Fiona, and she's gone, my awake brain decides she is the cause of the bacon smell. Throwing on some shorts I head to the kitchen. "Good morning handsome I made breakfast and coffee" and she hands me a cup of fresh coffee. This is nice, I could get used to this. "To what do I owe this pleasure?" I ask her. "The interview" then she goes back to finish cooking.

We have relaxing morning together watching a movie after breakfast. We discuss the party tonight since Halloween falls on a Sunday. I love the idea that Fiona came up with, plus its easy and comfortable for me so I am all about it. "Hey, I am going to head home and get ready for the party. I will meet you there?" I kiss her softly, "Yes babe, I will meet you there. We have early practice, so the guys better not get too crazy." She grabs her bag and hugs me before she heads out the door.

I spend the rest of the day studying and I also fit in a three-hour nap before I get ready. My Costume is easy I am wearing khaki pants, a Tampa Thunder jersey, and my Thunder hat backwards. I get the ease of being a traditional hockey player, I can't wait to see Fiona's part of the costume. I eat a quick peanut butter and jelly sandwich before I head out the door.

Arriving on frat row I immediately agreeing to come to this party. The parties here are always outrageous and it's not really my scene, I am more of a drink at the bar kind of partier. I find some parking a few houses down then begin weeding through all the people already drunk on the sidewalk. College really is a wild time.

I quickly find a few teammates and grab a beer from the keg in the backyard. Girls are swarming around us, puck bunnies and cleat chasers, alike. I move to the edge of our group feeling uncomfortable and not wanting to upset Fiona when she gets here. She texted saying she was on her way soon.

"Zane! Yo is that your girl. She looks smoking hot tonight. She can be my trophy anytime." One of the younger guys on the team says and I send daggers from my eyes at him making a noise that's almost a growl. He chuckles lightly backing up "I'm joking, I'm joking."

He is not wrong though Fiona dressed to the nines tonight. She was really excited to do these couple costumes, so I was happy to participate. She has her hair in the classic loose curl she does with a silver headband. She is in silver high heels that wrap silver rope up to her mid-calf. The dress is a short tight silver dress, and she has a sticker on it saying, 'Stanley Cup'. But my absolute favorite part is the 27 on her cheek.

"You look amazing Sunshine" I wrap her in my arms giving her a big kiss. "Thanks, I was really nervous about the dress, but I am glad you like it" she says leaning into my embrace. I lead her to the kitchen to get a drink, the guys start pouring shots and I already know its going to be a long night.

After a few hours of mingling and dancing with my girl I finally hear Fiona say, "I am exhausted, can you give me a ride home?" We start to make our rounds saying goodbye and making sure Lucy and Celisa don't need a ride home. Once we are sure everyone is safe and good to go, we head out. The ride is short with her not living far off campus. I walk her to her door, she unlocks it, stepping inside waiting on me to follow. I don't miss my chance I follow her and shut the door locking it before heading to her room.

NEED YOUR NUMBER

When I step into her bedroom, she is standing there naked. My heart starts pounding while I take off my shirt and start unbuttoning my pants. I am watching her as she climbs on the bed and spreads her legs. As I slide my pants down, I can see the glisten off wetness between her legs. She is ready for me, and I am so hard I don't think my brain has any blood left in it. I ditch my boxers right as she slides her hand between her legs and begins to rub small circles around her clit. I stand there staring and she starts to moan, my hand makes its way to start stroking myself as I watch her. She slides two fingers in still rubbing her clit and I can feel myself getting closer to climax. All it takes is Fiona orgasming with my name on her lips as she moans for me to follow directly behind her. I grab a towel from the bathroom and use it to clean us up.

"What do you want baby girl? You tell me what you want me to do" I climb on the bed and whisper in her ear. I hover over her giving her light kisses on her neck barely pressing my body to hers waiting on an answer. I am slowly growing harder, and I am sure she notices. She turns her head kissing me rough "I need you to fuck me babe. Seeing those girls crowding your table made me feel jealous, all I wanted was to shove you against the wall and kiss you until they realized the only person you were getting inside was me" and she reached down guiding me into her tight wet pussy. Taking her words to heart I lift us both up and pin her against the wall. I thrust harder and faster with every scratch she places on my back and each moan that she makes in my ear. I bang every jealous or insecure thought out of her head, I make sure to claim her as mine with each orgasm she has.

It feels like hours before we have exhausted ourselves and we both know we need to go to sleep. With an early morning practice, I tuck Fi in to bed and lay a kiss on her forehead before I leave. I am pretty sure she's asleep before I am out the door. Celisa is in the kitchen when I walk out "Hey have a good night, can you lock up behind me?" i ask. "Yes, I will. Thanks for making her happy Zane, I was jealous at first, I always crushed on you, but you and Fi it just makes sense." I walk out the door with a smile, hearing someone think we are good for each other always brings me joy. I go home and try to get some sleep before our 7 am practice.

Practice is miserable, most of the team is hungover and coach is making sure we take the punishment as a team. Mondays usually suck but this one sucks the most I am glad I didn't get drunk last night because I would hate to be the guys puking in the trash cans by the penalty box. My freshman and sophomore years that was me, when I partied the most, but I am glad that phase is gone.

I head up to see Fiona before I head to tape review. She is on the phone, so I wait on her couch that's against the wall. When she gets off the call, she looks annoyed, but she comes and sits with me. "Celisa wants to go out to frat row tomorrow night for her birthday, I don't want to go especially since its no boyfriends allowed" she rolls her eyes. "Its okay babe don't worry about me. Go have a good time with your sister and cousin. Call me if you need me." I kiss her to reassure her that I don't mind, and I trust her. We talk a little more before I head to tape, and she heads to a meeting with Marissa.

The rest of the day flies by without event. I go to class then go back to the rink so I can get a workout in. Coach says he is going to implement mandatory 'dry land' practices. Dry land sucks because its drills and workouts on the turf. It's usually hot and last forever. If the guys on the team would take gym time seriously this wouldn't be an issue. I decide not to let it bother me though. I knock out my workout then head home to study and get some sleep.

Waking up on Tuesday I decide to maybe see is Luke and Stuntz want to go to the bar tonight. They both text back agreeing to meet at Slapshots around 7 pm. With that plan in place I go about my usual daily agenda; practice, class, gym, studying. I do get to squeeze in a quick lunch with Fiona between her meetings and my class and practice. Looking forward to guy time I head home to get ready.

Since it's just the guys I wear a shirt, jeans, and my hat backwards per usual. After about 2 hours of drinking and eating random bar food we are about to head home until Luke's phone buzzes. "Hey guys I got to go help Lucy. Stuntz are you cool with dropping me off on frat row on the way home?" Luke asks looking stressed. Stuntz nods, I think he wants to see Lucy but that's just my speculation. "What is going on? Is Fiona ok?" I ask him worried. "Its fine. She is fine. I will have her call you" he doesn't make eye contact and starts to walk out the door. "Fuck that Luke tell me what is going on. I am going to head there now anyways so you might as well tell me" I almost yell at him.

"Fine. Lucy thinks that blonde puck bunny put something in Fiona's cup. Do not go in there hulk raging dude. It will only make it worse that's why Lucy called me she wanted to get Fi out without a lot of attention." He looks really upset and I am shaking at this point. I take off to my jeep and I am about to pull off when Luke hops in the passenger side. "Lets go together. Z man I know you are worried but you need to keep your head calm. She is my sister so I understand the worry but we need to be calm" he slaps my shoulder lightly as a sign of support.

When we arrive I see Lucy "Where is Fiona? Why are you not with her?" I yell at her. "Do not yell at me Zane this is why I didn't call you. You need to calm down. Celisa is with her keeping her dancing and moving. She doesn't want to leave but she is slurring, her eyes are dilated. Its getting worse so I want to get her out of here without causing a scene. It can ruin her career" as she glares at me. "Let me go in and get her. I will stay calm and she should leave with me easily" I plead. "Fine but we are coming too" and with that we all head inside.

Inside the party is in full swing drunk people dancing and making out everywhere. I spot Lucy with Celisa theres a group of guys standing way too close for comfort. I hear one tell Celisa that he can take Fiona off her hands for the night. I am about to shove my fist into his face when I feel Lucy touch my chest with her hand warning me to stay calm. Luke looks like he is about to commit murder at this point.

Fiona sees me walking up "Z you made it. Come dance with us" but it's all slurred. She tries to move to me but she trips and kind of just falls into me. "Lets go home babe" I try and guide her out. "No I want to dance" she backs away from me. "Sunshine we can dance at home and we can even get a mcdonalds coke on the way" I plead. "One dance Zane please" funny coming from a girl who cant even hold her own wait up. "Ok" I tell her taking her into my arms.

Slowly I sway with her while I hold her entire body weight up. With each sway I take a step back getting us closer to the doors. She is also getting more and more messed up. She can't keep her eyes open and is limp in my arms. I use that moment to pick her up wrapping her around me so it looks like a sexy moment instead of me taking my drugged girlfriend home.

I put Fiona in my jeep and turn to talk to Lucy "Should we go to the hospital?" She thinks for a second "Honestly I think its too late to pump her stomach, she just needs to get hydrated and ride this out." I tell her I an going to take her to my place and that I will make sure she is hydrated. I ask Luke to tell the coach I had an emergency so I will be missing practice tomorrow. On the way home I stop for Gatorade, Pedialyte, Powerade, any hydration drink I can find. I settle down for what I know is going to be a very long night.

Fiona

Waking up I feel incoherent, everything hurts, I don't know where I am. I start to try and get up; my head is spinning. "Hey, take your time getting up. You might still be lightheaded and weak" Zane tells me from the doorway. "What happened? Did I really drink that much? I remember trying to get you to dance with me. Why were you there is was boyfriend free? I feel horrible" I tell him reaching for a Gatorade on the side of the bed.

Zane proceeds to calmly explain the events of the night. How Lucy called Luke, carrying me to the car, spending all night trying to hydrate me. When he is done giving me all the details, I take a minute to contemplate everything. "Why me? I don't understand why she would do this to me. Is it because of us?" I ask him emotionally. I am scared because how could someone do this to another person.

Zane begins to explain that Celisa overheard one of the girls saying that Nicole was hoping she could get me to hook up with someone and he would leave me for cheating. What a stupid thing to do. How obsessed do you have to be to do something like this. I will not be going back to frat row anytime soon. All I want is to get some more sleep and forget last night happened.

Sleep doesn't come because my mind is racing. Thoughts of what could have happened if Lucy and Celisa hadn't been there. Where I would be this morning if they had been too drunk to notice me acting different. I am eternally grateful to them for taking care of me. Making sure they called someone, and I was safe. Zane took care of me which he didn't need to. He made sure I was safe and cared for. I have never had anyone protect me like this. "Can you hold me?" I ask Zane. "Of course, babe" and he pulls me into his chest.

I got an extra two hours of sleep. I felt safe with Z. "Thanks babe. I say waking up. Did you get any sleep?" I ask him. "Not really but its okay. My mind was racing about how scared I was for you. I am glad you were able to get some sleep when we laid down though, you need it" he says planting a kiss on my forehead. I get up and decide to shower and get dressed.

Coming out of the shower I see an outfit on the counter. "Fi there's fresh clothes on the counter. Lucy dropped them off last night for you" Zane tells me from outside the bathroom. I start crying feeling overwhelmed with love for the people in my life and how much I really appreciate them. My circle really showed up for me last night, I smile at that thought. I get dressed and go to the kitchen where Zane is making breakfast for us.

We eat breakfast and then we sit down to watch a movie. I don't want to leave. I love my apartment and my friends. But I really want to be here more than anything. I don't want to sleep alone but I am afraid to ask Z. I don't think he would say no but also things are still new I don't want him to feel obligated to take care of me. I don't want to be a burden to him with my lack of feeling safe.

"You ok sunshine?" Z asks. I think he can feel my unease while we are cuddling. "I just have a question but its embarrassing and i don't want you to feel obligated to say yes. I don't want to be a burden to you" I say with tears forming in my eyes. "You are never going to be a burden to me. What do you want to ask?" he says reassuringly. "Can I stay here a few days? I don't want to sleep alone. I also don't want to burden you." I say looking away. "Baby girl, I already planned on asking you to stay the next few nights, I would feel better having you close to me. Being there for you is never going to be a burden to me. We can go to your apartment and get some stuff and pick up something for dinner tonight" he says with a kiss.

When we arrived at my apartment Lucy was home, Celisa was at work. I explained to her I didn't feel like sleeping alone. She was so understanding of how I was feeling. She hung out while I packed for a few days of sleeping and work. I spent a good amount of time thanking her repeatedly, I wanted to be sure she knew how incredibly thankful I was for her. Once I had the basics for a few days we headed to target.

Zane gave me the best target trip ever! He took me on a shopping spree! I got a new brush, shampoo, conditioner, face wash, and some more random hygiene stuff. Then as if that wasn't enough, we grabbed some cute throw blankets and he let me pick out a few candles. We had so much fun joking around then getting a coffee before heading back home to make dinner.

Back at his apartment I light one of the new candles that smells like butterscotch and vanilla. I cuddle on the couch in the new blanket watching my favorite vampire show. I get up and help Zane cook dinner. Chicken parmigiana hit the spot while we watch my show.

It's not too late before we go shower then do our nightly routine. When we head to bed, I fall asleep quickly with Zane, laying in my arms gives my mind comfort. Our alarms come early, much earlier than I want. But we both missed yesterday so we can afford to be running late. Zane has dryland and I have filming I need to finish so it can get edited. We head out the door leaving early enough I can grab coffee.

Work goes smoothly, I get some content filmed with Stuntz and Davis. Luke comes to see me during his free time. I thank him multiple times for coming the other night. He asks all the normal questions about how I am feeling and if I need anything. To which I let him know I am doing better but I am staying with Zane for a few days while I get over the unsettled feeling I get when I go to bed. He is understanding and gives me the biggest hug before heading back to do team stuff.

"Hey sunshine, what do you want for dinner tonight? I was thinking of ordering in Chinese or something simple. Since midterms are next week I figured maybe we can put on your show while I study?" Zane asks popping his head in. I get up and give him a kiss "Chinese sounds good! I don't have to watch my show if you are studying I can edit that's less distracting. I am starting my training of the other sports next week so I am getting ahead on content so I don't get backlogged." He smiles and it gives me butterflies "Whatever you want to do, the tv wont bother me. I have a study session after class so I will be home around 7 then we can order." Then with a quick kiss he walks out the door.

I sit on the couch and zone out. I sit there for who knows how long thinking about Zane and I. I think I might be falling in love with him. That thought sends me spiraling into thoughts of what our future will even look like. Will we both be at Tampa Thunder, getting married, having kids who grow up on the rink like their parents. Or will he draft to a team farther way making me either move too or we have to do the long-distance thing for a bit. All the thoughts take over my mind until my phone rings.

"Hello?" I answer. "Hey Fi just checking in on you, I was so worried about you, but Zane seemed to have it under control" Celisa says sounding stressed. We talk about that night and my plans to stay with Z for a few days. I tell her thank you for helping me and let her know I am sorry her birthday was ruined. She isn't upset with me though. After we hang up, I get another two hours of work done before heading home.

I have some time to get showered and settled so that Zane has free use of the bathroom when he gets home. Once we are both showered, we get settled at the kitchen table doing our own things while we eat Chinese. I forgot how much I love sesame chicken and lo mien, It such a comfort food kind of night.

Heading to bed we lay down and get snuggled up. Right as I am about to succumb to my sleep then I remember that there is an away game this weekend. "Z you have an away game this weekend I will probably just head back home when you leave tomorrow" I say letting him know. "You don't have to leave babe, you can have Lucy or Celisa come stay here with you if you want" he says pulling me closer to him. We fall asleep not long after.

The next morning I text Lucy knowing Celisa has to work to see if she wants to sleep over with me here. Then I get up and pack a snack bag for Z to take on the plane. By the time Z gets up I have his snacks ready, and the rest of the apartment is dusted, swept, and mopped. I figured if I stayed this week, I needed to do my share around the house. "Thank you, babe, but I didn't expect you to clean up the house" he says pulling me in to his lap. "I just wanted to be helpful" I drop a kiss on his lap.

We have breakfast together, then I leave to head to work. We spent a decent amount of time making out before I left like two high schoolers. Once at work I try and get everything finished before meeting Lucy back at Zane's apartment. Zane shoots me a text that they are boarding the plane and I know I need to head home if I want to be there when Lucy arrives.

Arriving at the apartment at the same time as Lucy we talk up together. We both stop at the entry table where a vase of fresh flowers is sitting. Next to the vase is $100 with a note 'Have a great night! Here's some money for dinner and drinks. XOXO- Z'. "Okay that's so sweet, you are so lucky Fi. Who knew the resident grump had such a romantic side." Lucy says swooning over the beautiful daisies.

We spend the night eating sushi and drinking wine while watching the UK dating show that we love. I go to the bedroom to show Lucy the bathroom when I notice Zane changed the sheets and made the bed for us. He really knows how to win someone over.

NEED YOUR NUMBER

I call Zane before bed and check in let him know about our night and thank him for everything. I promise to watch the game when it comes on. Snuggling up with Lucy isn't the same but it helps a little. I am grateful to be still in Zane's bed, in his shirt, in his apartment. Safe where nothing bad can get me, and with that I go to sleep.

The next morning, I make breakfast and coffee while we sit around gossiping before Lucy has to leave for clinicals. I enjoy this time with her, but it solidifies that I think I might want to move in with Z at the end of the school year or get my own apartment. I don't say anything yet because we still have a long time before we have to decide on renewing our lease. Not long after breakfast Lucy leaves and I decide to lay down for a nap before the 3pm game.

I put on one of Zane's shirts and send him a picture of me in just the shirt and thong. I use the angles I learned from a TikTok to accentuate my ass. He calls me immediately "Sunshine! I opened that in the locker room, I don't need the guys on my team seeing you and adding that image to their spank bank. You look stunning though. Seeing you in my number is what I needed before the game! The blood rushed out of my brain seeing that photo, fuck you are so hot. I wish I was home the things I would do to you." I blush even though he can't see it. "Well I guess you better hurry home then hot stuff" and with that we hang up so he can get on the ice.

Zane

I am ready to get home to see my girl, but we still have a game to play. We are trying to keep our winning streak up. This is also our last away game for a few weeks, which I am most excited for. I want to be home again. The traveling isn't as fun when you have a girl waiting at home. Guys like Luke love traveling for games. It's 'fresh meat' as he likes to say. I just want to focus kick Tennessee's ass and get on the plane.

The game was rough. We definitely played a team that came in ready to fight for the W. I only went in the penalty box once during the second period. With a final score of 3-2, it was close. We all played hard and we're exhausted. It was a physically demanding game for the whole team. Even the bus ride to the plane was pretty quiet, especially after a win. Most of us fall asleep quickly once we board the plane.

I head straight home when we get off the plane. It's 3 A.M. when I get to the apartment and find Fi sleeping in a ball on the couch. I go set my stuff down and pick up Fiona to put her in bed. She is so light in my arms; she wakes slightly and cuddles closer into my neck. As I set her in the bed, I give her a couple light kisses. "Baby I am home. I'm going to change, then I will come to bed." She just murmurs in response.

When we wake up in the morning my sunshine is draped across me. The light from the window glows around her body like a halo. I move slightly to get comfortable and she begins to stir. Her leg draped over me makes me grow hard. I don't want to push her after the past week of her fear getting to her. I will let her tell me when she is ready again.

Slipping out of bed I head to the shower to take care of things myself. I begin stroking myself slowly with my arm against the wall, holding myself up. I moan out Fiona's name quietly and I start to stroke harder, thinking of her lips on mine. Her pink, plump, kissable lips are going around my cock and I imagine how they would feel flicking her tongue over my tip.

I look up to see Fiona naked outside the shower door. Without a word, she steps in the shower and drops to her knees. It's a literal fantasy come true with her on her knees and the water falling around us. Her mouth is around my cock, taking every inch. She moans as she begins to choke. Holding the back of her head, I keep her rhythm going until I am about to explode. She looks up at me and sucks harder, and I yell her name while she swallows every drop.

I pick her up, lifting her onto me. I slide in easily. Leaning against the shower door, I pound into her, slow and steady. Her pussy is tight as her hands scratch down my back and she moans. I reach my hand up and palm one of her tits. I rub her nipple between my fingers while I lick and suck her other nipple. When I can feel them both equally hard, I switch to the other side. I can feel her getting tighter and her breath becoming unsteady.

"Cum for me sunshine," I moan and then I pull her mouth to mine. We orgasm together.

We finish our shower and then get ready for our usual Sunday stuff. We have coffee and breakfast before settling into studying and editing. I have midterms this week so I am really trying to make sure I have it together. I want to be sure I keep my grades up.

Fiona takes a nap on the couch after lunch. Watching her cuddled up on the couch in a blanket, candle lit, and me studying, it feels right. It feels like home. This apartment has never felt like anything special to me; I just liked my own space, which is why I never decorated it myself and I let Penny do it. But her here makes it feel like something special. I like seeing her hair stuff in the shower, the blankets on the couch I never had before, the candles I never thought I would want.

I want to take her to Target on another shopping spree to decorate the apartment how she likes. I want to invite her to move in but I know that would freak her out because we haven't been together that long. I know how she is - she will spook if I ask now. I will take the time I get with her here right now and enjoy it.

She cooks dinner and then we settle in for the vampire show she loves. I refuse to admit that it's honestly not bad. If the team ever found out I watch these vampire brothers, they would never stop ragging me. I already get shit for going from grump to whipped. I am still grumpy with them, but since Fiona it's been slightly less. It's hard to be grumpy with that ray of sunshine in my life.

"I am heading for bed babe. I know you are studying, so no rush," Fi says, leaning over and kissing me. She walks away. Once she is in the room I get up, following her in. She's in the middle of changing, standing in her thong with a shirt in her hand.

"Keep it off, sunshine," I tell her, leaning against the door frame. "Go ahead and take that thong off and climb up on the bed, babe," I tell her as I take my shirt off. She lays down, staring at me with needy eyes. I let my shorts fall down and I step out of them, making my way to the bed. I kneel on the floor, pulling her to the edge.

Peppering kisses up one thigh and down the other. Spreading her legs, I drop a kiss right on her pussy lips. Using my tongue, I spread her apart and begin licking up and down. When I put her legs over my shoulder, I use my hands to help spread her out. I take my time blowing lightly on her clit. I can feel her shudder.

"Z, please," she whispers and she reaches down to touch herself.

"No ma'am, be a good girl and sit there nicely while I pamper this clit," I tell her before returning to give her some love with my tongue. I slide a finger inside her, then I move to two. She grabs my head, pulling me into her, squeezing her thighs around my head.

"Fuck Zane, please!" she screams as her eyes roll back.

I stand up and position myself between her legs. I give myself a few strokes, then I slide in the tip. Rocking in and out, just giving her a little at a time, keeping her on edge wanting more.

"Z, stop playing and fuck me," she begs, trying to pull me into her.

"Beg for it, baby," I tell her, moving the tip almost out for emphasis. It only takes a few more thrusts before she gives in

"Please, Z, please, I'm begging."

Before she can even finish the sentence, I slam into her. She is so tight and wet I have to focus so I don't cum instantly. I reach down to rub her clit, making her cum, pussy clenched around my dick.

I pull out. "Go ahead and grab the headboard," I say as she crawls up the bed and grabs on like I told her.

Her back looks sexy, elongated with her ass in the air. I take a second and smack her ass, hearing her sharp intake of breath.

"Good girl, keep your ass up just like that," I tell her,and enter her from behind. Thrusting over and over into her tight wet pussy, I can feel myself getting closer to climax. I wrap my hand in her hair, pulling her head back as we both get closer and closer.

"Now baby," I groan and we both orgasm together. I get a washcloth and clean my sunshine up. By the time I get back from the bathroom, she is passed out, naked in the bed.

Waking up on Monday morning, we both get ready. She heads to work and I head to my first midterm of the week. Midterm number one went well; only two more to go. We also have a home game this week, which the whole team is excited about. There is something special about having our game at home. The atmosphere is unmatched when you are on your home rink with your fans cheering.

This season we are close to securing ourselves a slot in the playoffs. Our hopes are high for a championship win because we are undefeated so far this season. This next game is an easy team with a weak offense but they have a great goalie. This is a good team to be coming back home to.

This game will also be the first home game Fiona comes to as my official girlfriend. I am excited to see her in my number again! I love the feeling of knowing my girl is there, cheering me on. To head to the penalty box and have someone to head nod to and let them know you are ok, the person in your corner no matter how you play, and is always there to support you, is a such a good feeling.

I swing by to Fiona's office after my midterm and drop off a McDonald's Coke. She thanks me by jumping in my arms and kissing air straight into my lungs. I love when she does this. I get a chance to grab on her ass without penalty. She tells me that she's heading home to get some stuff and then heading back to my place to start dinner. I almost get my feelings hurt that she doesn't consider my place home, but maybe she does. Even if she doesn't, I can't really be mad because it's not like I asked her to move in officially.

The rest of the week flies by between my midterms and practices. My midterms went well, and I am so happy to be done with them. Practices are fine. Coach is pushing us but it's, so we are getting into the playoff mindset.

Saturday I am ready to get on the ice the moment I wake up.

Fiona wakes up and heads to her place to get ready before i will see her at the game. She does the entrance tunnel photos, so at least I don't have to wait long before seeing her. I make a protein shake before getting in the shower. I put on my suit, making sure I bring an extra pair of clothes just in case Fiona wants to go out to the bar after the game.

I am in my suit, heading to the photo area in the tunnel when I see her. These are probably the best photos they have gotten of me coming in, because I feel like I look like a love-sick fool. She looks amazing! She is in tight black leggings, white Converse, and my white jersey. Her hair is in a high ponytail with a Penguin hair bow. She tosses me an Airhead and I pull one out and toss it to her. The Airhead exchange is my favorite part of this day so far. She drew #27 on her Converse for me; I see it when I really look. I pick her up, spinning her, and drop a big kiss on her lips, making her cheeks flush.

After that moment with Fi, I head into the locker room to a chorus of everyone mocking me for being whipped. I just roll my eyes.

"Don't you all have shit to do?" I grumble, refusing to drop my signature grumpy tone. I do smile though, letting them know I'm not going to murder them for joking with me. We get ready to take the ice and I eat my Airhead and prepare to head out.

Skating out, I laugh as I see all the Airheads and other random snacks being held in the air by fans. Fiona started that as a fun fact about me and the fans loved it so much, she made it a segment. She posts a player and their favorite snack. The next game we usually see fans holding it up. It's fun and it helps concession sales, too.

I skate past Fi, putting my hand on my heart then putting it against the glass. She repeats the same motion and my heart warms. Luke skates over, saying hi to her before we all skate off to get ready for the game. As we finish our laps around the rink, I think of how much I loved trying to beat out the guys for the most jerseys with my number on them. Now I could care less if someone is in my number. I have great teammates; wear their numbers. But I need my girl in my number. It's an absolute must.

We win in a shut out 1-0! Their goalie is really good. I ended up in the box once, and like I imagined, I found Fiona and we locked eyes and I nodded; so did she. I could hear her yelling when I got cross checked into the boards. I love when she stands up for me. She smiles at me all night whenever we lock eyes. I try to be subtle. I don't want any opponents using her to get in my head.

After the game I head to the locker room but before I am fully there, I hear my name being called. I turn around to see Fi flying and then landing in my sweaty, tired arms.

"Come straight home after the game, babe; I have something for you," she tells me before kissing me, then heading out the door. I take the fastest shower in history. I need to get home and see what she has for me.

Fiona

I told Zane I have a surprise for him when he gets home so I know he will be rushing straight here. He played a great game tonight and I am going to show him how proud I am. Things have been good between us the past two weeks; I feel like we have gotten closer and that we are even more comfortable together.

I hear the front door open and close, show time I tell myself. I have never been in a relationship where we were adventurous sexually, so this is all new ground for me. But I know Z is more experienced than I am, so I want to show him I want to do more. I want to trust him in all aspects of my life starting with our bedroom time.

The door opens and he is standing there in his button up and slacks on looking so fucking hot. "What's going on in here?" he asks without moving from the doorway. "I set all this up so we can experiment in the bedroom together. I have my safe word #27. I know you like being dominating on the ice and in the bedroom, but you have been holding back so let's stop holding back" and I motion my hand over the dresser holding some sex toys I got online, lube, and a whip. He smirks and begins to roll up his sleeves in the door way.

I stand there in a green lingerie one piece I got at the store this week waiting for him to say something. He leans on the doorframe one handed. "Ok sunshine lets experiment" he says in a voice that could melt my outfit right off my body. "Go ahead and crawl over to the bed and bend over" his eyes darken like he's been waiting to be more dominating with me. I crawl over and bend over the bed watching him cross the room. He grabs a few things then walks to the bedside table.

SMACK. I recoil slightly from the smack of the whip, I expected it to hurt but I didn't expect it too feel so good. I felt myself suddenly soaked between my legs. He spanks me again "That made you wet didn't it baby girl. You didn't realize how much you like it rough." He palms my ass lightly before dropping a kiss on each ass cheek. "Spread your legs" he sucks in a breath when I listen to his command "crotchless lingerie you dirty girl."

117

Suddenly I don't feel him behind me anymore, I turn around to see him stripping off his shirt and then laying down next to me. "Come sit down" he says, I think he can see the confusion on my face. "Come sit on my face I want to eat my dessert" he repeats. I hover over his face holding on to the edge of the bed. "I said sit not hover" and he pulls me fully onto him. My knees on each side of his head I shudder feeling his breath on me. He opens me up with his tongue, then proceeds to eat me like he hasn't had a meal in weeks. He nips at my clip sending me over the edge as I climax grinding my pussy against his face. He lifts me up a bit to say "Remember the safe word if you need it, you need to relax and trust me." I nod my head unsure what he's referring to. He goes back to licking and sucking my clit, he slides his finger inside me then pulls it back out almost immediately. I am confused as I moan my disappointment, then I realize why. His finger is now swirling lightly around my asshole. I have never done this, I immediately tense up. He gives me a smack on the ass murmuring against my pussy for me to relax. I try to listen as I feel the pressure but not pain. He takes his time and honestly the oral I am getting helps me to relax as I lean forward onto the bed to give him a little better access. When his finger goes in I feel a little pain and then an intense amount of pleasure. He keeps his finger still but I begin to rock wanting more. It only takes about a minute before I am panting and cum all over his face.

He lightly lifts me up off him into the standing position. "Such a good girl sunshine" he walks to the bathroom leaving me standing there in a wave of post orgasm high. He comes out of the bathroom naked his hands are wet he must of washed them. He sit on the edge of the bed "come show me what good things you can do with that mouth." How can me sweet caring golden retriever boyfriend talk like this, and how is it making me so incredibly turned on.

I walk over and drop to my knees I lick his length up and down spending extra attention on the slit making sure I get the precum. I proceed to take as much of him in my mouth as I can before he's hitting the back of my throat. I move my head up and down quickly, usually this is about all I do. I decide to spice it up a bit, I remember I used my teeth lightly last time and he liked it. So as I am coming back up his dick I let me teeth lightly touch him, and when we hit the tip I focus on just sucking there for a few seconds before dropping back down. I know he is about to cum because he roughly grabs the back of my head and begins to fuck my face. "Relax babe stop fighting it, you can be a good girl and take all of me right?" I am gagging but I nod anyway. I focus on trying to breath as he hits me in the back of the throat repeatedly. I look up at him with glossy eyes, he makes eye contact moaning out as he shoots his load down the back of my throat. Usually, I would just let it end here, but I keep sucking on him, until I can feel himself hardening in my mouth again.

"Get on the bed and spread your legs" he commands. I never thought I would like this but something about being dominated in the bedroom is incredibly sexy. He grabs the wand I bought, turning it on the sound already has me aching between the legs. He places the toy against my pussy rubbing it up and down my slit. "Play with your tits for me baby" I listen sliding my hands up and grabbing both my tits. The lace from the lingerie adding a little more friction making my nipples harden even faster. Its insanely stimulating feeling the lace on my nipples. Then the toy hits my clit, he rubs it in circles before sliding two fingers inside me while using the toy to get my clit. It doesn't take long before I am cumming on his fingers thanks to the added stimulation of the toy and the lace.

Zane reaches up and begins sliding my outfit off my body taking his time to let the lace rub down my body. I am breathing heavily at this point I am so turned on all I want is him. He lines up with my entrance and enters slowly, sliding in and out just barely. "Please I am begging you" with that he slams into me fully. I knew I just needed to beg for it. The sex isn't anything different but because of the extremely erotic foreplay the sex feels different. I feel closer to him. There is something about giving your body to someone sexually trusting them to not cross the line that makes your trust for them grow in many ways. When climax together, Zane takes my lips with his kissing me, as we ride out the high together with my pussy clenching around him as I can feel the warmth of his cum.

He carries me to the shower and proceeds to wash my hair and body for me, taking extra care when he washes my pussy knowing I am sore. He showers himself quickly while I get out and dry off. Getting out he brushes my hair for me and puts it in a loose braid. Then cleans up the room putting all the stuff into the nightstand after he cleans it. He climbs into bed holding me from behind. It hard to imagine the man who just washed me, brushes and braided my hair is capable of being so dirty but I loved every minute. It's not long before we both fall asleep.

I wake up in the morning to an empty bed, I head to the kitchen and find Z finishing up with cooking breakfast. "Morning beautiful" he says when he spots me. "Hey babe you let me sleep in?" I walk over giving him a kiss. He lifts me onto the counter. "Yes, I did babe, you needed it" and he kisses me. It quickly turns into making out with me moaning into his mouth I can feel him hardening between my legs. I reach down pulling my underwear to the side. He looks down before quickly sliding his pants down. He pulls me to the edge of the counter picking me up and guiding himself into me. He fucks me against the wall before walking us to the couch bending me over the arm rest. He wraps an arm around and starts rubbing my clit until we both cum.

"Go get ready for breakfast babe" and he pulls his shorts up drops a kiss on my lips and heads to the kitchen. We sit at the table and talk about our plans to go to thanksgiving at Penny's with their parents. I am super nervous to meet them, but Zane seems confident they will love me. Then we are all going to his game Saturday together. "Last night was amazing babe, and so was this morning" he tells me between bites. "It was great for me too I didn't know how much I would enjoy some of that stuff" I smile sheepishly. Then we finish our breakfast and spend the day watching movies.

The week flies by between work and Zane's busy schedule of practice and classes. I have been staying at his house for three weeks now. Its thanksgiving which i am excited for some time with Zane without work or practice getting in the way. But Last night at dinner I brought up after Thanksgiving dinner tonight I should probably start staying at my place again. Zane seemed kind of hurt but he understood that we should get back into a routine.

I get dressed in a burnt orange dress the falls right at my knees and pair it with some brown booties. I wear my hair in curls with the front twisted and pinned back. I put on light makeup accentuating my eyes. I try and keep my look simple and sophisticated. I am so stressed about meeting the parents. The drive is quick not giving me much time to mentally prepare.

Penny's house a cute two story in a little neighborhood on near the school she works at. We bring some flowers and wine for dinner. Penny opens the door ignoring Zane pulling me into a hug. "Ok don't suffocate her Pen"

Zane tells her chuckling. Hugging Zane, she then invites us inside. Zane's mom is beautiful she's tall with long strawberry blonde hair with hazel eyes. His dad is tall with short blonde hair and beautiful brown eyes. They take turns pulling me into a hug making me feel so comfortable.

We spend the dinner talking all of us exchanging stories of Zane. I learn about his obsession with pokemon as a kid. Or how he was convinced he would marry a Disney princess. I laughed about how Penny was the better skater for a while when they were younger, and Zane would pout over it. I laugh because Luke would do the same thing. I hear stories of him trying to sneak a girl in one night and getting caught. The conversation switches to me.

I tell them about growing up with my siblings and tell my share of funny stories. They are super supportive of my job and let me know they watch the content I post. Of course they are biased and believe that the Zane content is best. They gush over the Instagram posts we have made about each other. I am so excited to go to the game together all my worries gone.

I go to clean up the kitchen giving Zane time with his parents and Penny follows me in. "So Fi how long have you been in love with my brother?" She tells me looking curious. I almost choke on my spit. "Um what. I don't know what you uh.. mean. We haven't said.. I haven't said... um..." I stumble over my words. "You don't have to say anything girl you look at him like he hung the moon for you. You may not of realized it yet but you love him. He loves you but he will wait until he thinks you're ready. I can see it in his face and the way he is around you" She says confidentially. "Oh I am not sure Penny" I say. She hugs me "it's okay, I love you for him. You are the best girl to ever enter his life. Lets get dinner soon just us." She says. With that we clean the kitchen then go move to the living room for the rest of the night.

On the drive home I get lost in my thoughts thinking of what Penny says. Once back at the apartment I tell Zane I am going to shower, and I rush off. The last guy I loved broke me into a thousand little pieces. He destroyed me on purpose, and I am afraid of being vulnerable again. But if I take the fear away, I know I love him. I know I will spend the rest of my life with him if he allows me. I don't know why that word is sending me into a spiral.

After my shower I climb in bed "Sunshine are you okay? My parents love you if that's why are you upset." He tells me. "I'm fine just tired" I tell him leaning up to kiss him before laying down to sleep. I know I'm being a coward, but I just need to think. In the morning I feel a little better. Zane and I make out some and enjoy snuggling before we head to the rink. All my content is edited but I need to get a plan started for next week.

My day flies by with me focusing on working on next week's stuff. Heading back to my apartment I still Lucy on the couch. "Hey stranger how was thanksgiving?" she asks. "It was amazing I love them, but Penny asked if I love Zane and now, I am spiraling and pushing him away. I can't help myself because I know I love him I am just afraid of being hurt again. And if I am being honest I don't want to stay here, I want to be there sleeping in his bed." I start crying all of my emotions flooding in.

"Oh honey. It's okay to be afraid, don't ruin things with him over fear though. Did he tell you to leave? If not then go back there. Be with him. Show him you want him even if you aren't ready to verbalize it." She tells me. I cry for a little longer then I pack a bag with even more clothes for longer. I am terrified as I leave my apartment and head to Zane's.

I use the key to go inside "Fiona?" he calls out. "Hi Zane" I say sheepishly. "What's wrong babe? I'm glad you are here but what's wrong I thought you wanted space?" he asks me. I run and jump in his arms, and he catches me. He always catches me, he always will. I start to cry into his shoulder, he rubs my back until the tears start to stop.

"I am here babe when you are ready to tell me why you are so upset" he whispers as he rubs my back. I finally get my composure, but I stay in his lap for the support and comfort. "So, Zane just let me tell you everything before you interrupt, okay?" I tell him. "Ok babe you are scaring me just tell me" He says.

"I never wanted to leave I just didn't want to force my presence on you. I also realized I am not ready to say certain things, but I do feel them. I have really strong feelings for you and I don't want to lose you but I can't get myself to say that four letter word. I don't know how you feel or how you want to move forward. If you want me to only spend a few days a week here or back to just Sundays. But I want to stop running and make these decisions together. I love your family, and I just wanted to also tell you that. I probably should of called before showing up but here I am."

"Are you done?" he asks calmly. "yes" I tell him. "Good, my turn to spill my feelings, I have huge feelings for you. About you staying here, I was hurt when you said you were leaving to stay at your place because to me this is your home. What happened to you that night, when Nikki drugged you, showed me that without a doubt I want to be with you. I didn't ask you to move in because I didn't want to scare you off. Also never feel like you need to call to come here, in my mind this is OUR place. I know we just got together in early September, but I fell hard and fast." He confesses.

He didn't want me to leave. He has strong feelings too. He fell for me hard and fast. I never needed to be scared he was always going to catch me when I fell. We head to bed shortly after the confession with us both having to report to the rink early. I sleep so good after getting all those feelings off my chest.

I get dressed in a jersey and cute jeans with my hair in two space buns that I braided back. I put on my makeup and tell Zane bye then run out the door. I see my brother show up early to talk to coach, but we spend a few minutes catching up. I set up the tripod to record entrances and I hang out tossing candies and snacks to players. When Zane arrives, he stops short of me and digs in his bag. I assume for airheads but when he walks up he doesn't toss me anything. "Missing something Sunshine?" he asks. "No?" I say confused. He pulls out a paint pen "my number?" he says. I laugh "how could I forget?" I say and turn my cheek and let him add it. He gives me a kiss then hands me an airhead. "See you later babe" he winks.

I find his family easily up against the glass by the team. The glass seats are perks for family members of players. They don't show Zane's pregame routine of skating to me so I am interested to see if he does it in front of his family. As the team skates out, Luke comes by first and we fist bump through the glass, his family knows him already not making me have to explain anything. When Z enters the ice he comes right to us, he bangs the glass then tosses the usual airhead over. I smile, he slides his glove off putting his hand against the glass and I put my hand up against it. He then looks over and waves to his family before skating off.

Penny gives me a knowing look and his mom says "That was the cutest thing I have ever seen, I heard he did that but it was different to see. You are his calm before the storm. His penalty points are even down this season." I smile. The game goes good Zane ends up once for a minor and he nods letting me know he's good. His dad notices bringing it to everyone's attention

"He looks at you to reassure you he's okay that's really sweet" he smiles. Zane skates his best maybe because his family is there but i am super proud. He really showed off with his skills on the ice. He manages to stay out of the penalty box outside of the once for the rest of the game. He even has an assist to Luke for a goal which is super exciting for his parents. It is so cute the way they cheer for him against the boards when he is close.

They win the game 2-1, and the boys meet us outside. Where his parents take some time to congratulate everyone. They are really the sweetest people ever. We head to a group dinner with Luke and Stuntz joining us before we head home. We all enjoy tacos for dinner. The guys exchange their favorite moments from the game. Zane sneaks some little kisses to me its really sweet. Penny takes a picture with the guys so she can brag to her students about her future NHL brother and friends. It was nice and i am so lucky to be here with them.

Zane

Coming home from dinner Fiona and I shower and head straight to bed it's been along day. Thanksgiving is over so my parents will be heading back on the road soon. I am glad they got to meet Fi though. We are spending Christmas with her family which is exciting because I feel like meeting the parents is a big step. After Fiona's big confession I feel a lot better about where we are at in our relationship. I plan to ask her to officially move in around Christmas even though she technically lives here as it is. I want to do something special, but I need to talk to Lucy first.

Sunday after breakfast we head to Fiona's to grab some more stuff just to help her have stuff for every occasion. While we are there, I tell Lucy I need to talk to her and we make a plan to meet up on Wednesday afternoon. Heading home we unpack her stuff into the closet, and I clear a few drawers for her. Once she is unpacked, we lay on the couch and take a nap.

I wake up to her ass pressed perfectly against my groin. She is in a t-shirt and a pair of cheeky panties so I can feel her warm skin on me. I rub my hand up her thigh and lightly graze the hem of her shirt. She shudders pressing into me even more. "Baby wake up so I can fuck you properly and show you how strong my feelings are for you" I whisper in her ear. "Go for it" she says. I slide my pants down just enough to get my dick out. Pulling her underwear to the side, I feel she's already wet. I slide myself right into her. Slow and steady because she is tight especially at this spooning angle. It is not long before we both orgasm. I clean her up and let her fall back asleep while I order dinner.

Monday seems to drag on, but I did find time for coffee with Fi. By the time I come home she has dinner cooked and is sitting on the couch watching some chick flick. I am happy she didn't go back to her place this is where I want her to be. I like this domesticated lifestyle we have started.

Tuesday, I sleep in while she heads to work. Dropping off a McDonald's coke to Fiona's office while she's in a meeting. I go meet the guys after practice for a beer. Its our first night out since Celisa's birthday. "So I am in love with Fiona and I think im going to tell her soon" I blurt out after our second round. "No shit" Luke says like he's known. "We can all see that dude, you go from don't speak to me grumpy to target trips and braiding hair around her. Plus when the guys joke around with her you glare daggers at them" Stuntz says. Well that was easier than expected because they already know.

We enjoy the rest of guys night and I head home to my girl. At the apartment she is sleeping in bed peacefully. I go shower trying not to wake her up. Climbing back in bed she stirs slightly falling right back asleep. I lay there thinking of my talk I am having with Lucy tomorrow. Finally sleep hits me.

I wake up to kisses making their way down my chest, It's like a dream. I wake up fully when i feel lips around my cock. After bobbing up and down a few times Fiona looks at me and says, "Good morning handsome, just starting you day off with a little loving." She proceeds to give me the best head making me cum in record time. Then she just jumped up and got ready for work. I lay there for a few minutes; fuck I love this girl. I need to wait to tell her though.

I head to practice and then my early afternoon class. Meeting up with Lucy at the coffee shop on the medical side of campus. I am so nervous I am almost sweating. I hope she likes my idea and doesn't think I need to wait.

"Hey Luc" I say taking a seat with my coffee at the table she's at. "What's up Zane?" she asks looking intrigued by why I wanted to meet her. I tell her my plan for Friday night. I am going to have Fiona come home to a gift basket with a keychain, home décor stores, a mug, and a candle. My official will you move in. I also offer to help with her portion of the rent at their place, but I guess Lucy has a friend who is going to move in after she talks to Fiona. I really want things to go smoothly, and I am hoping this is the way.

The rest of the week drags on after my coffee meeting with lucy. I am so excited, and I think Fiona can tell I am planning something. I just want to wait until Friday when we are both home at a decent hour. During the week our schedules at night can be crazy.

Friday after practice I spend the day at Home Goods, Hobby Lobby, and Target getting gift cards. I find a cute mug and keychain in target too. I get this champagne toast candle at Bath and Body Works I think she will love. I arrange it all in a super cute basket I bought at one of the stores. Then I head home to surprise her.

Fiona is on the couch when I get home. "Hey where have you been? You left the rink before me I was getting worried" she asks not accusing but concerned. "I was getting you a surprise, close your eyes" I tell her overflowing with excitement. I put the basket on the coffee table and let her open her eyes. She looks through everything and starts crying. "Good tears or Bad tears" I ask concerned. "Good, definitely. Good. Yes, I will officially move in! I just need to talk to the girls." She says. "I already talked to Lucy before I asked to be sure they would be okay. But she is expecting your call I'm sure" I say giving her a kiss. "You talked to Lucy first that is so thoughtful of you" she says pulling me in for a hug.

We have chicken alfredo for dinner before we head to bed. Another home game means we have a busy day ahead of us. Tomorrow's team is physically abrasive they spend a lot of time in the penalty box. So, we know heading into the game we need to be physically ready.

Saturday Fiona leave before I am even awake. We have a later rink time due to coach knowing this game is going to be a blood bath. I smile seeing Fiona she's in her usual game day attire. My number is on her cheek, her hair is in a cute bun, her leggings and converse with my jersey. Before I can say anything, she's tossing a handful of airheads at me making me scatter to try and catch them. I am sure the footage of that is hilarious, but I hope she's ready for retaliation. Smirking I walk off to the locker room.

Heading on to the ice Luke, Stuntz, Davis, and I skate over to where Fiona is sitting. She looks confused as the four of us come to a stop in front of her. I press my glove to the glass and then when she gets close to put her hand against it all four of us toss a handful of airheads at her. I wink and we all skate away for warmups.

The game starts off rough but not too bad during the first period. The second period though, the other team is getting more and more aggressive. The minute one of their players check our goalie its fucking on. The unwritten rule in hockey is the goalie is always off limits. Racing down the rink, I shoulder check their player into the boards. Ripping my gloves off a full fight begins, helmets are flying until the linesmen break the fight up. I realize quickly that Stuntz, and Luke also got involved with other players from the other team. Three of us on each side in the penalty box right now. It was worth it though; I find Fi giving her the nod. By the time we are done in the box the second period is finishing up.

Third period immediately starts off violent, there is instant checking in to the boards from their team. O'Brien our left defenseman is in the box for fighting with one of their players. There is 7 minutes left in the final period when I get checked from the side. I hit the boards hard and before I even realize the player sends me and my helmet flying backwards. My head hits the ice hard I can't move it hurts so bad. I hear the team doctor talking to me, but it all seems muffled. I am conscious so I know that's a good sign.

I hear Luke next to me saying he's going to let Fiona know to head to the trainer's room. My head is killing me as I stand up to get off the ice I can feel the throbbing in my head. I look down and can see the blood, the trainers tell me to sit back down but I stay standing. Making my way off the ice, I head right to the trainer's room. I don't care about policy of not walking I keep going. I just want to see Fi and let her know I am ok.

"Yeah, he is up and they are getting him off the ice, Luke told me to head to the trainer area, I will call you when I talk to him. Bye Pen." She sees me walking up then. she's crying and her face is puffy "You are okay, I was so scared Zane" she tells me as I hug her tight. Before I can answer the trainers are shuffling us into the room. Checking over my head they recommend a trip to the ER for stitches and a concussion check. After trying to argue my way out of it Fiona speaks up "I will take him straight there."

In her car heading to the ER we make a few calls to my parents and Penny who apparently called Fiona to see how I was doing. They were watching on TV and it cut off with the trainer out there and me not moving. Not ideal when it's your family watching.

The ER was not too bad they got me back quickly the athletic director called ahead about what happened. I am waiting on my scan results, but the doctor does come give me 4 staples in the back of head. Fiona holds my hand the whole time. Three hours later we are out the door heading home. Concussion free and all stapled up! Concussions can be career ending so that was my biggest worry with this fight. I text coach the news on our drive home.

Getting home I go to shower and get ready for bed while Fiona runs back out to pick up my medications. I am exhausted and my head hurts so bad, but I am lucky this game is over, and we ended with a win. I would have been pissed if I got hurt and we lost. Poor Fiona was terrified today, I hated seeing her like that. I can't imagine how she felt seeing me on the ice unmoving. I drift off to sleep at some point while I am waiting for Fiona to return.

Its noon on Sunday when I wake up and I can hear voices. Coming out of the room I see Fiona, Penny, Luke, and Stuntz. They all came to see how I am feeling and brought over stuff. Penny brought chicken and rice casserole I love. And the guys brought coffee and muffins.

We hang out for a few hours before everyone heads out. It was nice seeing them and I am grateful for them checking in but damn my head hurts. Fiona heads to the kitchen to take care of heating up dinner. When she comes back to the couch, I pull her into my lap. Holding her against me I whisper in her ear "You are so special to me Fiona, I am so lucky to have you here." She smiles before saying "I was so scared, you laying there was terrifying, there was a lot of blood, and the lineman was struggling to get him off you." Kissing her cheek, I tell her "They went for the goalie, Fi, you know that is enough to clear the bench for a brawl. I couldn't let them get away with it. But I am sorry with how far it was taken. I don't even know how my helmet came off." We talk more about the fight and how it's going viral right now. Everyone loves seeing the team defending the goalie.

Dinner was good, Penny makes a great casserole. We watch a movie and then head to bed. I have no practice tomorrow, but I must report to the rink to talk to coach and the trainers. Then I still have to go to tape. Finals are in two weeks, Christmas Is in three weeks, with two games coming up one home and one away. We lucked out this season with no game Christmas week.

Fiona

Heading to bed it's the first time in the past 24 hours I feel like I really have to process how I feel. I have been on autopilot since the game. I knew the fight was getting bad the other players were all starting to brawl each other. But the second Zane's helmet flew off I knew something bad was going to happen. It was like slow motion watching him fall and hit the ice. The ice turned red slowly and he wasn't moving. I saw the team trainer head out to check him out and I knew it wasn't good. Luke skated over and motioned for me to head to the trainer area. So, I never actually saw Z get up. Penny was calling but I had no answers I was scared and so was she and her parents. Seeing him walk around the corner I have never felt so relieved. I was crying which is sad because he was the one hurt. But between the game, the hospital, and having visitors my mind hasn't been able to rest. It doesn't take long for me to fall asleep once I lay down.

Monday morning, I get ready for work giving Zane a kiss before heading out the door. He can't practice yet but he has meetings and team stuff he still needs to participate in. Coffee is my first task; I know we are going to have a lot of press stuff to do with Zane's injury. People are already asking if he's coming back to play the next two games. If we win this coming weekend, we will secure our spot in the playoffs, so fans are worried. We haven't made in comments publicly about Zane's condition except that he is back home and doing well. The college hockey league is going to want a full concussion report sent in.

Coffee in hand I meet Marissa to go over social media plans. We will have a press conference once all the admin stuff is done. I will do a live of that and then field questions from there. Zane is the team's best defender being without will cause a weakness in the team on the ice most likely. I also don't know how Z will handle not playing being only a few months from the championship, so hopefully if they bench him, it won't be for long.

The rest of my meetings for the day are quick, they schedule the press conference for 4 pm. I post on all the team socials letting people know we will be live with updates. I spend the rest of my afternoon creating reels and TikTok videos until it is time for the press conference.

Coach does a quick run through of Zane's condition, making sure to clarify he does not have a concussion. He does say he will be benched for the coming home game just to give his head an extra week to heal. There is no plan to keep him benched for the away game the following week. Fans in the comments are relieved and all express their support for Z and the team.

As I am packing up for the day my stomach growls. I forgot to eat, and I am starving, I text Z and he has study group, so I message Lucy and Celisa. They respond quickly with a girl's night in plan. Who can say no to wine and sushi, followed up by gossip from campus. Plus, I need to talk to them about me moving out.

When I arrive, I am swarmed with hugs and a glass of wine. The sushi arrives quickly, and we talk about the latest campus drama while we eat. It's nice because I don't go here so the drama is fun to hear but nothing for me to worry about. When we start our second glass of wine, I tell the girls about agreeing to move in with Zane. They both are excited and supportive, which is honestly such a relief. Lucy tells me about her friend Charlie. Who is interested in taking over my lease. She seems super nice and is a waitress downtown. She is finishing up her degree in business management. We make plans for the four of us to get together. After more chit chat I head out after reminding them that I will see them at our parents for Christmas.

Driving back to our apartment I think about all the stuff I need to get done before Christmas. I still need to get presents for Zane and Luke. Luke will be easy though I just need to run to the store and actually pick it up. Zane though I don't know what to get. He seems like he has everything he wants and if he doesn't have it he just buys it. When I get home, I need to bring up bills. I haven't had the chance. Maybe a cute doormat or something for the apartment. I need to figure something out soon I have three weeks to prepare. Pulling up to the house I see Zane is home from his study group.

"Hey babe" I say as I come inside. "Hey sunshine, have fun with the girls?" he asks giving me a kiss and pulling me into a hug. "Yeah we had a nice time. Listen I have a question for you, let me know if you don't want to answer" I tell him as I sit on the couch. "What's up?" he asks curiously. "We never discussed bills. Honestly, I'm not sure how you even afford all the stuff you do without a job and no scholarship. But I just want to know how you want to split the bills I don't want to free load." I tell him. He chuckles a little and I raise an eyebrow questioning him. "Babe I am not hurting for money because my grandfather set Penny and I up with a hefty trust fund. That's how a high school teacher has a nice house in Tampa with a single income. I only got this apartment because it's close to the rink. I don't need any money from you seriously. But if it you want to contribute you can help with groceries. Put the rest towards helping with the rest of your student loans if you want" he says.

With that conversation over I feel less bad about the dinners, target trip, gift cards, all the stuff he has somehow been affording. I can definitely use the extra income to pay off my student loans and maybe start saving for a new car. I am going to go sentimental for his gift for sure. That seems like the right thing to do. I just need to get a plan together this week.

Heading to bed we talk about him not playing this week "I am going to still be on the bench as their co-captain I need to be close to help them. I want to be able to help guide Walters as he steps up to my position. He is good but he hasn't gotten much ice time, so I want to help assure him" he says. I am so proud of how he is handling being off the ice this week. I know it's not easy. "On the plus side you are getting extra study time for finals next week. That is always good! Then you guys' head to Alabama and you will be back on the ice. I will be here cheering you on." I try to encourage him to stay in good spirits.

I must of fell asleep fast because I don't remember closing my eyes after talking about the game and finals. But its Tuesday so I am going to work with the basketball team today. Getting dressed I make sure to wear a school shirt with my leggings, so I don't go in all "hockey" is the best. I want to blend in as I help Stacy, the team's social media student intern, to get their socials tracking steadily upwards.

My day with Stacy is great. The basketball team is great, all the guys were friendly and willing to try all the things. I love when players are willing to participate in the silly TikTok's. She will be fine now that I have shown her the best ways to find sounds and ideas. I will also send her over a content calendar that should help to plan things. She will be coming to the game Saturday to learn my process for game day. By the time I leave the courts I am confident they will be viral before they know it.

Wednesday I go get Luke's gift and decide to use my gift cards from Z. Shopping Day is my kind of self care! TJ Maxx I get some picture frames, a few throw pillows for the couch, a few amazing scented candles, and a cute dress. Home goods I get some art for the walls, a new planner, and a cute little popcorn maker. I stop and get tacos for lunch. Target is my last stop and its also my biggest stop. I get some coffee first though my obsession with iced coffee is unreal. At target I go crazy getting a new comforter set, bath towels, bath rugs, a cute kitchen rug, and a cute matching loungewear set for us both. I also grab some groceries. Then with a car full of goods I head home.

It takes 5 loads to get everything into the apartment. But I hustle to get everything done before Z gets home. I text him to let me know when he pulls in. Everything is setup, hung up, and cleaned up by the time I get the text. I meet him outside the front door.

"What's up sunshine?" he asks looking curious. "I used those gift cards. I hope you like what I got. If you don't I have the tags and receipts." I say as I step inside letting him in. He looks at the kitchen now with matching mats and towels on the oven. "I like it" he says moving to the living room. The art is on the wall behind the couch, the pillows are on nicely placed and a candle is burning. "Looks good babe seriously" he says kissing my temple. He heads to the bedroom stopping to see the new comforter I got and the picture frame on the nightstands with photos of us in them. He then heads to the bathroom without a word. The matching rugs and bath towels are set out. There is a cute sign on the wall in here too. "You did amazing, and you obviously took into account my style when you got everything. I love it. The new bedding set looks great, and I love the art and photos" he picks me up kissing me.

He sets me on the counter and strips out of his shirt and pants leaving him standing in just his boxers. I pull my shirt off leaving my bra on. He kisses my neck, trailing kisses from my ear lobe to my collarbone. He reaches around taking my bra off and immediately take a handful. Lowering his mouth, he plays with one nipple while he palms the other one rubbing the nipple between his fingers. Switching side my nipples are sensitive and I can feel myself getting wet. I reach down attempting to stroke him, but I am at a bad angle. He realizes what I am doing and backs up letting me slide off the counter. Before I can do anything, he has my pants around my ankles and is spinning me around to look at the mirror.

He slides my panties to the side, then slides a finger in me. "Already so wet. I wonder if I can just slide in" he whispers as he pulls his cock out. He guides himself to line up with my entrance. "Be a good girl and relax" he murmurs before slamming into me from behind. "Look at how beautiful you are. Do you want to wear my hand like a necklace baby girl?" Z asks. I nod. He wraps his hand around my neck as he continues to rail me from behind. I cum with his hand around my throat and making eye contact through the mirror. I have never felt so sexy as I do when Z is looking at me.

He spins me around then picks me up and brings me from the bathroom to our bed. "Lets christen these new sheets" he growls as he climbs on top of me. I am still coming down from my post orgasm high when he is sliding into me. Reaching over to the nightstand I can hear him moving stuff around trying to find what he is looking for without stopping. I see him pull out the little pink wand from our last experiment night. I expect him to pull out and use it but no. He puts it on my clit while he is still fucking me. "Be a good girl and don't cum until I say so" he murmurs. "Such a tight pussy, so wet for me" he whispers. "Please Z I am ready. Let me cum. Please I am begging" I whimper as he starts thrusting harder and faster. "Not yet" he says. I am overstimulated, my clit is throbbing, my nipples are hard, my pussy is soaking wet begging to orgasm. He turns the wand up a notch, leans down into my ear whispering "Now baby" as he nips my neck. I have never orgasmed like that. I felt like I was reborn. I am catching my breath when Z gets up. He comes back with a washcloth "You were such a good girl, now go to sleep you have work in the morning" he whispers into the darkness.

Thursday is boring. I have no meetings. I have no impending deadlines. I spend the day walking around filming candid stuff. The guys playing hacky sack and throwing a ball. I get some workout footage; everyone loves a shirtless hockey guy in the gym. There's footage of them watching tape no sound just focused faces. Some on ice drills they are doing in small groups. I luck out and catch the guy's cracking jokes and get some really cute footage of just happiness. I come back to my office to see my favorite guy sitting on my couch with McDonald's coke. He hangs out going over plays while I work on posting some of my candid stuff I got today.

On our way out I see the Z everyone complains about being grumpy. It's almost comical to see how he is with people who aren't me. One of the freshmen comes up and says he is glad he is okay, and he barely grunts out a thank you. Like he uses all his words with me so he can't use them with others because he reaches his daily quota. Like in the bedroom he is the dirtiest of dirty talkers, with me he is just loving and golden retriever style absolute lover boy, with the team he scowls and speaks with grunts, but he is respected because of his drive and skill. A man of many faces, I guess.

When we get home Zane cooks dinner and we talk about the day a little bit. He tells me about how studying for finals next week is going. We discuss the plans for the game with him being on the bench I am going to try and film some good content showing his captain side since I never get much footage of that. Settling in to watch a movie after dinner I am reminded how happy I am right now.

With Justin it was like always walking on eggshells. I had to do what he wanted when he wanted. I didn't get to ask questions or have ideas. I considered this dream of owning a sports media company. I even had a business plan and all. Justin laughed in my face that it would never work and it makes no sense to try. So i let that dream die along with all my happiness. He was constantly crushing my soul. I don't know why I never left but its not for lack of wanting to. When someone treats you like that you begin to believe them. You believe you are a failure and that no one will ever love you. Its so discouraging that you don't want to try because what if they are right. Graduating college was the moment I realized I wasn't a failure and I wasted no time packing and leaving. I told him after I had started moving stuff. I didn't want him to be able to influence me.

I never told my family until after because I was so embarrassed. They reminded me that I am strong for leaving before it escalated. I am lucky to have a strong support system who helped me. Then meeting Zane who has shown me what its like to be truly loved and most importantly respected. He might be rough and dirty in the bedroom but I never question that he respects every inch of my body and mind. He allows me to be my own person by his side instead of trying to mold me into his ideal person. I think I might even be ready to tell him I love him but I am not one hundred percent sure. If he said it though I think I might say it back.

Zane

I am not sure what was going on with Fiona last night, but I could tell something was off. I hate seeing her like that. I know her ex did a number on her emotionally. I am trying my hardest to show her that there is a life that doesn't involve being controlled by someone else. Outside of the bedroom but she loves that. If she didn't, I would stop. I think she likes being able to give me control of her body knowing I respect her and the minute she says I will stop. I don't want her scared or upset ever. I am going to wait until the holidays are over, but I am going to tell her I love her.

Not playing has been super boring for me but I am getting lots of studying done. My four finals are next week. I will be done by Wednesday though giving me time to get some extra practices in before I am back playing at the away game. I only have three classes next quarter; I am almost done with this degree. I delayed entering the draft so I could finish school like my parents requested. Hockey is different than other sports because you can be drafted before college. I regret not drafting and signing with someone before I started school. But it's too late now.

Focusing on cleaning up the apartment before I head to the rink for dryland. I am happy that they are at least letting me do some stuff. My staples come out tomorrow morning before the game. Then I will be cleared to go back on the ice. My team has been supportive, and the trainers have been checking on me after the gym to see how my head has been feeling. So far so good on that front.

I need to finish getting stuff for Fiona's Christmas gift together. That is where my mind is at my whole drive to the rink. Christmas with the Campbells, I have met them but as Luke's teammate and friend. This is different and its Christmas time, so it just feels special and overwhelming. I know Fiona was stressed meeting my parents, but she wasn't best friends with my sibling before.

Dryland is tough with today's focus being on speed and agility. The guys worked hard though, I make sure to remind them they performed well. I also let them know it will pay off during the championships. Luke, Davis, Stuntz, and I need a championship win to put ourselves in the good graces of the teams we want to be drafted too. I know that the scouts have been watching all season but the next 4 games leading to the playoffs seem extra important. But in hockey you need to be ready as a team, you can't win with just a few people playing at their best.

After practice I head to finish up the things I need for Fiona's gift since it was on my mind from earlier. When I finally get home, she has dinner cooked and is watching her vampire show. We eat dinner and then I head to shower shortly after.

While I am showering I hear something and when I look towards the door I see Fiona stripping down. "Room for two?" She asks. "Always for you" I tell her. Stepping in she immediately drops to her knees. She begins stroking me before taking me in her mouth. The feeling of her warm mouth taking me inch by inch combined with the warm shower beating down on my back I am already close. I focus on not cumming early.

She cups my balls as she gags. Those beautiful green eyes staring up at me as I hear the sounds of her sucking my cock. "You like choking on my dick baby girl?" I ask her grabbing onto a fistful of hair pushing farther into her mouth. I hear her try and murmur a yes. "Be a good girl and make me cum and I will reward you" I tell her and begin fucking her face. She usually loves to swallow but I pull out this time and shoot my cum all over her chest careful to avoid her face out of respect. "You look amazing coated in my seed baby girl. Now let's clean you up so I can give you your reward" I tell her. As I begin helping her wash off.

I follow her to the bedroom spanking her right as she reaches the bed. "Lay down and spread those legs" I tell her. I kneel down as I stare at her pretty pink pussy I can she is already wet. I sprinkle little kisses on her inner thighs until she is wiggling trying to get me to kiss her clit. I laugh as I press my face against her slit. It must feel good because she moans. I blow lightly on her and she shivers. Sliding two fingers into her I begin to work her with just my fingers. Her moans are all the motivation I need to keep going. As she relaxes enjoying just the fingers, I start sucking on her clit. I lick up and down before coming back up and twirling my tongue around her clit lightly. Some men think you just lick it fast but that's not the key. You need to use good pressure alternating with sucking and licking. Its not a button you just press on. She grabs my hair I know she is about to cum, "being such a good girl by waiting for permission. Go ahead babe cum on my face" I murmur into her pussy. A few seconds later she is orgasming.

We both have an early day, so I clean her up and she puts on one of my shirts and her cute cheeky underwear that drive me wild before she goes to bed.

I wake up to her peppering kisses down the v on my stomach. God I love waking up with her. I pull my cock out wasting no time. I pull her up on to me sliding her panties to the side. I slip a finger inside, of course she is already wet. I guide myself inside her. She rides me like her life depends on it. We cum quickly and both hop in the shower.

"Thanks for starting my day out amazing babe" I tell her kissing her head as she does her makeup. "I know you won't be fucking anything up on the ice today so I figured you could fuck me before you head out" she tells me winking. Damn this woman is something else.

She looks gorgeous in a yellow penguin's long sleeve and bellbottom jeans in navy that she pairs with yellow converse. Her hair is down in curls, and she pins the front back. Her love for converse and bell bottoms makes me smile. I love her 1970ish style she has. She kisses me before heading out.

I get dressed and decide to do something different this week. I hope it will make her smile when she sees. I run out to the store before I head to the rink. She sees me and smiles. Then I see her fully take in my outfit; I am in a navy suit with a yellow tie and yellow converse. I bought them on the way to the rink so I was lucky they had my size in this color. Walking up I toss her an airhead and kiss her. I can see the tears in her eyes "Happy tears?" I ask. "Absolutely. This was so nice, most people make fun of my love for converse but here you are embracing it and even rocking them yourself. On a game day of all days, knowing we would get it on camera" she says tearfully adding in "Thank you Z." I smile and reassure her I love everything about her style before I head to the locker room.

"Dude are you serious?" Luke asks seeing me come in. "Fuck off dude. Your sister gets self-conscious about her converse because some people, I wonder who, give her shit. All I am doing is supporting her and showing her I love her no matter what she wears" I say then I catch myself "I love her style I mean." Luke looks at me knowingly "Just fucking tell her dude, I know you were waiting but damn you are going to slip up soon, so you need to just do it." I roll my eyes and let him know that I plan to once the stress of the holidays are over.

The game goes well I spend time encouraging everyone on the bench. Since I wasn't on the ice, I had the starts skate over and each toss Fi an airhead. They all love her so they were more than willing to help keep up the tradition. Not seeing her in my number hurts though. I didn't realize how much I love that, people knowing she is mine. My girl in my number, but I am not playing so I know that's why she gave her skin a break from the face paint.

We end up winning again. With three games left of regular season one next week and two in January, we have a chance of entering the playoffs without any losses. That would be a school first; our hockey team has never entered the playoffs undefeated. I walk out with the team and barely register that Fiona is running to me before she is jumping in my arms kissing me.

"GUESS WHAT Z?" she exclaims. "What babe?" I ask. "Coach pulled me aside, every home game has been sold out so far, and the January home game just sold its last ticket. I have done what I was supposed to when I started this internship. He is setting up my interview with the Tampa Thunder for January after the regular season ends" she tells me. "Babe that is amazing! You worked so hard and you deserve this! I am so freaking proud of you" I say spinning her in a small circle.

We head home and celebrate with sex against almost every surface of our apartment before we pass out. Waking up in the morning I find clothes all over the house. I laugh and start to get hard thinking about the activities last night. It was amazing but I need to cook breakfast and start my day of cramming for finals.

Halfway through the day Fiona runs out to help her mom with Christmas stuff while I study. By the time she returns its late and we are both ready for bed. We lay in bed cuddling talking about the upcoming week. Finals, getting back on the ice tomorrow, the away game. She is going to meet the girl taking over her lease at the away game watch party at Slapshots. Then we fall asleep.

Waking up I need to get ready quick if I want coffee before my final today. I kiss Fiona on my way out the door.

NEED YOUR NUMBER

The final goes well, I think. I am glad it's over though. I have two tomorrow and one on Wednesday. I head over to the rink eager to get back on the ice. I stop to see Fiona on my way, she tosses me an airhead wishing me luck back out there. I arrived early to check in with Stuntz but accidently use that time up making out with Fiona against the glass in her office.

Rushing down to get ready for practice. I am looked over by the team trainer who removed my staples Saturday in the locker room before the game. All is good, I step out on the ice. I look up at Fiona's office I know she is watching. It's like I can feel her support radiating through me. It must work because that's one of the best on ice practices I have had in forever.

Fiona beats me home and starts cooking dinner. She helps me study with some flash cards I made. Before she moves onto some stuff she needs to get ready to help the soccer team this week. We don't stay up too late with both of us having early days.

Waking up today knowing its Tuesday meaning I have two finals sucks. I rush out the door as Fiona is leaving to meet the soccer team. We exchange good lucks to each other before we kiss goodbye.

Both finals go really well, I didn't struggle at all. One more to go and this semester is over. I waste no time heading to the rink. Getting some extra time on the rink alone so I can work on my agility and mobility. I was only out a week, but my legs can feel the difference not used to going more than two days without skating at all. Even in off season I skate almost every day if not every single day.

Practice flies by and soon enough I am heading home. I beat Fiona home, so I cook us some dinner. We eat together then I study while she does some editing on the couch while she watches a different vampire show. How many vampire shows are there in the streaming world. It must be a lot I guess.

I stay up late cramming but end up finally going to bed around 3 am. Wednesday morning comes too quick, luckily, I am not rushing since this final is a little later in the morning. Fiona is gone before I wake up though but she left a note that should would be on the soccer fields and that she wishes me luck and knows I will do great.

Four hours after I wake up I am finished with my fall semester. Finals are done! I shoot a text to Fiona letting her know I was officially done. I am so happy to be done. I will spend the next 2 days prepping for our away game.

Coach said I can come in for extra ice time whenever I want this week. So I head to the rink now so I can practice before practice.

Chapter 23

I get the text that Zane finished his finals when I come back off the soccer field. I don't have pockets in the skirt I am in, so I left my phone on the bench. I am happy for him. I remember that post finals relief. Add on he is back on the ice so I know he is really happy right now. I finish up here before I stop to get us ice cream for dessert on my way home.

Starting on dinner I flip on the spin off for the vampire series I finished last week. I love these shows so much, they are my comfort shows. Zane comes home and immediately showers me in kisses. I love how loved he makes me feel. "Congratulations on being done babe!" I tell him as he sets me on the counter. "Thank you, baby," he murmurs against my lips. We make out like high school kids while we wait for dinner to finish. I insist on not going any farther because I really don't want dinner to burn.

Dinner is delicious and we have some ice cream for dinner. As we finish the dishes, I find myself being placed back on the counter. My skirt is pulled up and I hear Zane suck in a breath. I took off my panties between dinner and dessert hoping we would end up back in this position. "Babe tell me you didn't wear this short skirt with no panties outside with the soccer team today" he says looking up at me. This could be fun I think as I say, "I didn't have any clean panties It was fine there was no wind." He smacks my pussy "I will do your laundry if that's the case or where pants. Babe we can't have another man seeing this pussy. It's all mine to look at, to taste, to touch, to fuck" he says while he lowers his head to me. Licking my slit top to bottom he looks back up "do you understand babe?" he growls as he gives my clit the smallest nip sending me over the edge.

"Yes. Yes" I breathe out trying to even out my breath. He goes to town with his mouth, he is so fucking good at eating me out. He swirls his tongue over my clit before blowing on it slightly. I clench my thighs around his head and grab his hair pulling him into me. Moaning out "Please don't stop Zane, Please" and he doesn't stop he pulls me closer to him spreading me out before sticking his fingers in and I cum immediately.

He pulls his pants down, guiding himself in. He fucks me hard and fast on the counter before he bends me over our kitchen table. He smacks my ass right before he enters me again. Zane grabs my hand guiding it to my clit. "Come on babe let's do this together" he murmurs. Together we rub my clit and as I tighten about to orgasm. He removes his hand grabbing my hair and thrusts a few more times pulling my hair as we climax together.

We shower and head to bed, Zane holds me giving me light temple kisses until we both fall asleep. I am so spoiled by him.

Thursday we wake up and as we are about to head out the door I look up telling Z "By the way I took my panties off after dinner hoping we would end up fucking" and I take off to the jeep. He catches me tossing me over his shoulder and heads back to the apartment.

"Z we are going to be late, put me down" I giggle swatting his back as he brings me inside. When we get inside he pulls his down his pants and says "For teasing me like that baby girl you can give me something nice to think about during practice." I drop to me knees and he smiles. I see he is already hard thinking about me pleasuring him. I take him in my mouth I know how to make this end fast so we aren't late though. "Ok babe" I say.

I start sucking and using my hand on his balls. I slip my finger in my mouth "relax" is all I say before I get back to sucking him. He gives me a weird look then grabs my head and starts fucking my face. I reach around swirling a finger around his asshole. "What are you doing baby girl?" he groans obviously struggling to focus. "Relax trust me" I say before going back to taking mouthfuls of dick. I slip my finger in up to the first knuckle and he groans. "ready?" I murmur around his dick. I just hear him say "mhmm" before I make the come here motion with my finger. He instantly cums. I swallow every drop and lick him clean. "Let's go babe. Now that you have that to think about. I need coffee so I am going to take my car." I say as I wash my hands then I drop a kiss on his cheek. Speed walking to my car I see him taking his time walking to his car.

I grab coffee and head to the rink. I am filming content of the team practicing today. Which I knew but Zane didn't so I plan to use that to mess with him. I grab my stuff and head to the ice and take a seat on the bench.

When I see Z I give him a smile and a wink. His face flushes bright red. I let him get back to skating. I enjoyed taking control and being in control in a moment when he thought he was going to be in control. What is even better is he never took the control from me. He knew I needed that control in that moment and he let me have it. The bonus points is being able to mess with him while he is on the ice.

When he is getting water I lower my hand making the come here motion and he almost chokes sputtering water all over Luke. "What the fuck man" Luke yells. "Sorry man. Wrong pipe" he shoots daggers at me and I wink. He just shakes his head and smiles while he skates away.

My ex would never ever of let me do what I did. He definitely would never let me fuck with him like I did today with Z. When I get home Zane is already there. He scoops me up and kisses me. Sitting on the couch he keeps me in his arms. "Have fun today babe" he asks. "I did thank you for asking" I laugh as I respond. "I ordered Chinese tonight since I leave in the morning, I figured we could watch a movie and chill" he says. "Sounds perfect babe. Also, thanks for letting me have my fun and being a good sport about it" I saw leaning my head into his chest. "Of course, what fun is a relationship without laughter jokes and pranks" he says grabbing the remote.

We watch some action movie and eat our Chinese enjoying our night before he has to travel tomorrow. Friday on away game weekends suck. I hate him leaving but I enjoy those late Saturday night/early Sunday mornings when he gets back home. I am not looking forward to his pro career where they are gone for weeks sometimes. The pro teams play multiple games a week so it will mean he is travelling a lot. I hope we keep up these traditions of snuggling and movies though.

Friday morning comes quick, I drive Zane to the airport for the first time. I decide to shoot the guys loading onto the plane in their suits using that as an excuse to get extra time with Z. He stays by my side until the last player loads on to the plane. He kisses me so deeply I feel like we lose track of time until I hear his teammates hollering from the plane. I flush red before hugging him and hurrying off to my car.

I receive a text as I am getting on the road.

Zane: I miss you already sunshine. Have a good time while I am gone. I will see you soon. XOXO Z

Fiona: I miss you too Z. See you asap! Play safe. Bring me home another win!

I smile the whole drive. I am so in love with him. When I get to the rink, I get started posting content to help hype up the game. I make a cool montage of everyone loading on to the plane in their suits. As I reach into my purse to get my other memory card, I find a handful of airheads. I just burst into a full smile. Its time I need to tell him just how much I love him. But not until he's back I want it to be perfect.

Tonight, is boring I just eat dinner before i decide to head to bed early. While I am lying in bed I start thinking of Zane and I begin to feel that dull ache between my legs. Reaching over I grab one of the toys that has a vibrating clit stimulator that hits perfect while you also get the penetration stimulation. I start using it when my phone rings. "Hello?" I answer breathless. "Hey babe How are you doing? We just got to our hotel" Z says. I take a couple deep breaths "Im good" I say. "Are you sure you sound out of breath" he says before he follows up with "Fi are you touching yourself?" I moan then say "Yes to thoughts of you fucking me hard and fast my legs wrapped around your waist." I hear him grunt "Keep going baby tell me more." He says. "You have your thumb on my clit and my tight wet pussy is squeezing your cock as you continue to rail me" I whisper. I have never had phone sex before. I can hear him grunting as he strokes himself the phone echoing in the bathroom.

"You have your hand around my throat and whisper for me to cum" I say as I moan out "Zannneee fuck yes." I can hear him beating his dick more "Yes Fiona you are so tight and wet" he then moans cumming too. "well that was new and fun" I say. "Yes it was, next time don't start without me" he says chuckling. We talk a little before we both hang up heading to bed.

Game day morning is spent posting fun videos online and responding to comments. My day feels like it flies by. I text back and forth with Zane between their morning practice and him actually heading to the locker room for the day. I get ready for the watch party with the girls and Charlie. I wear a cute skirt with a shirt that says miller on the back with his number.

When I get there I have the girls take a cute picture of me showing off in his name and number. I post it online and tag Zane with the caption 'Hey @zanemillerofficial i need your number (winking face emoji)'. When the game starts, I see the starters all throw airheads at Zane and I laugh. "Was that your doing?" Lucy asks walking up. I hug her "Yes it was". I am introduced to Charlie who knows nothing about hockey but is happy to be included. I love her already she is super sweet and candid. She is a curvy brunette, and I am jealous of how her jeans hit her hips and ass.

We watch the game teaching Charlie as we go. She cheers when we cheer and boos when we do. Celisa shows up late but when she arrives, she slips right into the conversation with us. We win in OT 2-1 it was a tough game but they pulled it off. Both goals were from Stuntz and I notice Lucy looking extra happy with each point we got. But I am not saying anything until she does because I could be wrong about my thoughts.

At the end of the game a reporter comes up to Zane and he asks "Your team gave you some airheads on the ice, is that them welcoming you back?" Zane laughs before responding "No actually that's my girlfriend sending me a message to bring home the win. Its also her way of reminding me that's she cheering me on from home." Zane stands smiling "Do you think she was proud of your performance today? Is she a big hockey fan?" the reporter asks. "Well she's our social media manager and her brother plays on this team as a starter as well. So yes you can call her a fan. She will have her opinions on the way we played but she knows we played our hardest. Now if you will excuse me I have to get home to her." He winks at the camera with an airhead in hand as he walks away.

My eyes are tearing up when Lucy says "If you don't marry him I will I swear to god it's like he was written by one of those romance writers. He is absolute perfection." I laugh and say "Yeah if he asks, I will say yes. But first let's tackle me telling that I love him." We all giggle and talk about how I am finally ready. I give Charlie the cliff notes version of Justin and I's relationship. After I have a water, I decide to head home.

I climb into bed in one of Zane's shirts. I think about his interview and how much he loves me. I wish he was home so I could tell him I love him. I really want it to be special but at this point I think that anyway I tell him it will be special. We both know how the other feels we are just waiting to say the official words.

When Zane gets home, I am so out of it. He wraps me up in his arms as we fall asleep, I swear I hear him whisper "I love you sunshine." But I am not sure if that's my sleeping brain imagining it or if he actually said it thinking I was asleep. Now I can't get myself to fall back to sleep as I think of how to bring it up or if I should even bring it up to him. I finally fall asleep listening to his heartbeat and focusing on his breathing as he sleeps peacefully not contemplating everything.

Zane

Its Christmas Eve this week has flown by with practices being light since we don't have a game this week. I have been whispering I love you to Fiona at night when she falls asleep. I know I said I wanted to wait until the holidays are over, so I don't add her extra stress. But this doesn't count because she doesn't hear me. It's time to get up and get ready for all the Christmas eve things that Fiona has planned.

When I get to the living room, she has Christmas music playing and a Christmas candles lit. She kisses me before going back to baking cookies. She let me sleep in but apparently, I need to help get all the cookies baked and decorated. I am also in charge of wrapping the last few gifts for her family. I sneak a cookie coming out of the over its so good. I am going to gain ten pounds helping her with this.

A few hours later then baking and wrapping is complete. We decide to spend the rest of the day binge watching Christmas movies. We make it a mix of the classics and those new ones that always end the same with the city guy falling in love with the girl in the country or some variation of that. We have dinner and then continue our movie marathon. After 4 movies I call it quits and insist we head to bed. She snuggles up and falls asleep in my arms. I enjoy every moment with her in my arms as I fall asleep.

"MERRY CHRISTMAS" Fiona says climbing into my lap grinding slightly. I reach down to the hem of her shirt "Time to unwrap my present" I say pulling off her shirt. This girl is killing me "No panties again" I say. I slip my dick out of my boxers already hard. Guiding myself to her slit I let myself slide between her lips but not inside her. I move slowly letting the tip hit her clit over and over as she moans in my ear. She lifts off me a little and guides me into her. "Fuck me Z" she whispers. I quickly flip us and begin to thrust into her hard and fast. I lift her legs in the air onto my shoulders. "Z I think you are hitting my organs" she says breathing shallow. "Good" is all I say to her. I grab her throat and we cum together.

That was one of the best Christmas gifts I have ever received. We take our time getting up, showering, and getting dressed. Fiona looks beautiful in her red velvet dress and her hair flowing down her back. I wear khakis and a grey button up shirt. I help her get everything loaded into my jeep. Its eleven and we are finally on the road to her parents' house in clearwater.

Her parents are so welcoming and aren't treating me any different. Dinner is amazing! All the food and desserts probably made me gain twenty pounds. We are all sitting around about to exchange gifts and I suddenly feel nervous about my gift. I get her parents and siblings and Celisa all gifts. They love their gifts and now it's my turn to give Fiona her gift and my heart is pounding.

She opens her gifts one at a time starting with a new backpack for work with a nice laptop spot. "It's yellow Z I love it so much!" she says before opening the next gift. She opens the next gift and is speechless. "Do you hate it?" I say worried. "No, it's just too much. But I absolutely love it. I was saving up for a new laptop." She says holding up her new MacBook pro. "I have a trust fund babe seriously please don't over think it. I don't want money to be an issue with us." I reassure her.

Now it is my turn to open Fiona's gifts to me. "Mine isn't as fancy as yours but I put a lot of thought into it so hopefully you like it" she says. I lean over kissing her "It doesn't have to be expensive it's not about to money to me" I say. The first present is 5 different size frames full of pictures of us over the past 4 months. "These are for above our bed" she says. "Fi, I love it, I love sentimental stuff" I tell her. The next gift is a doormat that says, 'Unless you have airheads, alcohol or food go away' and underneath it says, 'Z & F'. "This is absolutely great I love it!" I tell her.

We spend some time watching movies and eating more dessert. We end up getting on the road around nine. I had such a good time and I am glad nothing really changed between Fiona's parents and I. The drive home Fiona holds my hand and sings quietly along to the Christmas music playing on the radio. I bring her hand to my mouth dropping a kiss on it. Thinking about how much I love her but I don't say anything. She gives my hand a gentle squeeze "me too" she whispers. It is almost like she knows what I was thinking.

Pulling up to the apartment we unload the jeep. I am bringing in the last load when Fiona calls me into the bedroom. She is naked and looks at me sweetly before saying "Make love to me please babe." I quickly undress and make my way over to her. I pick her up and kiss her slowly and sweetly.

The kind of kiss where time melts away and you aren't rushing you just enjoy every moment. Then I slowly lower her onto the bed. I take my time guiding myself into her. "You are so beautiful baby girl" I whisper as I brush hair out of her face as I ease myself in and out of her. I speed up a little but I continue to sprinkle her in little kisses as I thrust into her. "I am so lucky to have you Fiona" I murmur into her ear. "Zane" she moans. We take our time getting to climax. Filling our time with kisses, sweet words, exploring hands, and smiles. When we cum I take her cheek in my hand and I kiss her as I climax with her. I kiss her like she is giving me the breath of life. "That was amazing Z" she whispers. "You are amazing sunshine" I say as I get up to get a washcloth. I clean her up and pull her into me to cuddle until we fall asleep.

As soon as I hear her breathing even out I whisper, "I love you Fiona more than you could ever know, but I am going to tell you soon." I close my eyes after that as I am drifting off to sleep, I hear her murmur "I hope it is really soon." Then she is silent. I don't know if that was her sleeping and she won't remember it or if she actually just said that. I want to say something but if she is just sleep talking that would be embarrassing for me. It is a sign I need to tell her though there were a few times tonight while I made love to her I almost slipped up and told her.

In the morning she doesn't say anything, so I think she was sleeping. "So Z since the game is on New Years Eve this year is the team doing anything special?" she asks me. "No why?" I inquire. She has a very suspicious look on her face when she says, "I just have a small surprise for you that night, but I needed to know if I needed to change my plans." I wonder what it is as I finish eating my breakfast.

It is so weird that Christmas was a Saturday this year making our next game on New Year's Eve. I am grateful for it being a home game though. Then we have an away game the next week. Two weeks off before play offs start. Playoffs are broken up into 2 regional games, the semifinals, then the championship. We go from 16 teams to 8 to 4 to 2 competing for the championship. Its exciting and stressful. Championships will be the first weekend of March because we get a week of between semifinals and the finals.

This entire week feels like it lasts forever. I don't know if it is because we are so close to the end of regular season. Or because Fiona's surprise has me stressed. She has been working like crazy trying to get our first playoff game to be sold out since it's a home game. I don't get to see her much around the rink, but we do have dinner every night fitting in some TV when we can.

Waking up Saturday Fiona is gone before I wake up. She told me she had a lot to do to prep for our 'holiday' game. I get ready in my suit and converse heading to the stadium stopping for a coffee for my little caffeine gremlin.

Walking in I see why she got here early she needed to decorate. She put up signs and cute little signs for the new year. While each person she has an assistant shoot up with confetti cannons. I love it honestly it was super creative. "This is awesome Fi!" I say handing her the coffee. "Thanks babe I thought it was fun and different" she kisses me slipping my airhead into my pocket. I still can't believe we are still flirting with pieces of candy when we are going on five months together, but I love it.

"You look beautiful per usual; I will see you out there" I say walking to the locker room. Seeing her in my jersey will never get old. My number on her cheek brings a smile to my face. The locker room is decorated too with photo props and fun music and lights. She even set up a table with everyone's favorite snacks she asked about at the beginning of the season.

I start the game with my usual routine with Fi, tossing her an airhead and putting my hand on the glass. She blows me a kiss as I head off to warm up. I love it, the guys call me whipped but fuck that. I have a girl in the stands supporting me and cheering me on the whole game. I am lucky to have that, I didn't realize how much I liked that support until I had her. I miss it more than I should when I am at away games.

The game is a shutout, 3-0 it was easy. Davis is on his A game the whole time. I don't get any penalty points this game, but I got an assist to Stuntz for one of the goals he got. Luke scored once as well. One more game until we are undefeated. One more that is all that's in our way. The locker room is completely unhinged it is our last regular season home game! Everyone is partying and excited. Coach doesn't mind since it's a holiday and we kicked ass tonight. Luke starts a "ONE MORE" chant and we all yell along. The vibes in the locker room are amazing tonight. We hang out in there for almost an hour longer than normal.

I get a text from Fi, saying to enjoy the celebrations and no rush but she is waiting in her office. I shower then head to her office. By the time I get up there its 11 pm and her office is dark. "Lock the door" she whispers when I walk in. I do just that and she walks out in my jersey. Like just my jersey. "You once told me you wanted to fuck me against these windows and you also love me in your jersey why not all in one?" she says walking over to me. She drops to her knees starting to undo my belt. I help her get my pants off and she takes me in her mouth immediately. After I am hard as fuck she pulls out walking over to the glass and drops back to her knees "lets get you a better view" she whispers. She isn't wrong her mouth around my dick while I look down at her the rink in the background. Fuck this girl is perfect. I cum in her mouth as swallows every drop and I get to see her beautiful eyes glistening.

I pick her up and guide myself in and begin to rail her against the glass. Her pussy is so tight, and she is so wet. Her arms wrapped around my neck as I bounce her on my dick on the window. I can feel myself close to orgasm, so I pull out. I set her down and turn her around. "I want to see my name on your back as I cum in this pussy" I tell her as I groan thrusting into her. I smack her ass and she moans. "You look so sexy with my name on you back pressed against this window baby" I tell her. I pull her hair back and reach around and rub her clit bringing us both to climax. She kisses me and walks over to her desk getting dressed "be right back" she heads to the bathroom next door.

When she comes back in we sit down on the couch. "That was a great New Year's Eve surprise babe I loved it" I tell her. "What time is it?" she says leaning into me. "It is 11:55" I say checking my phone. "Want to be my New Year kiss?" she says smiling. "Maybe" I say laughing. She playfully swats my chest "very funny" she starts to laugh too. We snuggle up until the jumbotron flips on randomly "11:58" it says. "What the hell" I say getting up to move to the window. Fiona follows me over.

The screen starts flashing pictures of Fiona and me before the countdown begins. I look at her confused but she just says "watch please." Ten. Nine. Eight. Seven. Six. **I Love You Zane.** Three. Two. One. Before I can respond she is jumping in my arms kissing me like our lives both depend on it.

Fiona

This kiss says more than I think words could. We finally separate "Fiona" Zane says. "I know Z, I have heard you whispering it since before Christmas" I say. He pulls me into another kiss "You knew?" he asks. "Yes I just wanted to tell you in a special way, because this meant a lot to me. I wasn't sure I would ever feel this way again" I whisper into his chest. "I love you Fiona Campbell" he says. I just smile and keep holding him. "Let's go home sunshine" he grabs my hand, and we head home.

When we get home, I head to the bathroom to change. When I come out Zane comes over and leans on the door frame "Come here baby girl. Let me show you how much I love you" he says. I step up to him and he slightly cages me into the doorframe with one arm on the top and the grabbing my chin and tilting it to him. My heart is pounding, and I have an ache between my legs. Zane leans in kissing me sliding his muscular thigh between my legs. While we kiss, I start to rub myself on his leg trying to relieve the ache I have. "Are you going to get yourself on my leg Fi?" he murmurs against my lips. "If you don't do something about it soon" I murmur back with a smirk.

He picks me up and tosses me on the bed. "Get rid of those clothes" he says as he strips down. Once we are both naked, he looks at me with the most loving eyes before he pulls me to the edge of the bed and kneels. "So sweet and pretty, I love this pussy" he murmurs with his mouth on my clit. He starts delicately with just his tongue swirling and sucking on me. Before he adds two fingers to me. It feels so good my breathing is coming in shallow now. I grab his head and wrap my fingers in his hair. I can feel myself about to reach climax. "Go ahead baby girl" he whispers, and I let go.

Climbing on top of me he lowers himself slowly. Taking his time sliding into me. He grabs the headboard and begins to thrust deeper and deeper into me. He movements slow and controlled. Like he wants to savor every moment. He starts to speed up and we are both on the edge. As we both orgasm so deep in me my body shakes and I clench tight around him. "I love you Fiona" he moans mid climax and my eyes start to well with tears.

"Are you okay? What's wrong?" he says worried. "Yeah I am fine, just overwhelmed with emotions. I love you too so much" I whisper. "aw sunshine

155

its okay" he murmurs dropping a kiss on my temple. We both clean up and then we snuggle up and talk as we drift off to sleep. Things feel perfect right now I am so happy.

Sunday is our usual routine of breakfast and movies. Zane has no studying to do so we end up deciding to going out on a date for dinner. I put on a form fitting blue dress and wear my hair down straight with a pair of wedges. "Wow you look amazing Fi" he whistles out. "You clean up pretty good yourself" I say winking. He does look great in his khakis and sage green button up with the sleeves rolled. It might be January but its Florida and the weather is pretty nice. I grab a white cardigan just to be safe thought.

We go to a cute steakhouse for dinner in downtown and hit up one of the local speakeasy bars for drinks. We never go out with our schedules, so this is a fun change for us! I get some cute pics of us because what kind of social media guru would I be without my own personal social media profiles looking updated.

While I am updating my Instagram and I scroll past a post from a GU hockey player. He posted a pic of him, Justin, and another guy. The caption says looking forward to making it to the championships. #floridaherewecome

My stomach drops "where are the championships hosted this year Z?" I ask obviously upset. "At the Tampa Thunder arena. Remember everyone was talking about a huge weeklong party at Slapshots? Are you okay?" he says concerned. "I must have been half listening I remember the party but I didn't realize that the game is here" I tell him "Justin's teammate is posting about their return to Florida. I just haven't seen him since the parking lot and I am a little worried he might try something. But I know I am being ridiculous."

He pulls me into a hug "You will be okay, but you are valid in being worried. We will all keep an eye out on you babe. If you don't want to sit on the glass if you we end up making it I understand" he reassures me. I kiss him "Thank you babe, but I will of course be on the glass. I won't miss your championship game. I believe you guys will make it! I am sorry for ruining our date I just scrolled past when I made a post about us" I utter to him. "You ruined nothing. I will never be mad at you. Emotional abuse like Justin did isn't something you just get over honey. I will be here every step towards healing that you take. Now let's get some ice cream on our way home." he declares.

Zane makes me completely forget my worries; he is like magic when it comes to that. He is the definition of if he wanted to, he would. He is always there for me and supporting me. Never letting me get the best of myself. This is the kind of man that all those songs, books and movies are about.

I have my interview soon I am waiting on my email with the date. But I am starting to wonder what I am going to do if he gets drafted somewhere else. After Justin I always said I will not choose a man over my career. That was before Zane before the love of my life who I can't imagine not being around. I have a lot to consider. If he can get another Florida team or even a Georgia team, we can make long distance work. If not, I will need to consider if I want to interview with other teams and colleges wherever he gets placed. I am too happy right now in my life to stress. I am going to crush the interview and then after the draft we will address where we go from here.

Zane pulling up to the ice cream shop snaps me out of my thoughts. When we walk in I just grab his hand and smile. I won't let Justin or careers ruin this. We love each other and I have to believe that will be enough.

My positive thoughts are killed when behind us walks in Zane's ex Holly. I see her first but I don't say anything. He hasn't seen her but he does pull me in front of him resting his chin on my head and wrapping his arms around. "So what do you want sunshine?" he says. "I am going to get the butter cookie" I say praying we can get through this ice cream trip without incident. Holly scoffs behind us and when we look over she rolls her eyes. "No need to cling to him honey I am not after your man enjoy my sloppy seconds, he will leave you soon enough. Then he will crawl back to me when he realizes your innocent act isn't as fun in the bedroom. You will never be able to handle him and pleasure him like I can. He likes it rough not missionary" she giggles and turns to her friends.

"Fuck off Holly, I would never go back to someone who sleeps with the entire athletic department" Zane says. "Fuck you Zane I got tested and its not like you fuck raw anyways so get over yourself. You are only going to last so long being vanilla with your basic bitch" she says. I place my hand on Zane's chest to tell him I got this. "Well Holly I might be innocent but, in the bedroom, its different. I don't think Zane is thinking of you while I wear his hand like a necklace, and he fucks me raw yelling that he loves me as he cums. Since we live together, he has bent me over every surface and fucked me without a condom over and over. Going to sleep telling me how much he loves me each night. Claiming out in public. So just stop you lost him, and he won't be coming back he is plenty satisfied" I declare before turning back to order. I order my ice cream while the employee stares at me with his mouth wide open. I clear my throat and he apologizes and starts making my order. Zane kisses me "I love you even more now Fi. That was hot as fuck. Get your order so we can go home" he says.

Getting my ice cream, we head to the jeep. "I am so sorry I do not know where that even came from. I just am at my wits end with ex's messing with our date night" I tell him. "Babe, I loved seeing her get told off nothing is ruined. Let us head home and watch a movie we both have early days tomorrow" he says kissing me before closing my door.

Waking up Monday I groan not wanting to head to work. Zane starts his new semester today, so he doesn't want to get up either. "I will make Shepard's pie for dinner if you get up. You have class before dryland babe get up! It's your last regular season game as well. BIG WEEK! Let's go!" I tell him wanting to be sure he is up before I walk out the door. "I am up Fi, don't be late for your meeting with Marissa and coach" he groans still in bed. "Fine. I am leaving! Bye I love you!" I yell out walking out the door.

I head straight to the meeting room when I get to the rink. "Good morning" I say. "Good morning Fiona" Marissa says. "Morning" Coach echoes. "We just wanted to inform you that your interview is Friday morning. We will go with you for the first part before we head out to the airport for the final regular season game" coach says. "Oh wow so soon. Ok! I will be ready" I say excited. "Moving on to playoff season plans. We have two weeks off then our first game is at home. Let's be sure to get fans ready and hype. Are you planning on traveling with the team for the other away playoff games?" Coach asks. "That is the plan" I say. "Ok. I will plan to put you and Miller in the same room since you live together, and you will sneak into each other's rooms if I don't" he says stoic. I chuckle lightly "Sounds good Coach and I won't let you down with the fans and I won't distract him. I know room sharing and girls before games is usually a no go" I say. "I think you not being there with him will distract him more that boy is head over heels for you with you" he says a smile cracking his face. We finish the meeting after a quick review of the playoff ticket sales so far.

Friday morning comes so fast. The entire week flew by with Zane getting into the groove of his new classes. My playoff prep for all the socials. I feel like I have been glued to my laptop and iPad even when I am home trying to make sure I curated the perfect algorithm friendly posts. I haven't had time to prep with interview questions, but I feel confident.

While I get dressed Zane heads out to the stadium wishing me luck. Luckily the interview is at our rink thanks to coach, so I can breathe a little easier and feel comfortable in my own space. I end up wearing my hair half up half down in loose curls with some light makeup accentuating my eyes. I pick a navy-blue pant suit and white shirt with black heels embracing the colors of the Tampa Thunder.

Arriving at the rink I head to my office to drop my stuff and almost cry when I walk inside. There are two vases of flowers from Zane. There is also a pile of airheads. A hand drawn four leaf clover. To top it off he dropped off a coffee. I look down and see him and Luke shooting pucks on the ice. I send him a quick thank you text telling him I love him. Then I head downstairs to one of the most important interviews of my life.

Their head coach and team press director are so nice. They waste no time going over my profile for the team. Marissa brought the analytics from last season compared to this season. Coach discusses my professionalism with team and how I take the time to really get to know the players so I can adequately show them in content. He even is quick to note my relationship with Zane never effected my work with other players and I never showed favoritism. Which I was thankful for because I know that would have been a concern. An hour later I feel really good about how it went. They said I will hear back in 4-6 weeks because they have a few interviews left. Marissa says they want to watch how I handle the playoff content. That makes sense to me though, they could of waited to interview me until then so I wasn't stressed waiting. But I don't make the rules.

I head to the airport with Zane so I can get a little extra time with him. I tell him all about the interview and he listens to every detail intently. When we get there, he picks me up and kisses me passionately. "I am so incredibly proud of you sunshine! You deserve everything coming to you! I can't wait to stand behind you cheering you on" he murmurs into my lips. I tell him I love him and to kick ass because I will be watching! Another kiss then he is boarding the plan.

How crazy is it that my future professional hockey player boyfriend is telling me he can't wait to stand by my side cheering me on. I should be saying that to him he is the one that will be playing sports professionally. But I don't miss the importance of his support. A lot of women don't get support like Zane gives me. Time to head home and stay busy until my man heads home.

Zane

On the flight I try and nap but all I can think of is how well Fiona's interview went. I am happy for her, and I am so proud. But I am understandably scared what will happen to us if I don't get drafted to Tampa. I refuse to ask her to give up her career for me. This has been her dream and she is almost there. If I don't get Tampa hopefully another Florida team will pick me up.

My lease expires in May and I want to buy a house with my future wife and get a dog. I want to settle down. If I wasn't worrying about the draft, I would start looking at houses and rings now. I am ready to commit to forever with her. But right now, until I have draft answers, I need to focus on that championship ring.

It is late when we land in Texas so I just send a text letting her know we arrived safely. This is my last away game in college without her though. She told me that she is going to be travelling with the team for the away playoff games. I was super surprised when I found out coach offered for us to stay in the same hotel room. I guess he knew we would share a room with or without his permission. Plus saves the team from getting an extra room.

Waking up Saturday I head to the rink with the team for morning skate and light dryland stuff. Then we head back to the hotel. I use that time to take a nap then I call Fiona. She is heading to Slapshots to watch the game. She tells me to check my side pocket of my duffel when I do I find a bunch of airheads. We always seem to exchange airheads no matter how far apart we are. I love it. I love her.

Sitting in the locker room I get an Instagram notification. Fiona posted a new picture it's a picture of us on the tarmac kissing from the last away game. She is in my shirt with her back to the plane. Someone on the plane must have taken it and sent it to her. The caption says I got your number and you got my heart seems like a fairtrade. I set my phone down eat one of my airheads and get ready to win this game.

The game was a win but it wasn't an easy win. I went to the penalty box more today than I have the past few games. This team just couldn't stay away from our goalie so I had to be extra physical. We are officially heading into the playoffs undefeated. I had two assists today so my season stats are looking perfect heading into playoff time.

The locker room is unhinged everyone is celebrating being undefeated! Coach is even smiling. Luke stands up "TIME FOR PLAYOFF BEARDS" he yells. Everyone cheers. I usually keep my face clean shaven, so I am interested to see how Fiona likes it. Tradition is tradition though and she knows that. We all head to the plane in great moods. While I wait for take-off I see a text from Fiona telling me she was proud of me and she noticed my nod to the camera. I see our team TikTok playing on Luke's phone he tilts the phone to me. The video just went up and is already going viral. It's me going after the left wing from the vermont game after he slashed Davis with his stick. The comments are crazy with girls commenting about how hot it was. I laugh and roll my eyes. "I am sure my sister is loving these comments" he says before we both switch our phones off.

Arriving home Fiona is on the couch asleep. She wakes up when I get home and we head to the bedroom for bed. While I am changing she walks over and drops to her knees. "Those girls will never get a chance to have this cock" is all she says before taking me into her mouth. Possessive Fiona is hot. She cups my balls while she takes my whole cock gagging. Her eyes are welling with tears but the sounds coming from her mouth as she sucks is so fucking hot. I grab her head taking over the speed. Until I orgasm moaning out her name while she takes every drop licks her lips and climbs into bed. "Goodnight, Z" she mumbles snuggling up to her pillow.

Sunday we watch movies and go have lunch with her siblings, Celisa, and Charlie. It is nice catching up with them and getting to meet Charlie she seems nice. I can't help but laugh at how she all but drooled over Luke. He is naturally flirty with everyone so you can tell she was crushing though. Driving home when I brought it up to Fi she just laughed and said he has that charming boy effect on girls.

The next week flies by not having any games you would think practices would lighten up. NOPE. Coach is riding our asses much harder. We are living at the rink it feels like. When the weekend finally comes, I sleep almost all Saturday while Fiona is at her parents. I finally get up so I can meet Penny for dinner though.

NEED YOUR NUMBER

I catch her up on life. Fiona confessing her love on New Years Eve. To which she responded about damn time. I guess she has known we were in love before we ever knew. I tell her about my dreams of a house and a dog maybe even kids in a few years. We talk about the draft and my fears involving that. She is supportive and listens to everything. Telling me to communicate with Fiona about the draft now so it doesn't blow up in our faces when it gets closer. Pen tells me about school and how her students are doing. She is apparently ready to start dating again after her dick head ex. We make plans for dinner after the playoff game since it's at home and our parents are coming into town for it.

Getting home Fiona is in bed she says isn't feeling well and she falls asleep. She doesn't wake up until late Sunday. I make her some soup and get her some Gatorade. We lay down on the couch to watch TV when she makes a run for the bathroom. I follow her holding her hair back. Once she is done emptying her stomach, she brushes her teeth and crawls into bed. I get her some ginger ale and sit on the edge of the bed.

"Do you think it's the flu?" I ask her. She looks up "Yes Z it's the flu" she says annoyed. "I take my pill religiously if that was your concern" she follows up. "I didn't say that please calm down. Even if that's what it was, I wouldn't be mad. I am already trying to convince myself not to overwhelm you by asking you to go house shopping and dog shopping with me" I say sadly "So please don't make me out to be the bad guy. I was genuinely just curious" I say. I get up and dropping a kiss on her head and go to the couch.

I get up and comfort her every time she is sick in the night. I call out of practice to take care of her. But things are still tense with us. I sleep on the couch only going in to give her soup or drinks or hold her hair back. By Tuesday morning she is feeling better, so I go to class and practice. We still have barely talked. I text her letting her know I am crashing at Luke's tonight. Then I turn my phone off pulling up to his apartment.

He lets me in without question and gets me a beer. After we sit in silence a bit he finally says "I am grabbing you another beer then we are going to talk about why you are here, and my sister is alone at your apartment. I want to ask if you hurt her but from the look on your face, I think she hurt you." I down half the second beer before spilling my guts about everything. The dreams of a house and dog, the way I felt when she talked to me like I was the villain when I have always treated her like a goddess. "Not that I want a baby right now, but I have never given her any reason to doubt my feelings for her. Or my plans to have a future together including kids. It just hurt that after all the things I have said and done she still thinks I would be that horrible" I say with tears in my eyes. How embarrassing I am crying over his sister on his couch. "I am sorry Fiona isn't great with feelings I am sure you know that. But I don't think it's an excuse to hurt you either. Stay here a few days and let things calm down" he says slapping me on the back.

I turn my phone on in the morning to a few texts from Fiona and a missed call. All were nice and her apologizing for hurting me. Her last one asked me to come home. I send her a text letting her know I am going to stay here another night and we can talk when I get home that the time apart will be good for us to collect our emotions. I get up to head to class then practice.

Class goes well it's a cake class. I head to the rink stopping for lunch. I know Fiona probably hasn't fed herself so I grab her food too. I swing by her office she is meeting with someone which is perfect. "I just wanted to be sure you ate something" I say setting the food on the desk. "Please excuse me" she says to the person in the meeting. "Zane wait up" she says following me out. "Fiona I need to get to practice" I say without making real eye contact but I lean in giving her a kiss on the temple. "Z please" she whispers. "Fiona please give me space. I have always given you space. I have let you leave. I have let you take your time to sort your thoughts. I am just asking to hold off on this talk until tomorrow. I am not leaving you I just need to sort my thoughts" I say heading to the locker room.

Practice is fine but I am definitely not focused. Changing to go home Luke comes up "Go home Z, my home is always open to you. But you need her. You don't need a beer or time away. You need Fiona" he says. He is right I just need to talk to her letting this sit is only going to get worse. I get in my jeep grabbing Chinese because the girl probably only had wine for dinner.

Walking into the apartment I see Fiona on the couch drinking wine. Looking over she just stares at me not saying anything. "I brought Chinese. Let's eat so we can talk on full stomachs" I say setting the food on the table. Halfway through dinner Fiona says "How did you know I haven't eaten?" I smile "Well I know you probably better than you know yourself. You forget to eat all the time add in anything emotional you will go days forgetting food unless you are reminded. I told you I would always take care of you. Hence the lunch and dinner. Even if we are not getting along, I still wanted to be sure you were taken care of" I inform her. We finish the rest of dinner in silence. After we cleanup we sit back down at the table.

"What brings you home early?" Fiona says trying not to show her hurt. "Your brother made me realize that space and beer weren't what I needed. I needed my sunshine. I needed you" I state matter of factly. I proceed to tell her everything my dreams of a house and dog and future kids. A dream I had long before she got the flu. I tell her how badly it hurt being pushed away and spoken to like that when I have never given her an excuse to treat me that way. By the time I am done she is in tears. "Don't cry Fi. I love you please don't cry" I say. "I am just so sorry for talking to you like that. I was sick and I just didn't handle my feelings well. It's not an excuse though. I got defensive I am sorry. I also want a house and a dog. Kids in the future. I will follow you wherever the draft takes you Z. I knew that before this fight, but this fight just cemented in my heart I don't want to be apart from you" she confesses. I scoop her up and kiss her.

Fiona

Today is the first day of playoffs. I wake up extra early to prepare. Zane and I have been in a great place since our talk last week. I think the draft was weighing heavier on us than either of us realized. We are both much more relaxed and the sex has been amazing. I didn't even know it was possible to be this sexually satisfied. I look over at his beard he is growing out for the playoffs. The way that thing tickles me while he eats my pussy sends me over the edge. I did get beard burn one day though. Any way time to focus on getting ready for playoffs.

I draw on my 27 on my cheeks, put on a cute team beanie, putting on Zane's jersey, with a pair of bellbottoms and my converse. I am game day ready I kiss Zane while he sleeps then head out. I get the cameras all set up in the tunnel with my assistant I get this semester as part of her sports marketing internship. Her name is Hailey, and she is super sweet. The guys start arriving and we start taking pics and filming.

"Here comes your man" she says swooning. He was her crush before we started dating. "Sunshine, I got you coffee and a muffin since I am sure you didn't eat" he says his voice booming down the hallway. I set my stuff down and give him a kiss before he turns to leave. "Wait" I yell and when he turns around, I toss the airheads I had for him. He catches most of them chuckling as he grabs the rest. "Love you Fi" he yells walking away. Once arrival pics are done. I get to posting before heading to my seats.

I am seated with Penny and Zane's parents to one side and on the other is my parents, Lucy, and Celisa. Luke skates over and we all throw up the I love you sign. Shortly after Zane starts to skate over. My parents know our ritual but its slightly embarrassing for them to see in person. I don't know why though.

Skating over he knocks on the boards before throwing my airheads over. I don't catch all of them. He takes his hand out of his glove placing it on the glass. But different than normal when I place my hand on top, he changes his hand to a half heart. I laugh and follow suit. He mouths I love you to me and I shoot up the I love you sign. He smiles the biggest smile and returns the motion before joining the team for warmups. Both sides of me are a chorus of "aw how sweet" "how cute" and "the love is real". I love the support we have from our loved ones.

This game is against Tennessee we beat them last time, so the guys are going into the game confident. Zane ends up in the penalty box two times during the first period. The playoffs making both teams play more physically than normal. By the end of the second period, we are 0-0. This is causing both teams to get antsy I can see Luke starting to get reckless with his charges down the ice. The third period everyone is on edge the fans, the coaches, the players. Suddenly someone slashes at Zane and I stand up "what the fuck ref you didn't see that" I yell. The same player ends up smashed into the boards in front of us by Zane. It turns into a fight that has Rodriguez the left defender coming to help. I see Zane's helmet slipping off as the guy keeps grabbing him and punching. Zane is landing punched careful to avoid the helmet area. I smack the boards "Ref what the fuck break this shit up" I yell. Finally, the linesman gets it broken up, Z touches the boards in front of us nodding on his way to the box. With both of our starting defenders in the box, I hope to god we can keep control of the puck. Davis is doing great defending the goal. As soon as Rodriguez and Zane hit the ice again, they make a beeline for Davis to help him out.

With two minutes left Stuntz scores you could almost feel the bleachers shake with the roars from the crowd. We hold strong those last two minutes. All the players scramble to the ice jumping onto Stuntz in celebration. Z skates over to the boards and bangs and gives me the I love you sign. Then heads off the ice for media and then to the locker room. We all wait outside and cheer the guys on as they come out of the arena. I hug players give out fist bumps until I see my player. I jump and he catches me with a kiss. "You did it!" I murmur on his lips. He kisses me then puts me down and we walk over to our families.

We go out to dinner with our families. Stuntz joins us too which is always nice. We discuss travelling to Charlotte for the game next week. The draft is brought up but mainly because Penny offers to host everyone for the draft. So sweet of her I want to be with my brother and Zane, but I think my brother will go to my parents understandably. Zane's parents tell us they are staying in the area so they can be at the championships. Two games left and then they will be there. I know that they will make it. They are all playing at their very best I have seen all season.

When we get home we crash pretty quickly both exhausted for our own long days. Waking up on Sunday Z is already up making breakfast. "How long do we have?" I ask walking out of the room. He looks at the stove and says "enough for a quickie with you bent over the kitchen table." I drop my panties and bend over waiting for him. "Damn Fi you are so hot" he says pulling his cock out stroking it. "Hurry up before you burn breakfast" I say laughing. SMACK! He smacks my ass and then guides himself in.

In this position he is hitting me deep and it feels so good. "You are so tight" he murmurs as he reaches around rubbing my clit. "Z you are so deep. Fuck your cock feels so good. Like it was made for me" I moan right as I climax. He follows right behind me filling me with cum. As he pulls his pants up the oven beeps. "Food" I groan as I walk to the bathroom to get cleaned up.

After breakfast we watch movies while we both work on our laptops. Zane is studying and I am creating content for the next playoff game. I am excited to head to Charlotte though. My mind is distracted trying to figure out my plans for the week. My phone dings with a notification from Instagram. Opening it I see Zane tagged me in his story. It's a video of him panning from his computer to me on my computer next to him with the caption 'Easy like Sunday mornings'. "Okay that was cute" I say looking up at him. We spend the rest of the day doing our usual movies and work.

The week flies by with both of us being super busy with playoff prep. I have been in and out of meetings about trying to promote special merchandise and to help get season tickets sold for next season. Zane has been having two a days and dryland. They have also had tape every day this week. He also has his classes, so he has just been really busy.

Friday morning, I wake up excited and nervous. I get my bag packed and then shower and get ready to head to the airport. I end up putting my hair wet into two Dutch braids easy for travel and it will be curly for tomorrow's game. I wear navy joggers and a cute penguin's crew neck sweatshirt. Zane comes out in his suit, but I know they change on the plane into something more comfortable. He packed navy joggers and a long sleeve penguins t-shirt.

At the airport I get some pictures and then Davis decides to come take pictures of me. Also, some of Zane and I on the tarmac it was actually so cute. On the plane I close my eyes while everyone changes. Then settle into my seat listening to music while I edit. This time is perfect I get so much done. Some of the guys stop in the aisle to watch me edit. Loving the process, they ask questions and just admire my work. It was fun getting to include them in the behind-the-scenes part while Z looks over proudly. Even coach stops by watching for a few minutes.

Charlotte is cold but beautiful we are staying in a hotel in center city. Our hotel is nice, and the room is perfect. We have one king size bed but this time it's exactly what we wanted. "Remember our first hotel stay?" I ask. Zane chuckles "yeah you came back drunk, we had one bed, and the sexual tension was thick." I smile "How about we christen this bed the way we wanted to in cocoa?" I ask.

Without another word he is kissing me and trying to get his shirt off. I pull back giving myself space to get my clothes off. Once we are both naked he picks me up kissing me and walking me to the bed. "Now baby I need you try and be quiet my teammates are on the other side of this wall and I don't need them getting off to sounds of you" he informs me. I giggle and kiss him. He slides in and then uses one hand to play with my tit rubbing my nipple. Dropping his face to my nipple he gives it a little nip before sucking on it. Right before he switches side he blows lightly my whole body shakes from the sensation. The way he is fucking me right now you would think he was trying to rearrange my insides. Going as deep as he can hard and fast. Reaching down to my clit he has been on the edge and I think he knows that because he suddenly flips me over. "ass up baby" he growls into my ear. I spread my legs on my knees resting on my elbows he thrusts in but pushes my back upper back so I am lying flat on my stomach with just my knees bent to give him better access. "That's it baby girl. You are so tight with this ass up in the air and your pussy spread like this for me" he moans. He wraps a hand around rubbing light circles on my clit I am about to explode when he moves his hand to my mouth covering it "You are such a good girl" he whispers. I cum yelling his name into his hand against the pillow. He follows behind moaning my name lightly into my ear. Something about it is incredibly sensual and gives me chills. He gets up getting a washcloth to clean me up. Then we both climb in bed to sleep.

Saturday morning is hectic. We are both up early heading to the arena. I film their morning skate and some shots around the arena. We get lunch then head back to the hotel. Zane takes a nap and I make all my content and schedule it to start posting hourly leading up to the game.

Heading to the game I feel some stress Zane and I exchange our airheads before the game. I take my seat right next to the team bench. When he enters the ice, he comes straight to me for our pregame ritual. I say a silent prayer we win this game. The team is buzzing with energy I use this energy to film some more content.

The first period Luke scores and so does Carolina. They at least play a clean game they haven't been slashing or going for the goalie. I can tell Zane is relaxed knowing he doesn't have to worry about such a dirty playing team. Don't get me wrong they have scuffles but there is nothing penalty worthy or where the whole team has to focus on protecting the goalie. The second period ends with no points gained on either side. Its still 1-1. Zane did get penalty time, but it was only two minutes. Heading into the third period everyone is holding their breath. Their defenders are all over our offense they aren't getting to get down the ice. Zane ends up with the puck near the red line and sends a slapshot straight to the goal. He made it. Holy shit. He just made a slapshot from center ice. He skates by me on one knee his celly. I love it. We end up winning 2-1.

When I see Zane I jump kissing him! "You killed it! A fucking slapshot! Zane you were amazing babe!" I tell him. He thanks me and we get on the bus to head to the airport. The energy on the bus is high! They are all celebrating heading into the semifinals next week undefeated. It's a huge accomplishment. They only other team playing in the semifinals undefeated is GU. The other two teams both have one loss.

Heading on to the plane we all wait for the announcement for who won the Colorado v Alabama game so we know who they are playing next and where they are playing. Georgia beat Iowa so they are moving on to play the winner of Delaware v North Carolina. As the plane lands coach stands announcing that Georgia is playing NC at home. We will be playing Colorado in Denver. I am excited I have never been to Denver.

Heading home we are both exhausted, so we hit the bed immediately. I stay awake though thinking of what the championship is going to look like knowing Justin will be there. I am not looking forward to running into him again. There is a chance nothing will happen, and we can have a peaceful game. But I have a feeling that he is not going to let things go that easy. Things got bad on the ice last time they played each other and that was before we were even dating. If Justin says something Zane is going to kill him. The whole team also knows about Justin since Zane demanded to know how Stuntz knew about my anti athlete clause and I told all of them at the same time about my shitty abusive ex. I am close with the team, and they all hate him now so I don't need the entire team in the box because Justin sucks. I focus on Zane's breathing trying to clear my mind because I finally fall asleep.

Zane

Waking up on Sunday morning I am in such a good mood. My slapshot last night was amazing and it won the game. Fiona traveling with us was fun I liked her being there on the plane rides. We are heading to Denver this week which is exciting. I can't believe we are heading into the semifinals undefeated! Fiona stirs slightly in her sleep. I decide it's time for me to get up and make breakfast.

Fiona comes out looking sleepy but so cute. Walking over to me and planting a kiss on my lips. I smile and murmur "Good morning sunshine." She drops down pulling my boxers with her. "A prize for that slapshot last night" she says before putting my cock in her mouth. She knows just how I like it. She swirls that tongue over the tip and alternates taking me deep and just sucking the tip. I am getting close grabbing her head and she looks up at me with those stunning green eyes. I watch her take it all swallowing then licking me clean. "Is breakfast ready?" is all she says before walking to the couch.

Another Sunday full of studying and watching movies with Fiona. Luke and Stuntz are coming over for dinner though so that will be fun. Fiona picked beer and stuff to cook up earlier this week. I decide to take a nap after our second movie. By the time I wake up Fiona has the house cleaned and smelling amazing.

"You should of woke me up to help babe" I tell her. She smiles working on dinner "It was fine you were tired I didn't mind" she says. The guys show up about 15 minutes later and I get them some beers. "So we are leaving on Thursday coach said. He sent out an email something about in case of snowstorms." Stuntz tells us. "I took a nap so I haven't seen my email yet, I will check it out and follow up with my defense guys to see if they need help with reaching out to teachers" I inform them. "I will do the same for offense" Luke volunteers. Once all the important shit is handled. We all sit and eat. "This food is amazing Fiona thank you" Stuntz says. "yeah, Fi its great" Luke tells her. She thanks them both blushing.

We spend a few hours playing board games and drinking beer. It was fun I forget that I used to fill my days drinking at bars with them multiple times a week. I miss the time with them, but I do not miss the bar scene. They sing their praises to Fiona again on their way out. She hugs them both and tells them to get home safe. "Go shower and get ready for bed babe, I can clean up" I tell her.

I clean up and check my emails. I send out a text to my guys offering help and informing them of the travel plan changes. By the time I finish up and head to bed Fiona is passed out. All I can think about is how beautiful she is while I get her tucked in. I go shower and then crawl into bed beside her. Falling asleep is easy next to her.

I get up with my alarm and Fiona is already up getting ready. I take my time getting ready. She kisses me by then heads to work. I head to my class not long after her. We get the dates for midterms and by some miracle they are two weeks after the championship. I would of made it work, but that's a lot for the younger guys on the team who are in the thick of their degrees.

Practice is a bitch today. We do a bunch of speed and endurance training. Which alone would be fine but dryland a few hours later is speed and mobility. At least we don't have two practices today because I would die. I am exhausted when I finally get home. Fiona being the angel she is already has dinner ready. I scarf down my food before hitting the shower. I sit down on the couch and next thing I know Fiona is waking me up to go to bed.

Tuesday and Wednesday pass quickly. I am swamped with two a day workouts, dryland, tape reviews and my classes. I only see Fiona for dinner then I pass out. She doesn't complain though she makes sure dinner is ready and has been making sure I set my alarms before I fall asleep. She makes sure I have my shit together texting me reminders for things I need to before we leave Thursday. I am really lucky to have her.

Thursday morning, we have to be to the plane by 10 am. We don't have to wear our suits which is nice. All of us bundled up in team sweats. Fiona wears a sweat suit that's very similar except her is form fitting and her hoodie has 27 on it. It's going to be a long flight and I put my headphones on to sleep. When I wake up again, I see Fiona still teaching some minor editing to random players. I love how well she gets along with everyone. Holly never got along with anyone she thought she was better than everyone else. Or she was irrationally jealous and couldn't handle a simple conversation without acting a fool.

NEED YOUR NUMBER

Arriving in Denver it is fucking freezing. But it is breathtaking. Fiona is in love instantly. I guess we will be taking a vacation out here. The hotel room overlooks a snow-covered mountain and has a soaking tub. After we go get dinner in town Fiona comes back and climbs immediately in the tub. I sit on the floor next to her talking to her with my head back on the ledge. She rubs her hand against my scalp it feels so good I could fall asleep right there. When she is done, she wraps up in a fluffy robe before climbing into bed. We both fall asleep pretty quickly.

Friday we have the day to ourselves so we go explore in town. We play in the snow a little. We get back to the hotel by curfew which is 8 pm. We tried multiple restaurants and did a lot of shopping. Fiona got everyone a souvenir it feels like. I don't care I just find it so cute how she took time picking everyone the perfect thing. The view of the sunsetting behind the mountain is beautiful. Fiona is standing there watching it.

I come up and wrap my arms around her resting my head on her shoulder. "Its so beautiful" she says staring at the sunsetting. "I agree" I say while I stare at her. I grab her tit through her shirt and she starts to moan. I take her shirt and bra off and ditch my shirt. I continue to palm her tits in front of the window watching the sunset. Feeling her nipples harden as the blood rushes to my dick. She presses back and grinds her ass into me. Reaching between us I push my pants down letting my dick flop out hitting her ass. I slide her pants down. Lining up I guide myself inside her. Using my leg to help spread her leg a little more giving me a better angle.

Fucking her against this window with the sunsetting over the mountains is a literal dream come true. The pussy is tight, wet, and attached to the love of my life. She is bent over slightly giving me a perfect angle as she leans on the window. I wrap my hand around her throat "go ahead baby girl" I groan into her hair. We both cum. She is so tight, squeezing me over and over as she gets over her orgasm. Pulling out I go get a washcloth and we both strip down and climb into bed once we are cleaned up.

Saturday morning wake up calls come way earlier than I want. We all get up and head to the arena for morning skate. Fiona does some filming and then heads off to film around the rink. Once we are done, we head to eat lunch then back to the hotel. I lay down to nap while Fi sits and works on

175

getting the morning skate uploaded so she can post it before tonight's game. She wakes me up when we need to get ready to head to the rink.

We exchange airheads before I head into the locker room. She is waiting for me against the glass with my number on her cheek. We do our pregame ritual then I go warm up. We haven't played Colorado before, so this is going to interesting. To play a team we have never played in the semifinals have everyone a little bit nervous but we studied a lot of tape to prepare.

First period is uneventful with a lot of body checking going on there isn't anyone getting anywhere near either goal. I spend two minutes in the box for elbowing which I wasn't doing but whatever. As soon as the second period starts Denver scores. Then with a minute left on the clock in the second period they score again. Both small wrist shots but they were amazingly accurate.

Heading into the third period you can see the tension in the air. Something must of lit a fire in Stuntz ass though because he takes off after winning the face off. A quick wrist shot, and we finally make it onto the board. I am doing my best to keep players away from Davis. I get the puck with 5 minutes left; I pass to Luke and he scored. What a perfect play too. 2-2 we might go into overtime. The time is ticking down and with 3 minutes left Marshall scores 3-2. The next two minutes we all play defense trying to keep Denver as far away from our goal.

We finish the game at 3-2; we won! We are heading to the championship undefeated. The locker is fucking buzzing. Championships in our home city this is going to be fire! Slapshots is going to be partying that whole week! I can't wait to see how the next week off goes for training.

I see Fiona by the bus and when she jumps, I dip her low making her scream and giggle. "You did it babe" she cheers. "All of you fucking killed it!" she yells to everyone. Then we all load on the bus to head to the airport. I am talking to the guys while she sits with Marissa. They are working overtime on our championship bound posts. I watch her working hard and then nod at Luke, so he knows I want to talk to him. The bus ride is short to the airport. Thank the hockey gods because we are all exhausted.

On the tarmac Luke walks up while Fiona is distracted. "Hey, I need to talk to you about something. Beer on Tuesday while Fiona is with the girls?" I tell him. "Yeah, is everything okay?" he says concerned. "It's all good I just want to talk" I say nodding my head to Fiona walking up. "Congrats brother I am so proud of you! You absolutely killed it out there today!" she tells him pulling him into a big hug. Before we all load onto the plane.

I pass out the moment we take off. I wake up with Fiona leaning on me asleep with her laptop open. She is so damn beautiful. I still can't believe I landed this absolute angel. I hope the draft doesn't ruin things for us. But honestly, I think no matter what we will figure it out. I believe in us. I believe in our love.

As we start to descend to land, I wake Fiona up. She packs up her stuff and then cuddles back into me. We head home and I know we have a super busy week ahead of us. Once inside I laugh at the pile of airheads that say congrats, she must of set up before we left. "What if we had lost?" I ask her. "I would of ran ahead and removed the congrats sign. But I knew you would win. I believe in you." She laughs. We head to bed and sleep like the dead between the game and jet lag.

When she gets up, she heads to her parents to get some time with them. I use the time to clean the apartment before I shower and go back to sleep. I wake up and start dinner when she texts, she is on her way home. We only have one Sunday movie this week but that is ok. Family time is super important.

Monday we are both up and out the door before 7. The day drags by between classes practices, dryland, tape, and a mandatory yoga class we have to take. Tape sucks because the last time we played GU wasn't great for Luke or I. We lost our cool multiple times and I have a feeling Justin is going to fuck with us hard this game to get us rejected. As I think it coach says "Listen we all love Fiona and hate her ex, but you all need to ignore him. Miller and Campbell he is going to trying to get to you guys the most. But he knows she is close with the team so I won't be surprised if he tries to rile anyone up he can. Stay calm. We will get him back by winning the championship." Getting home I eat and pass out the minute Fiona and I get in bed.

Tuesday when I wake up, I let Fiona know I am meeting up with Luke at Slapshots while she has a girl's night. She gives me a kiss murmuring "Have a good time babe Love you." The day flies by I think because I am anxious to talk to Luke.

Arriving at Slapshots I grab a beer from the bartender and have a seat. Luke comes up moments later with his beer. "Spill it Miller, the past few days waiting has taken months off my life" he says. I roll my eyes at the dramatics and laugh. "I am going to marry your sister. You don't have to support that, but I wanted to ask you. I am also going to ask your dad, but your opinion matters to me too. I can't promise I won't hurt her. But I will try my hardest to keep her happy. I love her more than I love playing hockey which as you know is a lot. The moment she entered my life I knew she was it for me" I say full of emotion. He stares at me, and we sit in silence before he says "Of course I support you. I have seen how you treat her. You make sure she eats when we both know she will forget. You support her career and dreams. You wear those ridiculous yellow converses in support her. You aren't afraid to stand up for her even to me." And tears fall down my cheeks as I sit silent. "Congrats bro. She will say yes don't worry" he says.

Now to head home and decide when to purpose. The draft is coming up so I am not sure if I should do it then or wait until the summer. I want to do it when the moment is perfect. I already picked the ring after looking at her Pinterest and using what I know about her. Next is the talk with her dad on Sunday when we are all together for family dinner.

Fiona

I wake up Wednesday so tired. Girls' night was so fun though I am glad that I went. I can't believe what a perfect fit Charlie is in our group. Wednesday I don't have any meetings. I decide to sleep in a little so Zane is gone when I get up. With the championships next week, we so busy I am excited for a little breather today. I am pushing merchandise and championship tickers like crazy but trying to balance it out with actual team content. I don't want the page to get really sales focused or people will tune it out. Heading into work I focus on all my editing for a few hours. Zane comes and gets me to head home once he is done too.

Heading home I make dinner for us and he showers. Once dinner is over and we clean up I decide to be spontaneous since we have both been so tired and busy. I strip in the kitchen when he goes into the bedroom. I spray whipped cream on myself and head into the bedroom. Its dripping everywhere so this wasn't my best idea.

"Z" I whisper. He turns around and his mouth literally drops open. "Hungry for dessert?" I say. "Always" he says stalking to me. He drops to his knees. Starting with my tits he begins to lick slowly. Taking his time to clean one tit at a time being sure to suck until they are clean. Then he heads down my stomach licking making my body shudder from the sensation. When he gets to my pussy he says "Spread these amazing legs so I can get to my real dessert." I get wet from his words. I spread my legs balancing myself by holding on to his shoulders. He licks slow and plants kisses on my inner thighs. "Babe" I whisper. "Shh baby I am trying to savor my treat" he whispers onto my thigh where he currently kissing.

I feel his fingers spread my lips and I can feel his breath as he hovers over my clit. After what feels like forever, he dives in. He eats my pussy like I am his first meal after being on a deserted island. I am shaking by the time he adds in his two fingers. He reaches up rubbing one of my nipples. That's all it takes I cum all over his face not able to take all the sensations.

He removes his fingers from me, wipes his face on his shirt. Then strips down to nothing and picks me up. He holds me up while he lays back on the bed keeping me on top of him. I reach down and guide myself in after planting a kiss on his pouty perfect lips. As I slide down on him I watch his amber eyes flicker with passion. He moans as I take the last inch of him. I start to bounce and he grabs my tits playing with my nipples. It feels so good. I lean down moaning "Z you feel so good. My pussy was made to fit your big cock perfectly." He moves his hands to my ass palming them before giving them a slap. I moan leaning into his shoulder against his neck. "Be a good girl and cum with me" he whispers into my hair. Keeping one hand on my lower back and one on the back of my head keeping me against him. He proceeds to thrust into me hard and fast. Seconds later we both reach the brink of orgasm. I roll of him and go to get up and head to the bathroom. "Don't even think about it sunshine. I don't care how tired I am I will always clean you up" he commands getting up himself. After we are both cleaned up we pass out with me sprawled across him.

My alarm comes too early Thursday. I lay on Zane's chest thinking of my schedule for the day before I get up. My phone dings and I grab it. It's an email from the Tampa Thunder. Wouldn't they call if I got it? Maybe it's a rejection email. Fuck. "Zane" I shake him whispering. "What's up Fiona" he mumbles. "Sorry to wake you up on your sleep-in day. But I got an email. From the Tampa Thunder. I am scared to open it, I thought they were going to call. So, I think it's a rejection." I tell him with tears in my eyes. He sits up "Babe they would be stupid to reject you. Let's get up and ready then we will open it. You will regret not opening it on camera when you see they gave you the job" he says kissing my head getting up.

We get dressed and I put on my bellbottoms and my Tampa Thunder shirt. Zane sets up my camera for me then stands next to me while I open my computer.

"We are pleased to offer you the full time Social Media Manager position with the Tampa Thunder. You will see an attachment explaining the 4 weeks you have to respond. You have done an amazing job with the Tampa Penguins we hope you will join us. The contract is also attached if you have any questions or anything to discuss the people to contact are below. Welcome to the Tampa Thunder!"

I am crying when Zane leans over kissing my temple. "I told you babe! You are way too talented for them to pass up! I am so incredibly proud of you!" he murmurs into my hair. He reaches over shutting off the camera.

Then picks me up and kisses me passionately. We have to leave for work soon, but I tell Zane I am going to stop and see Lucy real quick then head in.

I tell Lucy and of course she is so excited and gives me the biggest hug. I can't stop crying about my dream coming true. My face must fall a little bit when I think about Zane and I because she grabs me hand. "Zane and you will make it work. He won't make you choose, and I know you both will make it through any distance if you have to." I talk to her for another few minutes. Before I head to the rink. I get a text from Marissa telling me to come straight to the press room when I arrive. Weird she must know I got the job.

Walking into the press room its dark but when I reach for the lights they turn on. "CONGRATULATIONS" is screamed at me as I scream. I am suddenly showered in confetti and airheads. Looking around it's the media team, all the players, the athletic director, and coach. Coach gives me a slight head nod before he tells the team "Hurry up and congratulate our season MVP. Then get your asses on the ice." Everyone comes and hugs me giving me their congrats and telling me how proud they are. Season MVP coach really has a way with work I giggle to myself. When Z finally walks up "thank you babe" I tell him. "You deserve to be celebrated. Season MVP though that was all coach. He is proud of the fan base you helped us to build" he tells me. Before he kisses me and hustles out to get out to practice.

My day flies by with all the excitement. My parents, Penny, Charlie, Celisa, and even Zane's parents text me congratulating me. I am so loved. It's crazy how much my life has changed over the past year. I head home at a decent time to cook dinner. When we lay down to go to bed Zane reminds me, he is so proud of me.

I feel him move under the blanket "what are you doing" I giggle. "I am just giving you a celebration gift. Relax for me baby girl" he murmurs. I can feel him moving my shirt up and moving my panties to the side. Thankfully I didn't put on shorts, I guess. He takes his time getting me to orgasm. Using all his favorite moves blowing my clit, twirling his tongue around it, sucking, licking me top to bottom, and of course fingering me while he eats me out. He makes sure I get a mind-blowing orgasm before he grabs a washcloth and cleans me up. "Time for sleeping sunshine" he says pulling me into him.

Friday morning is nowhere near as exciting. I do have a full day on the ice with the players individually and in small groups. We film player profiles to post as well as some fun dances and trending stuff. I make the guys where some of the new merch to help promote it. We have a fun time. Once everyone is on the ice in their scrimmage stuff for our team filming, I come up with a fun idea. When we are done with most of our filming I yell out "Anyone up for capture the flag?" and I hand two players flags and bolt. I speed skate between the teams and get some cool footage skating on the ice with them. After like an hour we call it quits. "Damn Fiona, we didn't know you were such a good skater" a lot of the guys tell me. "Well Luke is my brother I didn't have much of a choice to learn" I laugh.

At home Zane orders pizza and we have a relaxed night in with food and a movie. I go to reach for my computer to edit. "No sunshine. You are enjoying your night. The team pages will survive one night without you" he says pulling my feet into his lap. He gives me a foot massage that feels so good while we watch our movie. I must fall asleep because I wake up when he is putting me into bed.

Saturday Zane has a team building thing, so I hang out with Celisa before she has work. We get lunch and catch up on her life. She is enjoying single life and bartending right now. I guess she is making bank with the team doing so good. I am happy for her. I am glad to see her enjoying life. I tell her she should open her own bar sometime, but she always laughs me off. We say our goodbyes and head our separate ways. I will see her tomorrow at family dinner at mom and dads.

I decide that we should go out to dinner. We dress up for a celebration dinner at a local steakhouse. Charlie is working and we ask to sit in her section. She tells us about her last semester and talks about trying to find a job. I wish her luck and tell her I know a few people in the business world. I can introduce her too. Dinner was amazing so was the service. At home I get myself snuggled on the couch to watch my vampire show. Zane is on his computer studying but he is also texting a lot so maybe he is talking to the team.

I get up late on Sunday and Zane is up making breakfast. "Morning sunshine I am going to meet Luke for a workout then I will be back to shower and get ready for your parents" he says. After we eat, he gets dressed kissing me and heads out. It was so weird.

I text the family group chat.

Fiona: Zane is acting really weird should I bring it up.

Celisa: Maybe but what do you mean by weird.

Lucy: No leave it alone the championships are this week he is probably stressed.

Celisa: I agree that is probably it.

Luke: I am with him now. It's the stress of the game. Don't worry Fi.

Fiona: Okay Thanks guys I didn't want to start a fight or anything I was just worried. But I didn't even think about the stress of the game.

I shower and get dressed in a cute tank top floral jumpsuit with my converse. Zane showers and puts on some black shorts and a nice V-neck shirt with his converse. I smile because I can't believe I was concerned about this converse wearing man. Zane took the roof off the jeep. The drive to my parents is so nice. We blast my summer playlist and just let the wind blow in our hair. Well, my hair and Zane's playoff beard. I laugh out loud at that. "What is so funny in that pretty little mind?" he says. "I was thinking about the wind in my hair and the wind in your play off beard" I giggle. He just shakes his head and laughs.

My parents' house is in clearwater, so traffic is horrible, but we finally make it. Zane brought flowers for my mom and gin for my dad. I don't know why they love him either way. We sit around playing cards against humanity and having a drink. My mom loves this game and what better way to wait on dinner to cook than see who is the most fucked up in your family. We all laugh and have a great time.

Dinner is amazing my mom killed this meal. I need to get the recipe. Luke and Lucy are on their phones. I guess it's too much to ask for some family time. I roll my eyes at myself because we all know I suck at staying off my phone. "Hey, I want to celebrate your new job Fiona. Let's go to the pier and toss in a shell for wishes like we used to do" Lucy says. "Aw yeah that would be super fun" I say. Luke looks over then says "Just us kids though. Sorry parents. Also, Zane you have to stay to this is our little tradition." I am about to object and tell him how rude when Zane says "No worries I understand. I am going to help clean up then try and beat your dad at chess again." I look at him confused "Are you sure? I don't know why Luke is being rude." I say. "They just want this family moment. Babe I am not upset! Go have fun. He already texted me and asked if I would be offended and I said no. So go and have a good time" he kisses me "Take the jeep the roof is off" he adds.

We have an amazing time at the pier. It was some much needed just us four time that I didn't realize I was missing. When we get back to the house Zane and dad are having a drink while mom sits in the chair next to the chess table by them. Zane hugs them both goodbye. I say my goodbyes too and we head out. It's weird but the weird energy he had earlier seems to be gone. But maybe it was the alcohol I think as I drive us home. Not that he is drunk but we are always careful if one of us had more than two the other drives.

Zane

I wasn't sure that Fiona was actually going to leave. Once they are out the door Fiona's mom is by my side with a new drink. "Take a seat and tell us what is on your mind. Not that we haven't already been guessing since you called us" she says smiling. I take a big sip of my drink then proceed "I am in love with your daughter. I love her more than hockey and I know being Luke's parents you know what that means to me. I want to spend the rest of my life making her happy and supporting her every dream. I am not perfect, and I can't guarantee I won't upset her or hurt her. But I can promise to do my best to fix I when I do. Since she entered my life, she has made me a better man. I learned that I don't want to live a single day without her in my life." Her parents share a look then her dad looks to me. "We have seen the changes in you as a player more controlled more cautious of your actions. We have watched you turn into a leader on and off the ice. But we have also seen Fiona at her happiest ever. You have supported her in every moment. You defended her to Luke, yes he told us. You defended her to Justin but then allowed her to fight the battle with him. I am sure that wasn't easy on a protective man like you. You were converse and throw her congratulation parties. You love our daughter we can see that." he says. Then her mom takes his hand "Marriage is hard. It will be harder with you traveling for hockey. You will have to work harder than most to keep your relationship strong. You have to trust each other and be patient when the trust wavers. You will hurt each other but it's how you work to fix it that will matter. Our daughter isn't perfect, and she will make mistakes too" she says. Mr. Campbell reaches forward to shake my hand "We would love to have you as our son" he says. I can feel the tears falling while he shakes my hand. Her mom pulls me into the biggest hug crying herself. "We love you Zane we always have" she says.

After all the emotions calm down, we do finally play chess. Not long after Fiona and everyone gets back. We say our goodbyes and I hug both her parents' bye. The ride home is relaxed I feel an immense amount of anxiety lift off me knowing that everyone is on board with me proposing.

I have been texting with Lucy and Celisa about a ring. I finally ordered a lab created diamond with a simple silver band that has a small yellow diamond on each side. It will be here this week I just don't know when I want to ask her. Part of me wants to ask right before the draft or right after so we can start this next chapter together. I also want to ask her after graduation before I head to summer training with whatever team.

When we get home, I shower and lay down letting my mind rest. Fiona comes to bed shortly after and tells me all about their trip to the pier. She explains how much she missed their time as a foursome no offense she tells me. I understand what she means. I love the time I get just with Penny its special.

Monday when I get up, I send Penny a text letting her know I am going to be swinging by after practice tomorrow to see her. The whole day I can't stop smiling even during dryland I am just so happy with life. I get home after practice and Fiona has dinner ready. I enjoy every bite then I offer to clean up while she showers. When she gets out, I am waiting for her in bed. She looks at the clock "it's a little early don't you think" she questions. "I don't plan on going right to sleep sunshine. Now be a good girl and get your naked ass into this bed" I growl at her pulling the blanket off. "Make me" she says and goes to run to the living room. It takes me like three steps to catch up with her. I throw her over my shoulder and carry her to our bed. I set her on the bed and then start stroking myself. "Why don't you pay me back for making me have to carry you in here" I murmur and wink at her.

Standing at the edge of the bed she sits up and starts stroking me as I move my hand. She puts just the tip in her mouth letting her teeth lightly scrap across. I suck in a breath. Damn that felt amazing. She starts twirling her tongue and sucking only on the tip while she uses her hand to keep the rest of me stimulated. Right when I get used to her just sucking the tip she suddenly takes the whole thing. Fuck she is so good at this. I stare at her green eyes that are starting to glisten as she chokes on me. I grab her hair and she starts sucking harder and cups my balls. I explode right then shooting my load down the back of her throat.

Moving her up in the bed I climb onto her. Reaching down I guide myself inside her not wasting any time. As soon as I am fully in, I reach up and start playing with her nipples alternating between my mouth and my fingers. She is so sensitive on her nipples, I love it. It makes her super reactive to even the lightest touch. Or if I blow on her nipple right after I suck on it. She is about to cum i reach down and rub her clit lightly then I kiss her collarbone nipping her neck just a little and she implodes. I can feel her tight pussy squeezing my cock and the wetness dripping out of her as I thrust. I decide to spoil her with orgasms. So once she has caught her breath I reach over getting the wand out. I place it on her nipples first as I continue thrusting into her. I put one leg up over my shoulder. "Z this angle fuck I am already about to cum again" she moans. I move the wand to her clit and a few minutes later I feel her pussy clench around me wetness following seconds later. "Fuck Zane you haven't ever came yet" she groans. "I know baby I just wanted to spoil you" I say and pull out and flip us over. "Ass up like a good girl" I groan. She does as I say. Her back is so damn sexy all stretched out like this. I move my knees out a little spreading her legs a little wider before I slide back into her. When I am ready to orgasm, I grab a handle full of her hair tilting her head back just enough I can watch her face as she orgasms again this time with me cumming too. We crash after getting cleaned up.

I wake up on Tuesday morning slowly trying to get out of bed, so I don't wake up Fiona. I get showered and dressed before waking her up. "Babe time to get up. I am heading to the rink. Don't forget I am having dinner with Penny tonight, so I won't be home" I whisper. "Okay babe have a good time. See you tonight" she says while she stretches before getting up.

The day goes by pretty quickly but man the workouts are getting brutal. With the championship this weekend I thought coach might let up a little but nope. Once I shower, I get ready to head over to Penny's house. First, I stop by the mailbox at the apartment because the ring says it was delivered and I don't want it to be sitting there and Fiona check the mail. I grab the ring and head to Penny's. I open it in her driveway, its beautiful and unique. It fits Fiona perfectly I send a pic to Lucy and Celisa.

Heading inside Penny says she ordered some Chinese for us. "So, brother what's up?" she says. I toss her the box taking a sip of my beer. "Wow its beautiful. I assume her parents and brother said yes. I know you would ask them first before buying this. Right?" she inquires. "Of course, I asked. Everyone gave their blessing. Celisa and Lucy helped to pick it out" I say as she hands me the box. "Well, I love her and couldn't think of anyone better suited to put up with your bullshit. Do you know when you plan on asking?" she asks. "I am glad you love her. I don't know probably after the draft is

MARIAH GOODWIN

over. But I don't know I am going to have to plan the perfect moment" I say. "She doesn't want perfect Z. She wants you. No matter how you ask she will say yes. You can tell how much you love her based on the ring. It's perfectly Fiona" she tells me pulling me into a hug. The rest of our night is full of food and just joking around. Before I head home and go to bed.

Wednesday is weird the day passes quickly. I don't know why it feels like that because I have class on top of all of the practices we have going on. I get to see Fiona a few times around the rink though which is always nice. We even get to leave at the same time. At home we end up making dinner together and watching a sports newscast while she works on content. They play recaps of our season and GU's season.

Then they bring up the multiple fights the last time we played each other. There is no mention over the cause of the fights, but they do talk about if the game this weekend will be full of fights or if it will be controlled chaos like a normal game. I grab Fiona's hand shaking my head and turn the TV onto her vampire show. "Don't let it get to you babe" I say. "I'm not" she lies. We get up after an episode and head to bed. Tomorrow will be fun because we are filming as a team with Fiona. It will be our last time filming with her as the season comes to an end. Bittersweet feelings fill me as we fall asleep.

Thursday morning has nothing much going on except dryland and some tape. The teams' teachers excused us from class today with the championships in two days. Giving us all extra time to focus on plays and doing drills in dryland. We are all pumped to hit the ice with Fiona.

We are about an hour into filming when coach walks up to Fiona who is standing in front of the team bench "delivery for you Fiona" he says. She looks over to me "Thanks babe" she says with all of skating over to the bench. "Um they aren't from me" I say pissed knowing who they are from. I try and grab the card when I get close, but she already has it. Luke and I both jump the boards trying to get the card from her. "It's no big deal both of you back on the ice. We have one more shot to get" she tells us sticking the card in her pocket with the flowers sitting on the bench. Luke and I make eye contact and nod. "Okay sis if you are sure" Luke says. She turns to him to answer when I reach in her pocket grabbing the card holding it up reading it.

"Just read the fucking card so we can move on Miller" Coach yells at me.
Dear Fiona,

NEED YOUR NUMBER

Congrats on the new job. I knew you could do it. I expect to see you in my jersey this weekend. You have had your fun whoring around with Miller. But its time you stop embarrassing us both. Love you, Justin.'

The entire team breaks out in a chorus of fuck him and I am going to kill him comments. "Enough. All of you will head to the locker room practice is over. I will not warn all of you again. Do not engage with him during the game. Campbell and Miller get your heads right he will be using this to fuck with you. Scouts will be at the game. Do not chance your careers over him. Fiona, you deserve better than this. He deserves his ass whooped please ignore him. Easier said than done I know" Coach yells at all of us lowering his voice to speak with Fiona.

Fiona is home when I get home. She is crying on the couch with her wine watching Vampires. "I ordered Chinese. I know you had it with Penny but I need it" she says through tears. "Babe I am so sorry" is all I think to say. She cries in my arms for a while. Then we eat dinner before she returns to crying. In bed she whispers "Please don't react Zane. Don't chance your career. Kick his ass on the ice that will be the perfect payback." I hug her close kissing her temple "It's going to be a very rough game fists are going to be thrown but I promise to try my very hardest to keep a level head" I say trying to comfort her without lying. She falls asleep in my arms with tears falling down her cheeks. I am going to kill him on the ice. I hate him. Luke is pissed too. This game just got a lot more complicated.

Fiona

I wake up on Friday filled with dread about the flowers. I wish I could of hid the card from the team mainly Luke and Zane. They are not going to let this go and I already know it's going to be an issue going into the game tomorrow. But I still have a job to do so I get ready to head to work.

By the time I am out of the shower Zane is up. I blow dry my hair and put on my makeup. I pick a Miller shirt and leggings for the day. I don't usually wear Zane's name at work because I don't need to. Today though I feel comforted wearing it. He smiles dropping a kiss on my cheek when he notices. With that I head out determined to make today a good day.

The rink is busy with everyone trying to complete last minute plans for tomorrow at the Thunders rink. The players I run into don't act weird to me which I was worried about. They all respect me the same now as they did before the flowers. There are no looks of pity either. I hate nothing more than being looked at with pity. Tonight, we all plan to have an early drink at slapshots to celebrate the end of the season together. Coach has them all arriving later than normal tomorrow so they will be fine.

Heading home to get ready I straighten my hair letting it hang down my back taking advantage of the low humidity in March. I put on a cute romper that's green and makes my skin look amazing. I do some light makeup. Throw on my yellow converse than match great. "Damn girl you look amazing. Your legs look so fucking good in that" Zane says. I smile about to respond but he picks me up. Pressing me against the wall with my legs wrapped him. He kisses me neck "we don't have to go. We can stay here. You in this outfit is more than worth missing tonight. I am ready to get you into bed" he murmurs. I kiss him then I say "We need to go celebrate the season with the team before tomorrow." He whines and sets me down grumbling walking to grab his keys.

Arriving to Slapshots it is super busy with the entire team here. I go hug Celisa behind the bar and she gives Z and I a drink. Joining the team, we all share memories of the season. We take tons of pictures together posting them across our respective socials sharing the celebrations.

Lucy shows up shortly after and we head to the bathroom. On our way out a hand darts out grabbing me hard around the bicep. Looking up I see Justin "We need to talk" he commands. Lucy goes to step in, and I shake my head. "It's fine" I tell her. She walks away reluctantly.

"Stop with the bullshit Fiona. He is only with you to help boost his popularity before the draft. He doesn't actually love you. No professional athlete is going to settle for a converse wearing, loudmouth, "career" wanting girl. He's going to be swarmed with puck bunnies and models soon then he will leave you. Just stop embarrassing us both. You and I both know we are going to end up together. I am the only one willing to settle for you" he says trying to pull me into him. "Stop" I pull away. I step on his foot hard and rush back to Zane's side.

Tears are falling down my cheeks when I arrive back to the table. Zane immediately stops his conversation "Who the fuck made you cry?" he demands. "More importantly who the fuck grabbed you and left those marks?" Davis asks looking at my arm from across the table. Luke walks up "Why the fuck did Lucy just come tell me that Justin grabbed you and then demanded you talk to him. AND YOU AGREED!" he yells. Zane lowers her brows "First of all watch how you talk to her. Fiona you better start talking starting with the moment he grabbed you leaving those marks" he says pissed.

I tell all of them about him grabbing me and just figuring it was better not to fight it. When they ask what he said I just tell them that he was making a big deal over embarrassing him by not wearing his number. "No that wouldn't make you cry. I saw you tell him off last time. You wouldn't cry over that, so you need to just tell us the truth" Zane says. He knows me too damn well.

I tell them everything he said about my converse, my "career", the models and puck bunnies. I tell them about him saying I was being used to boost Zane's popularity for the draft. I finish by saying that he told me that he was the only one who would be willing to settle for me. That no one would lower themselves enough to actually marry me.

Everyone starts threatening to kill him and they all start looking around. "It's fine and he probably was smart enough to leave before I told you" I say. "Fiona none of that is true" Luke says pulling me into a hug. "Luke even you make fun of my shoes. I am weird he is right. Who would want a weird girl like me. I don't wear lots of makeup or dress fashionably. I am not a model. I am just a run of the mill girl who happens to be good at boosting a team and a player's fan base" I say tears falling down my cheeks. "Fiona please stop crying I am sorry I ever made fun of your shoes" Luke says. Zane goes to say something, but I shake my head with my chest heaving with sobs. Lucy grabs my hand "Zane I promise she will be fine. I am going to take her home though. Right now, she needs her sister. She doesn't need the teams pity looks. She doesn't need you telling her how much you love her. She knows that. She needs to drink wine and cry without judgement. I promise you will see her at the rink in the morning" she tells him pulling him into a hug.

Zane looks at me with pure sadness. Not pity just sadness. "Fiona I love you. I have known that I think since the moment I met you. I am sorry he hurt you. Have a good night with your sister. Please don't let him break your spirit though. You are none of those things. I love you so much" he murmurs into my hair while he hugs me. I lean up kissing him "I love you too babe. I will see you in the morning I just need this time with my sister" I tell him. He nods, offering to walk us out. I know shutting the car door and letting me leave with Lucy was hard on him I just need to be with my sister and drink without having someone pump me full of compliments while the look at me with pity.

We stop at Zane and I's apartment first to get clothes for tomorrow. I also needed to grab all my equipment for walk ins. Being here though reminds me that I want Zane and he wants me. If I was a pawn, he never would of treated me as good as he has been. Zane has loved me since the beginning I know that. To be sure he knows that though I send him a quick text before we leave. *'Zane, I love you. I know you love me. We are forever regardless of models or the draft. So please don't stress about me being with Lucy. I just need sisterly support. I will see you in the morning. DO NOT QUESTION WHERE MY HEART IS AT. I left it with you so take care of i. XOXO- your sunshine.'*

When we get to her apartment, I take a quick shower and put on some sweats. She has the wine ready for me. I spend the night alternating between crying and being so angry I can't cry. I don't understand why he had to show up. I can't stand how he thinks he has any rights to me. Or that he thinks he knows anything about Zane and me. I decide to be petty as fuck after my fourth glass of wine. Lucy and I laugh as I post a picture, I have of Zane holding me in bed obviously naked and we both sex hair. Our smiles show the absolute bliss we are in. The caption says: With happiness like this, I guess I can keep you forever. We giggle and know Justin will see it soon. Zane comments saying, "Forever doesn't sound long enough to be with you". My face flushes "FUCKING SWOON" Lucy says taking my phone to pin the comment to the top. Not long after the comments are flooded with Zane's teammates supporting us. One of them even wrote "That post sex bliss making you blind to Zane's stinky hockey gear?". I laugh so hard. "It's easy to ignore when you are that satisfied" I giggle showing Lucy my response. "You just confirmed you are in bed post sex in that pic, and you confirmed how amazing the sex is. Who is this drunk Fiona?" she questions laughing. We head to bed shortly after our comment fun.

I get up and am super relieved I am not hungover. I get do my hair in loose curls, but I put the top half up in a cute bun. I wear my makeup a little heavier but mainly because pictures will be taken regardless of if we win. Putting on my navy bellbottoms that hug my ass and yellow converse I smile at myself. I put on my white jersey with Zane's name and number. It fits me perfectly hugging me in all the right places. I ordered it online specifically for today. Lucy and Celisa tell me how hot I look and then let me know they will see me at the game.

I am waiting in the hallway with two assistants, I'm fancy I know, but not a single person from our team has entered. I am about to text Zane when I hear footsteps. Walking down the tunnel is the entire starting line up all in converse. Everyone hugging me and giving me an airhead. Luke whips his phone out taking pictures laughing at my face is what he tells me. I look at Zane pulling a face paint pen from my pocket "Hey handsome. I need your number" I smile handing him the pen. He adds the traditional #27 on each cheek before kissing me and dipping me low. I hand him his airhead and I stand there thinking I couldn't be happier. Then it gets better when the entire coaching staff walks in with converse on nodding to me while they walk by. "You did this?" I ask Z with tears filling my eyes. "Actually, it was Luke" he says. "I realized you deserve all the support for always supporting the team" Luke tells me and pulls me into a hug. The rest of walk ins are filled with converse wearing hockey boys in suits.

Luke posted the video of Zane and I online. That is going viral now with everyone saying they want to be as in love as we are. I post the walk-up montage of everyone in their converse and suits. The team floods the comments saying "We stand together against abuse and bullying. Being a hockey player doesn't excuse you." They just took a public stand without calling me out. I am crying when Lucy finds me. "Have you seen the response to their comments?" she says. I say no and open my phone.

The comments are full of support against abuse. People are duetting in their converse. Fans are tagging us in their game day outfits of them wearing converse. "This is amazing" I tell her wiping my tears. I can't believe the outpouring of support. I look down seeing her converse and tears start falling again. "Just a heads up our whole family and Luke's are also in converse. You single handedly just boosted the converse stocks" she says laughing.

Coach walks up "Fiona today is going to be hard on the team and you. I want you to know that I was told about last night and I am just as pissed as the team. I also will be contacting his coach after the game to tell him about Justin's behavior. I already told a few scouts I know who were interested in him just to warn them. No one wants a player who hurts women in any way. But especially in a way that might be violent and cause them negative press. Thank you for this season you have done amazing there will be a championship ring with your name on it" he says then walks away before I can respond.

Interns don't get championship rings usually so that is huge for me. "Holy shit he is going to ruin Justin's career" Lucy says. "He is. Honestly, he deserves it" I say shrugging my shoulders. I prepare mentally for the game ahead. I know things are going to be more violent than normal, so I take a deep breath then head to our seats.

We are seated with Penny and Luke's parents to one side. Then Lucy, Celisa, Charlie, and my parents on the other. All in converse "Thank you guys" is all I can say without crying. They don't push it everyone just claps my shoulder, or they nod at me. I am grateful for their support more than they know. Admitting how I allowed Justin to treat me was hard I was terrified of being judged for being weak. But everyone around me has continued to remind me how strong I am for getting out.

When the lights flicker, and the starters pictures start showing up as Georgia skates out first. Justin heads straight to us and Lucy and Penny both grab my hand. I turn my head, so I don't look at him. He hits the boards and yells whore before skating off to warm up. I focus on not crying. Zane cannot see me crying when he comes out. Our group of families are all grumbling about how nasty and shitty Justin is. I use that energy to help me collect myself. Then the lights flicker and our teams' starters show up on the jumbotron.

Zane

Sitting in the locker room my head shuffles through the past 24 hours. My mind starts and when Lucy and Fiona went to the bathroom. While they were gone, I tell Luke I am proposing after the game. He agrees it's a great time win or lose. I am excited I text Penny and ask her to hold the ring for me so when they enter the ice, I can grab it. I am so excited about this plan the guys are hyping me up. Then it all goes to shit Fiona is crying she has marks on her arm from that piece of shit. It was an intense night to say the least especially since she slept at Lucy's apartment. This morning was better though seeing her happiness as we all show our support in our converse even coach. Her asking me to write the 27 made my heart swell with so much love. Seeing her in my number makes me feel good as a man but having her let me add my number to her face fuck it felt good. Then the team supported her anonymously on her post they are amazing. Coach filled Luke and I in on what he did with the scouts. We both thanked him and let him know what it meant to us.

"Let's go Miller. Focus. Bring your girl the championship!" coach yells pulling me out of my head. I probably shouldn't have focused on the past 24 hours before the game but whatever. I grab a few airheads then skate out. Heading right to Fi I toss the airheads and then hold my hand against the glass much longer than I normally do. I needed that moment with her though. She blows me a kiss and gives me the I love you sign.

We have warm up then crowd the bench while Stuntz gives our pregame speech. "We made it this far undefeated. We have beat them before let's do it again. Don't let them use Fiona against us. She wouldn't want us to lose because of her. We also owe her this championship. On the count of three let's go kick ass. Three Two One" we throw our hands up and yell penguins.

Skating into position I am buzzing with energy. The first period is eerily good. No one scores but there is no shit talking. The hits are harder than they need to be on both side but nothing abnormal for a championship game. Heading into the second period Justin's teammates start dropping comments about Fiona. "She's a whore" "She is terrible in bed" "She gets around" "She is weird" all these comments they say as we play. Luke finally snaps but Rodriguez grabs him but the back of the jersey "Don't do it" he warns.

The rest of the second half is full of taunts. I shoulder check their right wing harder than I needed to but he wouldn't shut up. Luke is about to really lose it. It's just an echo around the rink of shitty comments about Fiona. I pull myself off the ice with two minutes left knowing my coverage is good and he will be fine for the two minutes. I regret it though because at the end of the second period Justin skates over to Fiona. He bangs on the glass and blows her a kiss. I go to jump the boards, but I am pulled back by coach. Luke is skating faster than I have ever seen to him, but Stuntz beats him there wrapping his arms around him from behind guiding him to our bench. Justin waves at us as he skates by giving us a wink. A chorus of fuck you goes out from our entire bench. I look at Fiona and she nods.

In the locker room we all take a breath and collect ourselves. "We are 0-0 you need to go back out there and end this shit. Beat him in the game. He is already showing how shitty of a man he is. Every single one of you need this win so I suggest someone gets that fucking puck down the god damn ice" coach yells. "Coach is right guys. We need to focus on the win right now. I am going to propose on the ice. It would be great to do it as a national champion ya know" I say shrugging. The team laughs we all slap each other's backs and head out. The fire has been lit so let's get this shit blazing.

The third period immediately becomes a shit show. As we line up for the face-off Justin looks over at his teammate and says "Wonder if I left a mark last night." Luke immediately says "When you grabbed her and dragged her through the bar? Let's not make it out to be any more than it was asshole." He laughs and replies "Sometimes a bitch needs to be put in her place." The puck is dropped Stuntz heads down the ice but Luke is headed to Justin. I am headed to Luke, but I am too late. They are already on the ground fighting gloves off. I try and grab Luke up, but I can't get him. I see coach telling me to back up. I skate back a little, so I don't get a penalty called on me for participating. Because Luke hit first unprovoked physically, he got a 5-minute major penalty and GU was provided a power play. Now we are playing 5 on 4 which is never ideal. Luckily in that time of us being down someone they don't score.

I get the puck right as the penalty clock expires, I speed skate down passing to Luke who moves forward uncovered shooting a perfect slapshot to the right of the goalie's hip. With the buzzer going off we have the point. It's hard to make a play with someone coming out of the box but it was a perfect opportunity with no one expecting Luke to be prepared for the pass. We have 10 mins on the clock when Justin finally starts trying to get to me. "You are going to get bored of missionary sometime. She is fucking boring in bed" he says loud. Luke's eyes flare with anger. "Weird because she never had a real orgasm with you. Yet I have her orgasming multiple times a night" I say. "Bullshit she doesn't even give good head" he says. "I have her choking on my cock every night. She loves when you stick a finger in her ass while you eat her pussy. Oh, and if you call her and good girl while you wrap your hand around her throat she squirts" I say chuckling. He doesn't realize it yet, but he will in 10 seconds. Arguing with me he let his team down and Stuntz is about to make a goal. BUZZ. The buzzer rings loud.

"Bro, I don't know how you got him distracted but go you" Luke says skating by. It's probably best he doesn't know. Before I can respond Justin is charging me. He rips off his gloves tackling me to the ground. I lay perfectly still taking the hits. He is about to get himself ejected. "You are a fucking asshole. She is a prude and shitty in bed everything you say is a fucking lie" he yells punching me. "Whatever you want to believe. I won't be thinking of you tonight while I call her a good girl and choke her. I won't think of you while she squirts. I won't think of you while I eat her delicious pussy. And guess what she won't think of you either" I say. He keeps hitting me even with the linesman trying to pull him off me. They finally get him off me, he gets a ten-minute major and we get the power play with only 7 minutes left we get to play 5 on 4 until the end.

Once the team trainer is done looking at me and wiping the blood off my face. I hit the ice nodding at Fiona. We end the game with Stuntz getting one more point with 30 seconds left. We all dog pile him. We just finished an undefeated season, won the championship in a shutout, and everyone I love is here. I couldn't be happier! Confetti is blasting everyone the families flood the ice. The fun thing is the other team stays in their box or on the ice for media while we celebrate. So when Penny sprints to me so she can get me the ring I smile knowing the nation will see this.

Fiona comes over jumps up and kisses me "My champion" she murmurs against me. I set her down carefully hoping she doesn't notice the circle forming around us of our families, my teammates, the media. "Fiona thank you for helping me get here. A few weeks ago I asked your siblings, Celisa, and your parents for their permission to marry you" she starts crying "They all said yes. My family said they already think of you as a daughter. I want to spend the rest of my life with you regardless of where that puts us geographically. I wasn't sure when to propose but last night prior to the incident I decided on tonight. I wanted to go into the next chapter as champions of love together. So Fiona Marie Campbell will you do me the honor by becoming my wife?" I drop to my knee producing the ring. "Yes of course. Yes" I slide the ring on her and stand up kissing her. "The ring is perfectly me" she says. "It is between your Pinterest Celisa and Lucy it better of been perfect. It was also lab created" I murmur into her lips.

Our families surround us in celebration. The team and coach come give their congratulations. The media come interview me, but I keep Fiona at my side. I want the world to see that yes I won a hockey game but I got the ultimate prize afterwards with my fiancé. Coach walks up and says "I know you have an amazing ring on that left hand but don't forget we have a championship ring for the other hand. To our season MVP!" The team cheers loudly.

Lucy walks up "There is something you both should know. Someone filmed Justin when he came out for warmups and when he came over at the end of the second period. They also posted it along with some audio they got from the game. It's going viral with the teams' comments about standing against abuse. People know" she says. I expect Fiona to freak out, but she doesn't. She stays calm and says, "Well maybe now other women will steer clear of him." I kiss her on her temple so proud of her.

t's time to head to the locker room and the ice is clearing our when Justin comes over. "You ruined my life you filthy whore. I know all the slutty things you do with him. You stupid bitch. I can't believe you would let people find out how you let me treat you. Aren't you embarrassed for allowing yourself to be treated horrible and manipulated?" he screams at her. She cocks an eyebrow at me about the sex stuff and I shrug. I am about to say something thought when she places a hand on my chest. "I didn't ruin your life you did. I am not embarrassed but you should be for behaving like this. You couldn't even make me orgasm I don't know why I ever stayed with you. I am marrying a man who respects me and treats me the way I deserve to be treated" she calmly tells him. "Oh, so letting him choke you is respecting you" he scoffs. She looks at me again and I shrug again. "I trust him 100% so yeah choking me is respecting me. He also cares for me after sex. He isn't a two pump chump in missionary either" she says turning to me. "You will pay for telling him that" she says kissing my arm. "I am offering two orgasms from oral before I fuck your brains out while you wear MY number" I say. "Deal" she says. "Good girl. Let's go!" I say and she giggles. When we are out of ear shot "I can't believe you told him about the choking" she says. "In my defense it's what distracted him while Stuntz got the goal" I tell her. "Fine I forgive you" she says kissing me before I head into the locker room.

This might be our last time together in our favorite arena, so I decide to be reckless. As we head to the locker room, we pass a storage closet. I quickly pull her in. "what the hell Zane its dark in here" she yells. "Shh baby girl I just want to fuck my fiancé in our favorite arena on my championship night" I say and start kissing her. I drop my helmet and gloves and begin pulling her pants down. I slide two fingers in her she is fucking soaked. "So, babe is it the dark closet and the chance we could get caught or is it rubbing your orgasms in Justin's face that made you this wet?" I tease. "Both I think. Shut up and fuck me fiancé" she says making my dick so hard I think it's going to break against my pants. "turn around and spread your legs" I tell her working on getting my pants down. Hockey pants are not easy to have a quickie in, note to self for the future. "Good girl" I whisper as I guide myself into her. She moans pushing her ass further into me. "I am so lucky to have a fiancé who takes my cock so good" I moan. I am about to cum already with the adrenaline from the day. I rub her clit and then wrap my hand around her throat. And we both climax together her pussy tightening around me. We get dressed quickly "I don't have anything to clean you up. But don't think I wouldn't if I had something" I saw before we slip out the door. She heads to her car and tells me she will meet me at home.

Fiona

I get in my car to drive home, and all the emotions hit me. I just sit in my car and process in silence. The entire hockey world now hates Justin that's a win. I am engaged to the absolute man of my dreams HUGE win. The team won the championship big win. The game itself, having my personal life on display, dealing with Justin; that was all losses in my book. The good outweighs the bad but I still deserve to grieve the bad. I think people get caught up in the idea of focusing on the good. Which I agree is important, but you need to grieve and heal from the bad or you will never be fully happy.

I start the drive home and realize when I pull in that Zane beat me home. I am sure he is freaking out right now. My phone is on silent in my purse. I dig it out that I have a bunch of missed calls and texts. I grab my bags and head inside.

"Oh, thank the gods you are okay!" he exclaims when I walk inside. "I am sorry I had my phone on silent in my purse" I tell him. He pulls me into a big hug kissing my head "Its ok I was just worried. After everything with Justin then I got home, and you weren't here. I thought maybe something bad happened" he says upset. "No, I am ok. I sat in my car at the arena and let myself feel all the emotions of the day. I didn't want to come home and not have handled them all personally" I say. "I understand. I am glad you took that time. If you need to talk about any of it, I am here for you always" he tells me. "Right now, I want to focus on my amazing fiancé" I tell him giggling. He picks me up and kisses me "I can't believe I get to marry you. Mrs. Miller" he murmurs against my lips. "That does have quiet the ring to it" I say kissing him.

When he walks me to our bedroom and sets me down I start to strip my clothes off. "Leave the jersey, I am not about to celebrate our engagement without my name across your back" he commands. I get my pants and panties off while he strips down. He goes and lays on the bed "Sit on my face but look towards my legs" he says. I follow his directions and lower my pussy against his mouth. I take his dick in my mouth and begin to twirl my tongue on the tip. He begins to twirl his tongue on my clit. I begin to suck him inch by inch until I have his whole length in my mouth. He slides a finger in my pussy and alternates between sucking my clit and swirling his tongue around it. I start to suck harder and faster I grab his balls and he thrusts slightly in my mouth making me gag. He adds another finger and continues his tongues assault on my clit. A few moments later he is filling the back of my throat with cum while I grind my pussy into his face cumming on his tongue.

I climb off him moving up to lay by him. He is immediately rolling over caging me in with his large body. "I love you future wife" he murmurs kissing my neck. "I love you too future husband" I say back. He reaches down guiding himself into me. He takes his time fucking me tonight. His thrusts are deep and hard. I moan into his shoulder as I reach my climax. He kisses me as I come down still fucking me. When he finally gets ready to orgasm, he rubs my clit getting me to cum with him. "Four orgasms in one night if you include the broom closet. My future husband spoils me" I giggle into his neck. He gets up and grabs the washcloth cleaning me up. "You deserve every single one of them" and he kisses my pussy. Tossing the washcloth in the laundry he climbs into bed pulling me close to him.

Zane wakes me up asking if we can go to Penny's for breakfast to see his parents before they leave. Of course, I say yes then get up to shower and get dressed. Zane is wearing nice khaki shorts and a button up with the sleeves nicely rolled. I decide to dress similar with in a white sundress with a subtle floral print. With my converse and my hair down in its natural waves. "You look stunning sunshine" he says. "Thank you. I didn't know if we were supposed to dress up you look super nice, so I decided on this" I tell him. "There is no dress code babe I just grabbed something" he says. We grab our stuff then head over to his sister's house.

When we walk in everyone yells surprise and again, I scream. I am not good with jump scares. I look around at all our friends and families. The balloons and congratulations sign. "How did you guys do it so fast?" I ask crying. "When Zane told Luke he was asking at the game we used the phone tree and TA DA we have a surprise engagement brunch" Lucy says. "We wanted to do it before our parents left" Penny adds. "Plus, everyone knew you would say yes" Luke says. "Thank you all so much this is amazing" I say through tears.

After we greet everyone, I grab a mimosa and we all sit and talk. The food is served buffet style, so everyone is able to kind of graze and socialize.

NEED YOUR NUMBER

It was exactly what I would plan myself. Something simple, intimate, and low stress. We take lots of pictures and every compliments Zane on the ring. I cry looking at the pictures and videos from the proposal. He really did an amazing job. Our families already know each other and like each other which is great because I couldn't imagine tension in the family.

People ask us if we decided on a date, but we haven't discussed it yet. We talk about the game and how amazing it was. No one mentions Justin but I know he is on everyone's mind when we talk about the game. I haven't checked online or any sports news, but I am sure it's not looking good for him. After a few hours we head back home promising to see everyone soon. With the draft in two weeks, I know most of us will be together soon.

Driving home I snap a picture of my hand on Zane's on the gear shift. I decide to post that, and a few people took of the proposal with the caption: I got your number now I need your last name. I laugh because I know Zane loves when we joke about that moment in our first interview when I asked for his number, but I meant his jersey number. He checks his phone at the light and sees the tag. He chuckles "that joke will never get old" he says. I knew he would love it. I am ready to get comfy on the couch after a long few days.

Getting home I head straight to change when I come back out Z is watching the sports channel. They are doing a segment on Justin they don't say my name and they bleep out everything sexual. They talk about him being cancelled and his career being ruined. Then they have a segment on our team. There is a part about our engagement and coach calling me the season MVP. "This girl is going to be in demand in the sports media world just watch. This won't be the last we see of her. The things she has done for a small college team. The pros are going to be begging for her" the anchor says. Zane looks at me and says "He is not wrong you know. You could open a business where you go and train sports social media managers. You could host speaking events. You could offer more than just hockey and you can even offer college/pro/etc." I laugh "That would be fun but let's be realistic here" I say.

"Check you emails and tell me you aren't blowing up with interview requests" he says confident. HOLY SHIT "I have over 50 emails from teams asking to interview me" I say breathless. "Told you" He says. "There is football, basketball, hockey, soccer, even a nascar team. It's not all pro either there are some college teams here" I say overwhelmed. "You are amazing I am

205

not surprised" he says. I text our family chat with our parents telling them about the news and the emails. They all agree with Z that I should form a media company.

I shoot an email to Marissa asking for a meeting then I relax. "No hockey or work talk" I say. "So when are we getting married?" he says. I don't answer thinking. "I would prefer this weekend, but I can wait" he says with a huge smile. I laugh "I don't want anything big but I would like an actual wedding" I say. We go over things we both do and don't want in a wedding. We decide on September 8th so we can honeymoon before the hockey season begins.

We discuss venues and we decide on trying to rent out the ice rink at the school. How romantic to get married where we met and where our love story began. Where our love developed and grew. I shoot an email to the athletic director asking for a meeting so I can ask her about the possibilities of this. We are being so productive right now. My engagement post is blowing up. Everything is just perfect.

Monday morning Zane has class so I start looking at wedding stuff until I get an email from Marissa, she can meet this afternoon. I start getting my thoughts together to talk to her about. I want to be sure I cover all my bases. I text Z and let him know where I am heading.

"Hey Fiona. I hear congratulations are in order" Marissa greets when I walk in. "Thank you so much" I say. We gossip a little about wedding and engagement stuff. I tell her about my idea for venue and she loves it and wishes me luck with my meeting. I tell her I have it set up for tomorrow morning and she tells me how excited she is.

"Are you here about the news segment on you? I assume your email is blowing up?" she says. "Yeah how did you know?" I ask. "Who do you think gave out your email?" she says laughing. "I was wondering but I was too excited to think into too much" I say. "Are you wondering who to work for?" she asks. "No I actually want to start a full sports social media company" I tell her. I give her my ideas and plans. "I love it. Please let me know if I can help at all. I think your initial plan is perfect. Get everything official quickly then send out emails from your company to everyone requesting interviews. Don't forget to add the university to the list we could use someone to help train the others" she says. We say our goodbyes and I walk out determined to make all my dreams come true. I will marry the man of my dreams and work in hockey social media management.

When Zane gets home, I cook dinner and tell him about my meeting. He offers to help me financially to get my business going but I decline. I want to do this without his money, but I will take his support. I let him know about the meeting I have with the athletic director tomorrow. He offers to come but I think it will be best just me. I stay up way too late getting my business plan together, but I am just so excited. I was able to find an old business plan i made for my capstone in college. My dream of one day owning a sports media company. Justin crushed that dream quickly. So i focused on the Thunder and working for them. But Zane is amazing to help me build my dream career. I knock out a bunch of details on it. Finally, I crash on the couch.

Tuesday morning comes quick with my uncomfortable on the couch. I get up and put on a cute but professional outfit for my meeting. Giving Zane a deep long kiss I then head out the door. Stopping for coffee and arriving ten minutes early. I down my drink take a deep breath and knock on her office door.

"Good morning and Congratulations" she says. "Thank you and Thank you for making time for me today Mrs. Baker" I tell her. I explain my business plan to her and go over all the services I plan to have. "Sounds amazing we are definitely interested. Send me over the prices and we can discuss further" she says. "Well actually I was willing to offer to train 3 people for free in exchange for something" I inform her. "Oh, what would be worth all that free work for you" she inquires. "I want to have my wedding in the ice rink on September 8th. We will hire a clean-up crew and I know we have covered the ice before for events." I tell her. She picks up the phone and makes two phone calls going over everything. "You have yourself a deal" she says. We shake and I let her know I will be emailing her with my information.

I walk to my car crying everything is falling to place. I send a text to our group chat with both our families 'September 8th we are getting married on the ice at the Penguins Arena". My phone blows up with everyone excited over how unique and perfect that venue is.

When I get home Zane has flowers on the counter for me. He gets home and dinner is ready. We talk about the venue and the deal I made. He isn't exactly happy about it but that's okay. "The draft is next Thursday are you excited?" I ask him to distract him. "I am but I am more excited to take you house shopping once we get a location" he says. "We can rent babe" I say. "No I want to own a house with my wife. Please don't fight this. I have enough money. I am struggling not going to buy you a new jeep of your own" he says. "My car is fine babe" I say. "The minute it asks up we are heading to the dealership that day" he says serious. "Fine. You are incredibly annoying when it comes to wanting to buy me big things" I say laughing. We spend the rest of our night cuddling and watching TV before heading to bed.

Zane

Its Monday morning on draft week and I am anxious. I stayed busy all weekend helping Fiona get her business stuff together. We got her business name 'Sunshine Sports Media' and she set up her bank accounts. She made a website and spent all Sunday sending out information to everyone requesting an interview. She even emailed the information to the Thunder. I am proud of her. I think she is going to love working with a lot of teams across a bunch of different sports.

I hit the gym with Luke after class. He talks about how worried he is to be drafted away from his family. I tell him my worries about going somewhere I hate. I don't have to worry too much with parents who travel full time and a fiancé who is opening a business what will have her traveling so she doesn't need to be anywhere certain. But the thunder is and always has been my first pick.

I head home to Fiona looking stressed over her computer and planner. "What's up boss lady? I say. "I have gotten 16 teams interested including the Thunder. I am trying to schedule my info meetings over the next week. I just want to do good" she says. "Take a deep breath. You will do amazing sunshine. These teams would be lucky to have you." I say. "I am going to start dinner. I want you to put the work away and flip on your vampire show while I bring you some wine" I also tell her. She nods her and reluctantly closes her computer. Bringing her the glass of wine I give her a big kiss "You need to create work hours and boundaries, or your business will eat you alive" I tell her.

"If I get 4 or more teams to sign up I am going to hire Charlie if she is interested. Maybe even Celisa. Celisa can handle scheduling and traveling plans. Charlie is a business major so she can help more on that side" she says thinking out loud. "That is a great idea babe" I tell her. "They will just work remotely if we have to move. If we stay in Tampa maybe, we need to get an office? I am excited and nervous." She says. "I never really wanted my own business like this, but I loved helping the other sports and this is such a unique opportunity for me to have this business. I never allowed myself to dream this big. Now it's like there is no limits on my dreams thanks to you and your support" she adds.

We talk more about her plans, and I can tell listening to her deep down she hopes I draft to the Thunder. She doesn't want to leave Tampa, but she will if I have to go. I love listening to this version of Fiona. She believes in herself, and I love it. We head to bed, and she tells me about her plans to go wedding dress shopping next month. We fall asleep talking about our wedding parties.

Tuesday morning when I get up, I hit the gym before class. I have my midterm, but it is open book so I'm not really worried. Fiona is meeting with three teams this morning, but I am meeting her for lunch after. She is heading to the bank to apply for a loan after that, so I am going to meet up with Luke, Stuntz, and Rodriguez. I am going to ask them to be my groomsmen over beers at Slapshots.

My midterm was easy. I beat Fiona to the restaurant. She comes running in face flush. "Hey babe where's the fire? I say joking while I get up and kiss her. "Ha ha babe. I just was running late and didn't want you waiting on me" she says. We order our lunch then I ask her "How did it go?" She smiles "I sent contracts to a pro soccer team, pro baseball team, and a college will be getting back to me" she tells me excited. "That is amazing sunshine. I honestly think you should hire Celisa and Charlie soon. You are going to get busy faster than you think. Just my selfish opinion since I want as much time with my fiancé before training starts up" I tell her. We laugh and talk about my plans with the guys. I tell her to swing by after her bank appointment.

We go our separate ways and I head home to change before meeting the guys. Celisa is working so I chit chat with her waiting on the guys. When they arrive, we all go sit in a booth. "So, I wanted to see if you guys would be my groomsman? Luke, I want you to be best man." I ask sipping my beer. They all say yes, and we order a round of shots. We tell Celisa the occasion and she takes one too. "Congrats Zane I am so happy for you guys" she says.

Shortly after shots Fiona comes in ordering another round of shots. "What's the occasion now?" Celisa says. "I got the loan" Fiona exclaims! "That's amazing girl" Celisa says hugging her. We all give our congrats and take our shots. Big things are happening in our lives. The draft is in two days I am praying it doesn't mess anything up for us.

Fiona heads home before me wanting to get some work done. I kiss her goodbye and promise to be home soon. "I am so proud of her" Luke says. I smile "Me too, she has so many big things happening. I just hope the draft doesn't ruin anything" I tell the guys. "Her business is remote you will be fine. She would prefer to be here in Tampa, but she can easily work from anywhere. Don't stress over something that hasn't happened yet" Stuntz says. After another thirty minutes I head home.

Fiona is asleep in bed with her computer in her lap. Grabbing her computer from her I see she is looking up how to stay organized working from home. It makes me smile knowing she was looking up how to make things work if we need to move. It sort of soothes my soul knowing she is committed to us even with the idea of moving. I kiss her goodnight and whisper I love her before I go to sleep.

Fiona wakes me up Wednesday by climbing under the covers and beginning to stroke my dick. I moan and then touch her cheek saying, "Good morning sunshine." "Morning Z. Today is your last midterm and the day before the draft I can only imagine the stress you are under. I want to help you relax" she says right before she licks my entire length. She starts lightly sucking on the tip while she runs her tongue across the slit on the top. Then she begins to take my entire length inch by inch. Taking all of me into her warm and wet mouth. It feels so good I am not going to last long. She sucks on just the tip and then takes all of me hard and fast. I grab the back of her head shooting cum down her throat. She takes every drop before licking my tip and sitting up with a huge smile. She crawls up the bed plants a kiss on me "Have a great day babe" and she is up getting ready for her day.

I get ready and head to my midterm stopping at the table to tell Fiona I love her and will see her tonight. My midterm is simple I am confident I did great. Then I head to the gym with the guys. Feeling better about the draft I relax a little knowing that it's going to be okay. I really hope all of us get placed in Tampa, but I am not sure how many slots they have available for the team.

On my drive home I text Penny confirming the draft party at her house. By party I mean we are going to watch the draft as a family. Fiona is going to live stream it on my page for me. It will be nice to have footage of me getting the call to look back on. My parents will be with us too which is amazing. It is a huge night for my career. It is also a big moment in my relationship with Fiona where we find out if we are uprooting our entire lives.

I get home and Fiona has dinner cooking while she works on the counter. "First thing we are doing after the draft is house shopping. You need a home office so you can be organized." I tell her. "Oh good because I may have talked to someone about a litter of puppies that will be ready to go home in the middle of May" she says giving me a megawatt smile. Grabbing her phone, she shows me the puppy she is in love with. It is a bernedoodle; Bernese mountain dog and Poodle mix so its hypoallergenic but still a big dog like she wants. "The breeder is a little expensive, but I figured you wouldn't mind spending a little on this sweet girl" she giggles. "Anything for you sunshine" I say and look at the dog again. She is a cute puppy.

After dinner we scroll through our phones looking at puppy stuff. Careers, a puppy, and a home soon. I am so happy to have met this beautiful woman. We clean up the kitchen and then I get ready to go to bed. I fall asleep with Fiona in my arms.

"ITS DRAFT DAY" Fiona exclaims wearing my penguin's jersey! "I have two meetings then I am heading to help Penny set up. She took the day off so we can set up. You go get your haircut and trim up your playoff beard. Get camera ready. Then the guys are coming here for a drink with you. Before you head to Penny's house" she informs me of my day schedule. I chuckle. "Thank you for planning everything, babe. Especially the drink with the guys. You keep me on track, and I appreciate it" I tell her giving her a kiss.

I get my haircut and beard trimmed; Fiona made it clear she didn't want it shaved off. When I get home, I make sure I have my khakis and button up set out. Shortly after the guys arrive there is a knock on the door. Fiona had pizza delivered with a note taped inside the box saying "CONGRATULATIONS GUYS! I AM SO PROUD OF YOU! HAPPY DRAFT DAY! XO- Fi". We all take a picture of it. "Your girl is amazing" Rodriguez says. "He is not wrong. She planned all this out great" Luke says. We eat and have a few beers before we all go our separate ways to get ready. Our goodbye is a little emotional because after tonight all of our lives are about to change.

Penny and Fiona set the living room up with streamers and balloons. They have food and a little bar area set up. Behind the TV Fiona's iPad is on a tripod ready to begin the livestream. Fiona is dressed in a cute black dress. She makes me a drink and we all sit down flipping on the correct channel. Its time.

Tampa picks third we are all holding our breath then we hear "our first-round pick is Blake Stuntz." We all cheer so excited for him. I shoot off a text to him. The waiting between draft rounds is long and anxiety fillled. I can't seem to stop bouncing my leg or fidgeting. I know that they have to let the teams circle through each round but I wish the draft was done team by team. Fiona rubs my back and tries to relax me Tampa's coach stands again "Our second-round pick is Luke Campbell" We send him texts of congratulations. We continue to wait when Tampa comes back up at the end of the second round after a trade we have another second round pick available. Our next pick is Zane Miller. The whole house erupts in cheers while my phone rings with a welcome call from coach. When I hang up and turn to look at Fiona. I see her in a Thunder jersey with 27 and Miller across the back. She knew I would make it, she always believed in me. "We did it sunshine. We are staying here!" I say full of emotion with tears in my eyes. She throws airheads up in the air and then jumps in my arms as we both laugh. A round of congratulations happen from my family. My phone going off with texts. But Rodriguez drafts to Tallahassee we are still happy though he will be in Florida still. After a big round of celebration, we head back to our apartment.

When we get inside Fiona heads to our bedroom, so I lock up then follow her. She stands in the Thunder jersey and says, "Tomorrow we have a meeting with a realtor to get ourselves a house." Everything this season has led us to this moment. We are getting married on center ice where we met. We are getting a dog. We are both beginning our dream careers. Life is perfect all thanks to a beautiful brunette converse wearing social media intern that waltzed into my life and we both never looked back.

I toss her on the bed and begin to worship her pussy with my tongue. Alternating between sucking and blowing on her clit then adding in a few twirls of the tongue she is cumming on my face quickly. I climb on top of her guiding myself in and begin thrusting. I lift her hands above her holding her hands in place with my hand. She moans and I can feel her clenching as I fuck her harder and deeper. I wrap my other hand around her throat lightly and she orgasms again. I let go of her hands and throat letting her catch her breath. I flip her over "I want to cum with you wearing my last name in the thunder jersey. A literal dream come true" I murmur as I guide back into her from behind. When I am about to climax, I grab her hair and tilt her head back wanting to stare into those beautiful green eyes as I fill her with my cum.

I get up and clean her up. We lay down to go to sleep her head on my chest. "How did you know to get the jersey and make a realtor appointment?" I whisper into her hair. She sighs "I never stopped believing in your dream. I never stopped believing in you" she says kissing my chest. I kiss her head and we fall asleep together. I don't dream tonight because all of my dreams just came true.

Fiona

4 months later July

Zane is outside mowing the lawn, so it is finished before he heads to training camp for the week. Tilly, our puppy is sleeping in my office. Zane picked Tilly since that's another word for fight in hockey. I didn't fight it though because it is a cute name. We found the most beautiful home on the outskirts of downtown. It has a decent yard and is 4 bedrooms with an office. We moved in last month and finally are completely unpacked. In May I picked out my wedding dress before I had to fly to train a football teams social media team. So, it has been a very busy few months.

Once the lawn is mowed and I am caught up on work we decide to have drinks by the pool. One of the best things about this house is the pool and yard. We are lounging on pool floats when suddenly I am in the water. I come up for air and feel Zane grabbing at my bathing suit to pulling the string and it falls open. I pull the string on the top taking it off completely. He pulls me into him, and I wrap my legs around his waist. He tilts my chin up and we start making out. I grind against him feeling him growing harder. He pulls the strings on my bottoms and the go floating away.

He buries his head into my neck kissing me while he guides himself into me. I will never get tired of how amazing sex is with Z. Backing us up against the wall I can feel my back scraping while he pounds into me. I grab a fistful of his hair he reaches down to my clit. "Fuck Z this feels amazing" I moan into him. We both climax before he pulls out be keeps holding me to him. "I am going to miss you sunshine" he murmurs into my hair. "I will miss you too babe. But we will stay busy to fill the time. You with practice and me with work and I have a doctor's appointment" I say. Hoping he picks up on the doctor's appointment. We have talked about wanting kids and they say you need to give your body time off to get rid of the birth control and it can take around a year to get pregnant. I decided to come off now so we can start trying after the wedding.

"Doctors appointment for what? Is everything okay?" he asks concerned. "I am fine" I tell him. "Then what's up?" he says. "I am getting some blood work done and letting my doctor know I am going to stop my birth control"

I inform him. "What! Really? I am going to be a dad?" Zane asks. "Calm down it will take some time and lots of practicing but yes hopefully in the next year we will be parents" I say smiling. He twirls me around in the pool so excited. This man is going to make an amazing dad.

We have dinner and sit out watching the sunset having a glass of wine. The puppy playing in the yard in front of us. I can believe this is our life. We fought hard to get here though, and we deserve every ounce of this. I head up to shower while Zane finishes packing. Climbing into bed he wraps me in his arms the same way he has done for months. Sleeping without each other sucks because this is our normal. I fall asleep as he sprinkles little kisses on my head.

The next morning, I wake Z up with my lips wrapped around his cock. "Good morning, Sunshine. I love waking up like this" he moans. I know he has to get up soon, so I make sure to use my time wisely. Twirling my tongue then giving the tip a little suck before I take the whole thing. He wraps his hand in my hair and I take my hand cupping his balls. I begin to choke as he fucks my mouth faster and harder. It's not long before he is shooting cum down my throat.

I get up to head to the office and he gets ready to leave. He pins me against the wall giving me an extremely passionate kiss. He pets the dog and heads out the door. I grab coffee and load Tilly up and we head to our office in downtown. When I arrive, Celisa is at her desk on the phone but Tilly runs right to her. I head to my office to start my day. My computer is just turning on when Charlie walks in to talk about the 3 new teams interested in hiring us. Working with them is amazing and It has been such a journey. "I got three interviews including Stacy who was a student intern with the Penguins' basketball team" Celisa says. "Keeping it local I love it" Charlies tells her. I smile and we all get down to business focusing on our tasks for the day while Tilly runs around.

My business is taking off we have 5 pro teams, 4 colleges, and 1 sports TV station on our client list. We don't need to advertise anymore because our clients are walking billboards. I do miss my time actually doing the grunt work with the teams filming, bonding, and editing. But the trainings I offer are making huge strides in sports media.

I even got the chance to work with the Savannah Bananas on a campaign to help raise funds to help domestic violence survivors. It was sponsored by Converse and had an amazing turn out of professional athletes who came and donated. It was beautiful to see the turn out and have it sponsored by my favorite brand alongside the inspiration for my career.

We order some lunch and while we are sitting in our conference room eating someone delivers flowers. 'I miss you already sunshine. I will see you soon. XOXO- your future baby daddy' Celisa reads the card out loud. Then they are both jumping up "omg you are pregnant" "what". "I am not pregnant I said we could start trying after the wedding, but I have an appointment tomorrow to come off my birth control. He knew you would read the card and wanted to fuck with me." I tell them.

The rest of the week passes without incident. My appointment goes great I stopped my medicine yesterday. I am meeting Lucy and my mom tomorrow to go over some wedding stuff. Zane gets home tomorrow afternoon which is the most exciting. I can't wait to see him. I head to bed knowing tomorrow is a busy day.

Leaving my mom's house, the next day I head home to start dinner. When I get home, I see Zane's jeep in the driveway. He got home early! I sprint inside to see him. He is standing in our bedroom unpacking him bag when I run over and jump into his arms. "Welcome home babe" I murmur into his lips. "Glad to be back sunshine" he says. Walking us to our bed he sets me down. "I believe I owe you for how you woke me up before I left" he says with a wink.

He lifts my dress and loops his finger on the straps of my thong pulling down quickly. He runs his tongue across my pussy lips. "So wet and ready for me already babe" he says. He licks me and sucks on my clit. It doesn't take long before I am cumming on his tongue. Fuck he is so good at pleasing me. We end up having mind blowing shower sex before I go cook dinner.

The rest of July flies by and its now the first Friday in August. We leave for our respective bachelor/bachelorette parties today. I am excited as I drop Tilly off with Penny to be watched while we are gone. We are headed to Jamaica for the weekend and the boys are going to Vegas. Getting back home Zane sets me on our kitchen counter making sure we leave for our trips satisfied.

He moves my sundress up and my panties to the side. "Such a pretty pussy" he says. Then he bends down licking me from top to bottom. I shudder from the stimulation with the cold counter and his warm mouth on me. Once he has me about to climax I grab his hair holding his mouth to me as I cum. He pulls back and smiles "delicious" he says winking. I go to sit up but he stops me "be a good girl and spread those legs again sunshine" he moans while he pulls his cock out stroking it. "Touch yourself baby" he whispers. I reach down rubbing my clit with one hand and my nipple with the other. I let out a quiet moan then Zane is sliding into me. He fucks me hard and fast making me have to grip the edge of the counter. He lifts me up and pins me to the wall still inside me. He proceeds to rail me so hard you would think the wall was going to come down. He finally puts his fingers on my chin lifting it and kissing me. We both orgasm as he kisses me on that wall.

Charlie, Celisa, Lucy, and I have an amazing time relaxing on the beaches. We drink and eat lots of food. I didn't want anything crazy, and this was perfect. We don't do any excursions opting to enjoy spas and massages instead. Monday morning comes way too soon as we board our flights back home. I am excited to see Zane and Tilly though. I can't believe our wedding is in one month.

The next three weeks fly by when we get home. With working and trying to make sure the wedding plans are finalized. Zane is acting like having sex is his new career. The man has fucked me on every surface of our house more than once. I am not complaining but that keeps me busy at home. I am slammed at work with hockey and football starting up. I am working on wedding stuff whenever I can. I feel like this time leading up to the wedding is more stressful than it should be. I guess most brides feel like that though. Zane is trying to help but he is so busy training for the season about to start. I tried not to travel much so I could be here handling things.

I am taking this week off to get ready for the wedding this weekend. Then week after the wedding off for our honeymoon. We are flying to Turks and Caicos and staying in one of those cute bungalows. It looks so relaxing out there and why not spend some of our hard-earned money. Our bridal parties have been amazing at making sure that we have all the help we need. I am hoping that maybe something happens with Lucy and Stuntz. She has always had a crush on him, and weddings tend to bring people together.

I spend the week making sure to get every single thing handled. I pick up my dress leaving it with my mom. I get my nails done with Lucy. I pack my honeymoon bag and I supervise Zane packing his because he will forget. I make sure I have Tilly's stuff together for her stay Penny's house. Zane and I pick up our marriage certificate at the court house. Then I make sure to put our rings in my day of bag or else Luke or Zane will forget them. I am making sure we are ready for our start of forever.

Friday morning, I wake up to Zane under the covers lightly licking my slit. I fell asleep after sex, so I am naked already which is convenient for him. I moan and he begins to lick my clit. The feel of his beard on my thighs is extremely stimulating. He flicks his tongue on my clit then switches to sucking on it while he slides two fingers in and out of me. I squeeze his head with my things yelling out his name with my hand wrapped in his hair. While I come down, he lays back on the pillow and I climb on to him. I guide his cock into me slowly riding him. I toss my head back bracing myself with my hands on his chest. I bounce up and down while he plays with my nipples. When he is about to cum he smacks my ass then starts rubbing my clit. We climax together. "The next time we do this it will be as husband and wife" he moans into my neck.

He gets up and packs his bags. He will be staying at the hotel next to the college where we will spend our wedding night. I help him get his bags loaded up including my honeymoon bag. He also is going to take Tilly to drop her at Penny's on his way. "I love you sunshine. I can't wait to make you Mrs. Zane Miller" he says before picking me up and kissing me like it will be our last kiss ever. The way he holds wraps his fingers in my hair and uses the other hand to cup my ass holding me up makes my insides flutter. Him holding me like this never gets old and I hope he never stops.

I tear up as he drives away knowing when I see him again will be at the end of the aisle. The girls will be meeting me at the rink around 11 we are getting ready in the locker rooms. I make a glass of wine and go relax in the hot tub as the sunsets. After some time in the hot tub I head inside to shower and hopefully get a good night's rest.

Zane

I wake up and it's my wedding day. I have never been so excited for something in my life. I wake up in the hotel feeling refreshed and ready to see my wife. She has been working so hard to make everything for today perfect. I hope it is everything she imagined. As a wedding gift I got her a tricked out new jeep. She has been working so hard with her business, getting our new house to be a home, and on helping me with my transition to pro hockey. Her dream is to own a yellow lifted jeep with blacked out windows. Now she owns it and it's parked in front the arena so we can drive it back to the hotel tonight.

I send her a good morning text before I get up and take a shower. I make sure I have everything I need for the day including my suit before I head over to the arena. I grab coffee and a muffin on my way I don't want to be tired or hungry on my wedding day.

We are getting ready in the home locker room at the arena. While the girls get ready in the away team locker room. We will get married on one side of the ice. The other side will be our reception with even a dance floor. We will have an open bar and buffet style food. Fiona was sure to include pieces of our story in every detail. The table assignments are pinned in the corner on a surfboard in honor of the beach clean-up. There are airheads on top of a hockey puck at every seat. She also skates and a pair of converse hanging off the DJ booth. There are pictures of us everywhere around the party area. The photo booth has a "pose like us challenge" that shows everyone 10 photos of our signature pose of me holding Fiona in my arms with her legs and arms wrapped around me. The goal is to recreate it the best. Our guest book is a polaroid camera set up with pens to sign the picture.

The guys arrive and we all pour a shot. We get ready taking our time drinking beer while we wait to enter the ceremony area. I want to see Fiona but there is no way she will allow that. Luke comes over and claps me on the back "I couldn't imagine anyone better to marry my sister. Welcome to the family brother" he says and I nod. We both know if I answer the emotions will take over. The wedding coordinator comes and tells us its time.

The bridal party goes first with Celisa and Rodriguez, Lucy and Stuntz, then Charlie and Luke. We don't have the maid of honor and best man walk together since they are siblings. Plus my wife is trying to play matchmaker. I walk my mom down the aisle looking at all our family and friends who made the journey. Coaches, teammates, classmates, and extended family members we don't see often. The music changes and everyone stands. I feel Luke place his hand on my back as my eyes fill with tears.

Fiona is stunning she looks like a princess. Her dress is off white with a floral lace overlay. It hugs her in all the right places. I am crying now. Her hair is down in curls just the way I love it. Her breathtaking green eyes stare emphasized by her mascara. When her hands are placed in mine, she winks then shows me her converse under her dress. I chuckle and so does everyone who sees. That's my girl always winning over the crowd.

The ceremony is short and sweet unlike our kiss at the end. I dip Fiona and kiss her like absolutely no one is watching. Her dad clears his throat, and everyone laughs. I throw our linked hands up in victory as we make our way down the aisle. When we reach the end, I pick her up and hold her in our signature pose, our foreheads touching, "Hello Mrs. Miller my beautiful wife" I whisper. "Hello husband" she murmurs back. I put her down and make our way to the area to meet the photographer.

After a million hours of photos in about a trillion different poses we finally head to the reception part of the arena. We sit at our table and listen to speeches from loved ones and friends. Some speeches are funny, some are embarrassing, but they are all full of so much love. Dinner is served "eat quickly I have a surprise for you" she tells me. I am starving so that is not an issue. Once we both finish we quickly get up and sneak through the side door. Fiona drags me by the hand upstairs to her old office. She opens the door and lets us in. "We only have a few minutes, better make them count" she whispers.

I don't have to be told twice. Making quick work on my pants while she pulls her dress up around her hips. She leans against the glass pushing her ass out revealing white crotchless panties. My breath catches at how sexy they are. I slide into her "This pussy is mine for life now that you are my wife" I mutter. "It was always yours husband" she says. I rail her from behind while we look down at our wedding below. We orgasm together for the first time as husband and wife. She grabs some napkins and I clean her up. We fix our clothes and head back down. Surely everyone noticed we were gone and knows what we were doing but we try and cover it up.

The cake cutting is fun we both attempt to cover the other in icing. We have all the dances be the first part of the night. I would be lying if I said I didn't cry during our first dance. I realized before tonight we never really dance but it was nice holding her in my arms. My mom cried the entire mother son dance as expected. Fiona and her dad cried during their dance. So it's safe to say that tears were shed a lot tonight.

The DJ opens up the dance floor and everyone has an amazing time I see Luke and Rodriguez trying to recreate our pose. Lucy and Stuntz are doing dancing and hanging out. Celisa is flirting with one of my new teammates. Everyone seems to be having an amazing time. I can tell the bridal party is definitely wasted. Fiona decides it's time for the bouquet and garter toss. Everyone crowds around Fiona sits in the chair and I go up under her dress. I take my time dragging the garter down her leg knowing she is super turned on. The DJ has the single men crowd around and I flick the garter landing right in Stuntz hand who wasn't even trying. Next Fiona turns around and throws the bouquet with Lucy catching it. What a coincidence I throw a wink at Fiona. Stuntz slides the garter onto Lucy not going too high to be respectful. But both of their cheeks are flushed red. Fiona has been trying to set them up forever.

The rest of the night is filled with dancing and lots of drinks. We all take crazy pictures and tell stories of all the fun times. Finally, the wedding planner tells everyone it's time for us to go. After one last surprise she has everyone line up outside with sparklers and we run under them stopping to kiss. Luke walks up and hands us the keys. I click the lock and say, "Happy wedding day Sunshine". She starts crying and runs over to the jeep admiring every inch. "It is perfect exactly as I wanted it" she tells me. "I know I put the details in my notes app anytime you would talk about it" I said.

We say our goodbyes to everyone. Lots of hugs and tears later. We are on the road to the hotel. Fiona is still obsessing over the jeep while we drive. I am happy she loves it. When we walk through the lobby people cheer and congratulate us. It is really nice but right now I just want my wife in bed with me. When we get to the honeymoon suite door, I scoop her up "Crossing the threshold as husband and wife" I say while she giggles.

She has me help her unbutton her dress then goes into the bathroom insisting she needs to make sure she is careful so she can preserve the dress. But when she comes out of the bathroom, she is wearing the sexiest piece of white lingerie I have ever seen. It accentuates all her curves in the best ways.

She climbs into bed and I take my time worshipping every inch of her beautiful body. While I eat her pussy I play with her nipples the lacy adding extra stimulation. She cums on my tongue for the first time as my wife and fuck is she sexy. I strip the lace off her piece by piece before I spread her legs and thrust into her. I lift her legs so I can go deeper as she yells out "Fuck yes show me how good you can pleasure your wife." That amps me up I shove a pillow under her ass and fuck her. I give her no chance to catch her breath as I deliver orgasm after orgasm to her. When she gets on top all bets are off she rides me and cups my balls it sends me over the edge and she falls forward as we both come down from climax. I get up and clean her up and we fall asleep in each other's arms as husband and wife.

Our alarms come way too early in the morning. But we have our flights to get to, luckily its first class so we can sleep on the plane. We were these shirts that say bride and groom that Fiona thought were funny knowing I hate matching shirts but that I wouldn't tell her no.

The flight is long, but we sleep the whole way. Once we finally arrive to the island and get into our bungalow. We hang out on the overwater hammock having drinks. Talking about the wedding and how amazing it turned out.

The week flies by with drinks and adventures. We go snorkeling and on a sunset boat ride. But we spend most of our time laying out on our bungalows' porch. We also spend a good chunk of the week having amazing mind blowing sex. I even fucked her doggy style on the window in the floor so we could both look at the fish below us.

On the last day we are laying on the hammock after lunch when Fiona bolts up the bathroom. I hear her throwing up. "Are you ok?" I ask concerned. "I am good I must of ate something bad" she says. We spend the rest of the day swimming. We end the night with an amazing candlelit dinner on the water watching the sunset.

The plane ride home lasts forever Fiona is still not feeling great. We try and sleep the whole flight home. Lucy picks us up from the airport and the minute we get home Fiona is running to throw up again. "I knew your boobs looked bigger!" Lucy exclaims. "What" Fiona and I say at the same time. "Oh, I guess I am wrong. I thought your boobs looked bigger because you are pregnant" she says. "When did you have this thought?" Fiona says annoyed. "Um your wedding day your dress was tighter in the chest, and you weren't on your period like Celisa and me. I thought you were having someone slip you sparkling grape juice or something. My bad though I shouldn't have assumed" she says. I grab my keys "I will be right back we will get the answers now" I tell them kissing Fiona.

On my to the drug store I start thinking about Fiona throwing up, she felt super tired, her boobs did look bigger. When I get there, I grab 10 tests of different kinds. The guy at the checkout looks at me super weird. I shrug and pay then I walk out. When I get back to the house Lucy says "Dude did you buy them out? We only needed one box." I shrug and reply, "I didn't know so I came prepared."

Fiona pees in a cup and the three of us dip the tests in and turn our backs. "No matter what I am happy Fiona" I pull her into a hug. Lucy steps out to give us some space for this. The alarm rings we hold our breath and turn around holding hands.

MARIAH GOODWIN

The End

Epilogue

Four years later

"Hadley Grace Miller get a move on we need to get to dad's game" I yell to my 3-year-old daughter. I get my 1-year-old son, Hudson into his car seat. Finally, Hadley comes out to the jeep, and I load her up and go lock up the house. We walk into the stadium and go up the family box where we see my parents, Zane's parents. Celisa, Charlie, and Lucy. My kids in their matching Miller jerseys that match mine. All of us with 27 painted on our cheeks. Ready to cheer the Thunder to becoming Stanly Cup champions!

The kids are all playing together sweetly not paying attention to the game at all but that's okay. I love our family and how close the kids are. Lucy has 2-year-old twins a boy and a girl, Celisa has a 1-year-old son, and Charlie has a 2-year-old boy and a 6-month-old boy. All of the kids are decked out in their respective dads' jerseys.

My business has expanded we have over 100 employees allowing me to be a hands-off owner and a hands-on mom. We have a new office in Portland Oregon for our west coast teams. Charlie, Celisa, and I all work from home very minimally. It has been amazing to grow this business with them.

Zane is going into his second Stanley cup championship. He has worked so hard the past four years. He never lets the sport overshadow his kids. There are missed events, but he does his best to be present and when he isn't he always calls in.

Our extended families have grown the past few years. It hasn't been easy for anyone their relationships have struggled but we are all here now.

For more from your favorite Tampa Thunder players join my newsletter so you can have up to date information on upcoming releases.

Next up is Lucy and Stuntz how does her long-time crush turn into a one night stand that becomes her enemy. A second chance romance with our favorite little sister and the Tampa Thunder team Captain.

About the Author

Mariah Goodwin is a nurse in Tampa, Fl. She is a mom and a wife. She is obsessed with Harry Potter and Disney.

She recently wrote her first novel after deciding she had enough stories in her head she should share them with the world.

She has had a love for reading since childhood.

My favorite romance book genres are:

Dark romance, sports, billionaires, and small towns.

My favorite tropes are:

Marriage of convenience, one bed, grumpy sunshine, fake dating, enemies to lovers.

Read more at https://www.mariahgoodwinbooks.com/.

Printed in Great Britain
by Amazon

35839405R00136